THE GIRL WITH THE SILVER Star

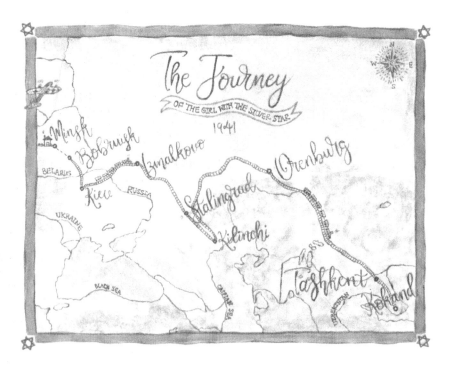

The journey of *The Girl with the Silver Star* was over 2,500 miles across the Soviet Union through Belarus, Ukraine, Russia and Uzbekistan

THE GIRL WITH THE SILVER *Star*

RACHEL ZOLOTOV

Text copyright © 2020 by Rachel Zolotov

First Edition

ISBN: 9798696529783

For Sasha & Lia

In memory of Raisa & Abraham Tsalkind

To all of those who fought to survive, protect and most importantly, love - even in the darkest of times.

Raisa & Abraham, 1925

CHAPTER ONE
THE CLUTCHES OF WAR

23 JUNE 1941
Minsk, Belarus, USSR

Sofia sat with our packed bags next to the door, her head down and jet-black curls covering her face. I made my way over to her and asked if she was alright, knowing what the answer would be before I asked it. She looked up, and with tears swelling up in her chestnut-brown eyes, she said, "Mama, I'm scared. I don't want to leave home. Where will we go?"

"I know Sofia, but you heard your Papa, it's not safe for us here. The Nazis could be headed our way. Come get into bed, tomorrow morning we will leave for Bobruisk. You'll get to see your Baba and Deda. Wouldn't it be nice to see your grandparents?" I asked as I shuffled Sofia to her bed.

Sofia didn't answer. Instead she walked past Abraham with her head lowered and went over to Luba's bed and snuggled up to the warmth of her big sister. Luba embraced her and tried to be strong for her little sister, but I saw her fear nevertheless.

"Good night girls. I love you," Abraham said as he pulled the cover over them.

"Good night Raisa," Abraham whispered into my ear and pulled me close. "I love you, my sweet little bird."

"I love you too." I listened for the rhythmic breathing of the girls. They had already fallen asleep. Abraham tossed and turned next to me, the burden of his thoughts keeping him awake, as were mine. "Abraham," I whispered, "Are you sure we need to leave? I think we should wait and see if the Nazis get pushed back."

Abraham turned to face me and took my hands gently into his own. The silver streaks in his wavy hair caught the moonlight as it trickled through the window. His soft face began to change as the words pushed free. "It's not up for debate. We are leaving!" snapped Abraham.

The certainty in his voice was not surprising, it was his harsh tone that nudged me away from him. I knew Abraham would do anything for us, but why was this decision only his? I would bring it up again in the morning. Perhaps a good night's sleep would help us both see things clearly. I closed my eyes and tried to relax. I wanted to drift away into slumber, but instead my body pulsed with uneasiness. The shadows of our packed bags loomed over my mind. Had I packed everything we would need? Where would we go after we got to Bobruisk? I thought about the news Abraham heard from his manager. Was it really true the Nazis had rounded up and killed hundreds of Jews only three hundred kilometers away from us in Lithuania? As I nodded in and out of sleep, I tried to push away the thoughts and questions, but they rushed towards me like a tsunami.

Suddenly, the air raid signal roared in our ears, jolting us out of bed. Abraham instinctively grabbed my hand to let me know he was there. He lit a candle, tied on his shoes and went to gather the bags, while I rushed to Sofia and Luba. The piercing sound scared Sofia into a fit of tears that hit the floor like heavy raindrops. Abraham opened the door. Neighbors scattered around and rushed to get into the bomb shelter, their yells echoing through the streets. We dressed quickly, grabbed our bags and hurried outside. I wasn't sure how I was even moving; my brain was paralyzed with the suddenness of it all, but the overwhelming need to protect my family and get to safety kept me focused.

"Girls, stay close! Don't leave our sides, and hurry," Abraham shouted, as he led the way to the shelter. We held onto each other as we ran through the narrow, uneven cobblestone street with sounds of sirens and exploding bombs ringing in our ears.

Inside the cramped shelter, the hours ticked by slowly and the thunder of explosions became so frequent that I lost count. Sitting in the darkened chamber, my senses were more acute than ever and the damp, moldy smell of earth filled my lungs, making my eyes itch.

My ears rang with every cough and shrieking cry of our neighbor's baby. Even in the faint flicker of candlelight, I saw the sweat bead up and run down Mrs. Gutman's face as she attempted to calm her sick baby by rocking him and pacing in endless circles.

Once tears would no longer flow from my tired eyes, I looked around, taking a mental note of the neighbors I could see. Pavel the butcher was there with his wife, their faces drained of color as they held each other closely in the corner. The Kagan family huddled together next to them with Haim keeping his wife and five kids as close as he could manage.

Across from us crouched the red-nosed Mr. Shulman. He was silent at first, while his bottle of vodka kept him company. "Be quiet already! Get that baby to stop crying, or I will come over there and shut him up myself!" Slurred and wet his words sprayed out. His shoulders hunched over as he glared into the empty bottle looking for more. When he realized there was none left, his eyes widened in terror, or maybe in realization that soon he would have to face what was happening.

It seemed as if we had been locked away for days when everyone finally hushed and Sofia gave in to sleep. I stroked her curls as she slept, tightly in my embrace. Without warning, an explosion nearby shook the earth around us. Sofia awoke with a cry and Luba jerked closer to me. Abraham towered over us, doing his best to shield us from the dust raining down.

I leaned against the moist wall, trying to stop the quivering from taking over my entire body. I put my hand over my necklace, feeling the six points of the star cold against my skin and prayed that we would be able to escape the clutches of war before it was too late.

CHAPTER TWO
WEB OF WORRIES

24 JUNE 1941
Minsk, Belarus, USSR

We waited deep beneath the ground until we could no longer hear the blasting of the bombs and the wailing of the sirens. When the doors were opened, a flood of light rushed in, awakening us. I stepped out after Abraham and the girls, and when I looked around, confusion overtook me. I grabbed Abraham's hand.

We stood in silence and took in our surroundings. No matter which direction I looked, I saw destruction. Our city burned, homes destroyed, and bodies lay lifeless on the street. I wanted to cover the girls' eyes to shield them from the horrific images, but it was too late.

Abraham broke the silence. "We must leave now. We need to go to Bobruisk and pick up our families, then decide where to go."

As we walked down our street towards the train station, we discovered that some houses remained untouched, while others were completely destroyed. "Was that the Kagan's house?" I asked, pointing to the pile of smoldering rubble on the corner of the street. "*Oy vey iz mir.*" They have five children to care for and nothing left but the clothes on their backs, I whispered to myself. Abraham quickened his step as we passed by the butcher's family home. It had been somewhat spared. Half of it still stood and the brick oven peeked out from underneath the debris.

The Karnovsky family home stood whole as though a magic blanket had been shielding it from harm. I ran over to Ita, who was kneeling over something in front of her house. "Ita, what is it?" I called, as I approached, but she didn't respond. Had she heard me, I wondered. I rushed over and put my arm around her as soon as I saw. Her little boy, Aron, only ten years old, glared back at me with spiritless, unmoving eyes. My body went into shock mourning for my friend and her loss. I could have never imagined the feeling of losing a child until now. I couldn't move.

Slowly, the loud thumping of my heartbeat quieted in my ears and I drifted back into reality. I was about to ask where Moysha was when I spotted the crease of his top hat a few meters away; his matching dimple chin jutting out beneath. I held Ita as close as I could, trying to keep her shaking body from falling into a thousand pieces. Abraham's shadow caught my attention, and without saying anything, I felt him urging me to keep moving. "Ita, come with us. Abraham, our girls and I are going to Bobruisk," I said, looking into her empty eyes.

"I can't leave them here. I will stay with them… even if that means… even if it means my death as well. I would rather die here with them, than with… without them." She managed to get out between sobs. "I won't leave them. I can't, Raisa. You understand, don't you?"

I did sympathize. If I were her, I wouldn't leave either. "I know, Ita. I won't make you leave, but Moysha and Aron would want you to live on for them. Be careful my friend." I squeezed her once more and turned to Abraham and my girls, letting them know it was time to go. I didn't want to leave her there, but I knew she wasn't ready to say goodbye yet, and we had to find the rest of our family.

"Look Mama and Papa. It looks like Masha's house is partially standing," Luba said, focused on our neighbor's house. Her cheeks had several streaks of dried tears, and her eyes were red and puffy in the corners as she stared into the distance.

"Thank goodness Klara and Masha left for their country house," I exclaimed. "Yasha was supposed to meet them there. I hope he left already," I said, glancing around to make sure I didn't see him among the fallen in the street.

Further down the street, I spotted a familiar tree. It took me a few minutes to realize that just beyond it was our house, or rather what was left of it. The four of us stood hand in hand looking at the rubble that was our home only a few hours ago. As tears slid down our cheeks, Abraham knelt down and looked into each of our eyes. "Those were only walls and possessions, our memories which we shared in that house will live forever inside our hearts. We are together and safe, my girls. Dry your tears. We must be strong for each other."

He was right. All that mattered was our safety and that we remained together. Still, no matter how hard I tried, I could not wish away the rush of sadness as I stared back at the fragments of our belongings scattered amongst the debris. Walking through the devastation, I realized we were luckier than most. Those who were caught off guard had lost not only their homes, but all of their possessions. I was grateful that we had packed before the sirens went off. I made myself hold on to this thought as I moved one foot in front of the other.

My thoughts fragmented as I looked at the faces of those around us, searching for our friends and neighbors. My soul felt torn and my heart ached for my children, for Ita, and for all that was lost in a matter of hours. Walking further, I wondered how I was going to make it through the rest of the day.

We headed to the station and joined the thousands of others trying to leave Minsk. My entire body was tense and overwhelmed from the sheer number of people. Every trace of space was taken up by someone or something. Children cried uncontrollably, men and women shouted with fear, and the elderly begged for help. My ears rang with each shriek and plea that darted past us. I wondered how we would get out of the disarray that extended in every direction. The few trains going to Bobruisk were fully packed with women, children, and the elderly. As they passed by, I could see the reflection of our glassy stares in their eyes.

People rushed forward like packs of wolves, pushing to get into the already overcrowded trains. Desperation started to set in as the station felt like it was closing in on us. Panic was no longer an emotion I merely felt, rather I embodied it as it raced through my veins.

I tried to close myself off from the chaos and focus on Abraham, who was the one person that always made me feel safe. I grabbed his hand and pulled him closer. Luba wrapped her arm around his, and Sofia held onto my other hand tightly, her grasp just as firm as it was hours before.

Abraham's furrowed eyebrows held concern when I looked up at him for reassurance. His shoulders seemed broader, as if they had grown over the last few hours to make room for our burdens. Even his voice wavered as he spoke. "You girls must be tired from standing. I see an area down by the end of the station where we can sit down for a few minutes and decide what to do. Follow me."

My head throbbed as I tried to make sense of the last few days. I knew that our life had changed, but I didn't want to believe it. I still hadn't processed the loss of our home, our neighborhood, and our town.

◆ ◆ ◆

I thought back to the day before yesterday, when I had admired the sky out of the kitchen window. It had been a mix of light grey, blue and white, and for a moment, it looked like a painting I once saw. The clouds hung low like puffy cotton balls, with the sun just barely peeking out. The trees stood in full bloom, and vibrant flowers filled my view as birds flew gracefully across the sky.

It had begun as a normal Sunday afternoon. Luba had helped me make lunch, while Sofia colored quietly. We were making soup with potatoes, carrots and leftover chicken when Abraham had turned up the radio and our routine life quickly faded away with the broadcast. The voice of the foreign minister, Vyacheslav Molotov flooded the room with news that the Nazi troops had attacked the Soviet Union. He named the cities that had been bombed and listed the number of people killed or wounded. My heart thumped in my throat and grew louder as the seconds ticked by. I wondered if Minsk was next. Soon, the beating of my frightened heart became so loud that I had to strain to hear the radio. I wondered if Luba had picked up on the panic which had crept into my thoughts. I tried to distract myself and opened the lid of the soup to give it a taste, while continuing to listen to the radio.

Abraham rotated the radio knob until it had clicked off, and suddenly the room felt too quiet for my racing heartbeat. I turned my attention to Sofia, who was now reading, immersed in the world of her favorite fairytale, *Thumbelina*. The smile on her face as she turned the pages, reminded me of her innocence. I wondered if the news we'd just heard would take that innocence away. How many more moments of childhood would she have left?

Had that really only been two days ago? Even yesterday morning felt distant in my mind. My head had weighed heavy with concern while I stumbled out of bed. As I glanced outside, the birds no longer soared gracefully, but rather seemed to be flying away in a hurry. Something was different all around me, and I couldn't help but feel it in the depths of my soul. The confusion mixed with uncertainty hovered above us like a dark rain cloud.

Abraham had headed out for work, trying to act as if nothing had changed. He kissed us goodbye and left with fear lurking in his uneven footsteps. The three of us watched him walk into the distance. I had tried to push away the concerns that rolled around in my mind, but they swirled around like a tornado, picking up speed and destruction. I wished my worries had been merely a nightmare hiding in the depths of my imagination, but instead, they came tumbling down on top of us soon after.

My thoughts drifted to last night when I was preparing dinner. Abraham had opened the door with such force that he startled us all. His breath was heavy, his cheeks flushed, and his smokey grey eyes were filled with worry. "Raisa, girls, we must pack our things and leave early in the morning. My manager heard from a relative in Kaunas. The Nazis are rounding up all the Jews. The Fascists were bombing the airfields near Minsk today, and soon they might be taking over the city. We need to pack and get to a safe place. Grab your rucksacks and fill them only with necessities, and then come help us gather as much food as possible. Who knows where we will go and for how long, so pack warm clothes as well."

We had all stood staring at him in shock. I tried to move, but couldn't; my body was frozen in place like a bronze statue. When I turned, Luba and Sofia also stood motionless. Abraham shouted this time, "Hurry girls, get started. We must pack, eat and get some rest!" This was the first time I had ever heard him raise his voice, and we had been married for over sixteen years.

Quickly, I motioned to the girls, "Sofia, Luba, listen to your Papa. Pack your clothes." With a frightened expression smeared across their faces, Sofia and Luba hurried to do as they were told. Luba started with her clothes. She put aside her favorite warm sweater. I loved how the burnt orange color complemented her fair skin and sandy brown hair. The girls seemed to be fine on their own, so I walked to the dresser to pack for myself and Abraham.

I reached into my drawer and looked through the clothes, but my mind was panicked and torn. I hoped this was all a bad dream. The room spun around me as I tried to focus. I paused and took a breath. I needed to move; there was no time for unraveling the web of worries and questions collecting in my mind.

First, I folded a few winter outfits and placed them in my bag. I added my favorite simple summer dress, guessing it might be useful and wouldn't take up much space in the bag. Then, I laid out what I would wear for the trip and fetched my low boots. My boots were the only pair of shoes I had left that didn't have any holes in them. Each of us had only a single pair of shoes, and we felt particularly lucky to have them. Shoes had become hard to come by these past few years, and the shoes you could find were expensive and fell apart quickly. Lastly, I added a warm scarf and undergarments to the bag.

It was hard to decide what to take. I had many possessions that I held dear to my heart, but we couldn't possibly carry them all. I tucked my favorite pictures into a sturdy brown leather envelope and threw it into my bag. Then, I hurried to my sewing table and put together a small sewing kit. I took a minute to think about leaving our home and friends. Looking all around, I wondered if we would ever come back home again. My hands trembled uncontrollably and my heart beat to a terrified rhythm.

Pushing aside my fears, I stuttered, "Luba, are you finished, my love? Could you go help Sofia finish packing?" Her ability to remain so calm and brave at only fifteen had given me a brief moment of satisfaction.

"Yes, Mama. I just finished. I will go help Sofia," Luba said, rushing over.

"Thank you, my love." I saw Sofia struggle out of the corner of my eye, but I knew I needed to pack a bag for Abraham. Sofia was much more interested in clothes than Luba had ever been. She longed for new clothes to wear and frequently sacrificed her comfort for looks. Her love of fashion had started about two years ago when she turned eight. I often spent my days sewing her something special.

"Sofia, you can't carry all of these clothes in your bag. Let's pick out your warmest outfit, one summer outfit and something you can layer for the trip," Luba said hurriedly, her soft hazel eyes pleading with Sofia to obey.

Sofia tried to decide, but went back and forth, talking Luba through why she preferred this shirt over that shirt, even though the obvious choice was right in front of her. Luba tried to reason with her, but they both became more frustrated as Sofia continued to add more clothes to her pile.

"Mama, Sofia needs your help. She isn't listening to me. She can't possibly take all these clothes!"

I hurried over, and after a few moments, without saying anything, I divided the pile and packed it into Sofia's bag. I could tell Sofia was upset, but she knew it was no use arguing with me. Sofia had also put aside a few pictures, so I tucked them carefully into an envelope so they wouldn't bend.

I rushed around packing the last of the clothes for Abraham, while Luba and Sofia collected the little amount of food we had left in the house.

"Girls, take all of the preserved food and bread, and divide them among our bags," I shouted over my shoulder.

Abraham came over to my side. "Raisa, I gathered the important documents and money, let's put them together in my bag. We need to take our most valuable possessions and only the ones small enough to carry. We can't risk leaving them and we might need them if the money runs out. What can we carry with us?"

"Grab your watches and my jewelry and put them inside this pouch. We can take our silver spoons and the kiddush cup given to us on our wedding," I said trying to think of our most treasured belongings.

I had finished packing the last few items and diverted my attention to dinner. Usually, standing over a pot of simmering food calmed my nerves, but not this time. Tension was in every corner. Sofia's face was somber as she sat on her bed pretending to read. Luba helped me set the table and Abraham finished placing the packed bags next to the door. There was fear then, but not the panic I had now.

♦ ♦ ♦

"Mama, Papa, how long will we be gone for? Will we be back in time for the start of school?" Sofia asked with a frown. The brakes of an approaching train hissed and screeched as it slowed to a stop, snapping my thoughts back to the present.

Abraham let out a long breath. I imagined the parts of his brain working like a well-oiled machine as he pieced together a response. "We don't know, my dear. We could be gone for a while. No one knows how long the war will last. What we do know, is that Minsk isn't safe. I know it's hard to understand, but we need to get as far away from here as we can," Abraham spoke calmly, but I knew better than to believe his composed demeanor.

The trains came and left. I gazed up as the blanket of slate clouds shifted across the sky. Everything was moving and changing faster than I could process. A long train sped through the station, sending a rush of wind through my silver-streaked brown hair. There was a brief moment of silence until I heard the trucks pull up and the soldiers march into the station.

"All able-bodied men between the ages of eighteen and fifty-one line up. Have your papers ready," the Red Army officer shouted into the crowd of people.

My mouth went dry as I looked over at Abraham. I read the look in his eyes. The fear of what would happen next was written all over him, starting from his ghostly white face all the way to his trembling fingertips. In that moment, I didn't want to admit it, but I knew somewhere deep inside that I was about to be separated from the love of my life.

"Do you have to go Papa?" Sofia cried out. Her eyes pleaded with him for a different answer.

Luba stared down at her feet while shifting her weight. She began to bite the tip of her thumb before she finally looked up at Abraham and asked, "What will we do without you? What will happen to us if they take you?"

"I have to go. It will be worse if I resist. I will be back, wait here for me."

My body drifted into a state of numbness and my legs shook as we watched him join the line of men. The closer he reached the front of the line, the tighter the girls' hands grasped my own. I tried to imagine how difficult this must be for them at their age. Their love for him was unmistakable. From the moment he held them, they shared an instant connection. Every day when Abraham came home from work, I saw a sparkle in the girls' eyes. They lit up like fireflies as he scooped them into his embrace. I wished I could tell them that everything would be alright.

Abraham finished showing the soldiers his papers and turned toward us. With each step he took, sadness followed, casting a dark shadow over us. Soon, he stood before us, and with our hands locked together he took a deep breath and explained what we already knew, but didn't want to accept.

Suddenly, we walked through a door which led us to an entirely different world. In an instant, pieces of our shattered life began to fall all around me. Abraham tried to be strong and put on an iron mask for us, but the fear in his eyes cut through my heart like razor blades.

"My train departs in three hours, where we will be taken straight to training. I have been drafted to protect our motherland. Let's take a walk and have some lunch before I leave," Abraham suggested. He tried to sound positive but the unsteadiness in his voice didn't fool me.

As we walked away from the train station in the direction of the park, the girls held on to Abraham tightly, not wanting to let go. I walked behind them, watching as they interacted with each other. Abraham glanced back, as if to check on me, but I looked away. My mind was filled with too many thoughts and questions. I tried to push my feelings aside and focus on Abraham. I needed to memorize each wrinkle, every curve, and how his curls lay just right. We had spent sixteen years looking at each other every day, and now I somehow felt I had taken those years for granted.

"This bench is in the shade. Let's sit down and have a bite," Abraham called back to me, shifting my gaze back to reality. I reached into my bag and pulled out the cheese and bread as Abraham took out his pocket knife and cut them into slices for sandwiches. Together, we made four equal sandwiches, one for each of us. I tried to eat, but my body refused. My stomach turned with fear and with each attempted bite, it grew more uneasy.

"I'm not too hungry," I said. "Would you girls like to split the rest of my sandwich?"

"I would," Sofia answered and Luba nodded in agreement.

"Could you play in the grass while Mama and I talk?" Abraham asked. "I see some flowers. Can you find some pretty ones for a bouquet?" The girls nodded and walked slowly towards the open field, knowing better than to argue.

"Raisa, we must transfer the food from my bag to yours, and I want you to take the silver and watches. You will need them. Here are your documents and the rest of our money. I want you to be careful. People will do whatever it takes to survive, even if that means stealing. Don't let your bags out of your sight, ever. Sleep with them under you and in-between you and the girls."

"No, no Abraham. You keep some of the money. What if you need to buy some extra clothes or food? You don't even know when you will get any payment from service," I said, worried. I knew that he was perfectly capable of taking care of himself, but the thought of not being the one to do it for him tugged at my heart.

"I have everything I need for now, and if I need more, I will figure out a way. You will take all of the money. Please don't argue about this, my dear," he said as he pushed the money back into my bag.

"How should we get to Bobruisk? I am so worried about my Mama and Papa and my sisters; I hope they are safe."

"You should leave on foot. You must get out of Minsk as soon as possible. When you arrive in Bobruisk, take your family and leave as quickly as you can. Head east or south. Try not to travel north. If the war drags on, the winter in the north will be miserable."

"I agree. I hope I can convince my family to leave. You know how Papa can be. Thank goodness your Papa and Manya left for Moscow last week to visit their friends. At least they are far enough away from here. What about your brothers and sisters? Did they go to Moscow as well?"

Abraham thought for a moment before replying. "They went with Freyda and her three girls. Leia and Malka should be in Bobruisk, as should Sander. Sander will probably be taken to the army before you even arrive though."

"Should I go to them and have them come with us?" I asked.

"If you could, I would only ask that you go and tell them to go to Moscow and join my Papa and the rest of my family. They should stay together, and you must go with your family," he answered with a softness in his voice that assured me he had his reasons for this plan.

"How will I get in touch with you?" I asked.

"Once you are able to, send a letter to the military post with my name on it. I would also include my date and city of birth and it will be forwarded to my regiment. Once you get a letter from me, you will be able to send mail directly to my unit so it will reach me faster," he explained. I wondered how he knew this, but I didn't care enough to ask at this moment.

I leaned over and nestled my head in his chest. His arm wrapped around my shoulders, protecting me for the last time. As we watched our girls pick flowers in the distance, I sat, not wanting to say anything else. I only wanted his warmth and to breathe his scent a little longer. I looked up and into his eyes, trying hard not to cry. "Oh Abraham, I will miss you. I'm scared to be without you, but I will do everything I can to keep our girls safe. I will think about you every moment. I never thought I would be lucky enough to know such a pure love that you have shown me. You will forever carry my heart no matter what happens."

Before he could reply, the girls swooped in with their flower bouquets. "This one is for you Mama!" said Luba.

"And this one is for Papa!" Sofia exclaimed. Abraham hugged them both and the three of them ran off playing and laughing together in the grass. Abraham took advantage of every minute he had left with his girls; neither his departure, nor the suffering taking place all around us could ruin his time with Luba and Sofia.

I watched them, wishing I had a way to hold onto these moments. After Abraham leaves, I know Luba would have to grow up even more, and her childhood years would float away as quickly as a balloon set free into the open sky. Sofia might hold on to her youth a bit longer, but her outspoken and charismatic personality would not get the chance to shine as brightly.

We walked in a row, hand in hand, back to the train station. Rain came down in large drops as if someone from up above were crying right along with us. I was thankful for the downpour, so I didn't have to say anything. Instead, the awkward silence was replaced by the sounds of our boots splashing through the puddles. The train station buzzed with people, but the only face I saw was Abraham's. We stopped to face each other, glowing with emotion. Abraham gazed downward, holding me in his giant embrace. His muscles tightened as he fought to hold his emotions together. I looked at him like the hero that I already knew him to be and then I smiled and got up on my tippy toes to whisper in his ear.

"Abraham, you are my one and only. I love you more than I have ever loved anything in this world. You be safe and come back to us. We need you."

Before I could continue, tears began to flow and Abraham softly wiped them away. "My dear Raisa, I promise you, this is not goodbye. We will meet again. I want you to write to me every day and take care of yourself just as much as you take care of these girls. I love you more than you know. Don't worry about me, my love."

Then he bent down and whispered a few words into each of the girls' ears. Whatever he said made them both smile, even as tears streamed down their frightened faces, and I couldn't have loved him more in that moment. He always knew the right thing to say. He held the girls close and gave them each a kiss before standing up to kiss me one last time. My throat tightened and as more tears formed, I said one last "I love you" before he turned and walked away. When he waved back at us, I could barely make him out from the tears clouding my view. He stepped onto the train and waved one last goodbye before the train disappeared into the distance.

CHAPTER THREE
DOOR NUMBER SEVENTEEN

28 JUNE 1941
Bobruisk, Belarus, USSR

It was the three of us girls now and we had no choice but to continue. I had to be strong for them and for Abraham. Now more than ever, I longed to see my Mama, Papa and sisters and make sure they were safe. Our only choice was to walk to the next station if we ever wanted to get out of Minsk. As we escaped into the unknown, danger loomed in the darkness ahead, but turning back was not an option as blazing fires lit up the skyline behind us.

After the first long day of walking, my body ached, and my feet formed blisters. We had to keep moving, as we heard news from other evacuees walking near us that the Nazis had advanced further. I knew we needed to get ahead as quickly as possible.

Letting nature envelop itself around me was the only way to escape my aching body and keep the girls' attention away from the pain they were enduring. The bright white and yellow patches of chamomile flowers became my rays of hope, and each time I came across them, cheerful memories from the past snuck into my thoughts. Watching the girls run through them made me remember our walks to the park near our house. Sometimes, when we stopped for a break, I would pick the chamomile blooms and show the girls how to tie them together into crowns. All around us, seemingly protecting us, grew a forest of birch trees. I never truly had the time to notice their beauty until they became our shelter. They stood tall and slender, but united like a family. They were my favorite type of tree because of their unique trunks, and while we stopped to rest, they were a fun distraction for Sofia and Luba. They went from tree to tree and carefully peeled away sheets of curling bark, and whoever was able to get the biggest piece won. Watching the sky move and change above us was perhaps the most beautiful to look at. The three of us enjoyed looking up at the ever-changing clouds as we tried to find different animals or objects. The night sky was a wonder, and before bed, we gazed at the sparkling stars. I pointed out the stars and planets that I remembered, and the rest were left to our imaginations. One night we even saw a shooting star rush across the sky.

On our journey to the next train station, we walked for a few hours and then stopped to rest for an hour. If we were lucky, we found a bench to rest and have a small bite to eat, otherwise we found a patch of grass nearby. At night, we huddled together on the ground when it was too dark to continue walking. As Abraham had suggested, we held our bags in-between us so they couldn't be stolen while we slept. I kept our money tucked away in a secret pocket inside of my blouse that I had sewed when we were resting. The more stories I heard of people waking up to find that they were left with nothing, the more paranoid I became of losing our only possessions. At night, Luba and I tried to take turns sleeping so there was someone to watch the bags, but it was hard to stay awake after walking the entire day.

We came across all different types of people as we made our way through the woods and villages. There were some people with good hearts who helped where they could, even if they had little to spare, and of course there were those that made their thoughts about Jews perfectly clear.

On our second night, as we passed through a village, we walked along a row of small houses. An old woman was outside sweeping in front of her doorway. She cautiously eyed us as we neared.

"Mama, I'm hungry," Sofia announced.

"I know dear, but I already told you, we have to save what we have left for tomorrow. Maybe when we stop for the night, I can give you both a small piece of bread to hold you over."

Sofia slowed her pace a little and rubbed her belly before she continued down the street. "Yes, Mama," she said sadly.

I felt defeated. My own pains of hunger suddenly overtaken by the agony of not being able to keep my girls fed. A moment later, we passed by the doorway and the sounds of the old woman sweeping stopped.

"Come over here!" She motioned as we turned back to face her. "Wait a moment, I'll be right back." She disappeared inside and emerged a few minutes later with a wrapped parcel outstretched towards us. "Take this, you and your girls need it more than I do. I heard the Nazis are close. You need to go quickly. They are killing all the Jews." She looked back and forth down the street as if to be sure none of her neighbors had overheard and quickly shut her door, leaving us alone in the strangely quiet street.

We darted into the nearby woods and found a tree to lay under for the night. We opened the parcel and found bread, cheese, dried meat and even a few squares of chocolate. I divided the food between us and wrapped three portions for later. We ate underneath the shimmering stars and among the quiet rustle of the vast forest.

My belly was finally satisfied. The rumblings of hunger hushed as we huddled together on the soft grass. I thought about the old lady for a moment, and even under the cool breeze of the night sky, I was warmed by her goodness. Her kind act had me smiling inside, even if it was for only a short time. My moment of comfort was quickly overshadowed by her harsh warnings. They sent a chill down my spine. Just then, a small movement rustled through the leaves nearby, and I caught a glimpse of a tiny rabbit. It stopped as soon as it caught sight of me. The rabbit's heart beat noticeably from its chest, and its glassy eyes focused ahead, as if hoping that if it doesn't make eye contact, then maybe it can get away unnoticed. I looked away, releasing it from my watchful eye, and letting it run back into the safety of the forest. I knew what it felt like – being hunted, vulnerable and exposed. Too scared to close my eyes, I watched Luba and Sofia sleep and imagined them having sweet dreams.

The next night, unfortunately, we found out that selfishness was much more common than the generosity we had encountered only the day before.

We walked by a farmhouse with a small house and barn next door. The sun was minutes away from setting and we had exhausted our legs for the day. A man was tending to his horses when we came closer.

"Are you looking for a place to sleep for the night?" he asked from a distance.

We picked up our pace to get closer to the man. "Yes, we would appreciate a place to lay down," I answered.

His face scrunched up as he stared at my necklace which had come out from under my blouse. "We don't take in Jews. Find somewhere else to stay."

My face stung as if I had been slapped. My stomach turned with anger. We rushed away trying to leave behind the hate, but it followed us like a fast-moving storm. I wanted to push away from it, but there was no way, it was now all around us.

"Mama?" Sofia called, when we had gotten far enough away that the rush of adrenaline no longer kept my legs moving.

"Yes, my dear," I answered pushing back my tears, overwhelmed with sadness.

"Why won't he take us in? Why does it even matter that we are Jewish?" Sofia asked.

I wished I had the innocence of a ten-year-old. I also wished I knew how to answer her. I sensed the hole inside of me that started when Abraham and I parted, grow wider now. He would have known what to say. He would have bent down and looked her in the eye and said something perfect.

Taking in a deep breath, I tried to think of what Abraham might say. "Well, honey, some people don't understand that even though we all have our unique qualities, as a whole we are no different than them. Just because we are Jewish, doesn't make us more or less, it just makes us all human beings. Sometimes, when people are scared, they try to find someone or something to blame to make themselves feel better," I explained.

"But why are they blaming us? We aren't Nazis." Sofia exclaimed.

"No, we aren't, but the Nazis are killing the Jews and some people feel that they are only in the middle of a war because of us. Does that make sense?" Sofia nodded, but I knew she wouldn't understand until she was older. At least for now, my answer would do. Luba had been quiet, walking with her head down. I wondered if she understood what I was trying to say.

"So, when the Jewish schools closed a few years ago, that was because others think we are too different?" Luba asked.

"That is one way of thinking about it, yes. I can't explain why some people dislike us for being different. Maybe it's because it's easier to hate than love, especially if that's what you were taught. Whatever is happening around us, know that you still must love, always. If you lose the ability to love and let hate take over, then you will be no better than them," I answered. I assured myself that this was as close to what Abraham would have said, and we settled once again for a long night amongst the trees.

Women, children and older men walked alongside us. The distant dialects of Mother Russia and our neighboring countries melted together as we helped each other to keep moving. We stopped to take a rest the next afternoon. A woman sat by herself on a bench as we approached. Its rigid wooden planks called to us like warm fluffy beds. I wondered if I would be able to get back up this time. I wasn't sure, but I had to sit down. My eyes rested on the woman at the other end of the bench when I heard a sniffle.

"My name is Raisa. These are my two girls, Luba and Sofia," I said, noticing her arm lifting to wipe away a stray tear.

"I'm Ester. It's nice to meet you," she replied in Russian. I could tell she was Polish instantly from her accent.

"What city are you from, Ester?" I asked in Yiddish, knowing it would be easier for us both to use our universal language.

"I was born in Warsaw and lived there all my life. This is the first time I have left my home city. What about you?"

"We are from Minsk. We fled a few days ago, when the bombs started to drop." Ester fixed her eyes into the distance as I spoke. "You are alone?"

Still focused on somewhere faraway, she replied, "Yes. I'm all alone now. I need to get as far away from here as possible. As far as my legs will carry me. I have already come so far…" Her voice trailed off to meet her stare.

"You are not alone anymore. You can come with us for as long as you like."

She turned towards me, looking me in the eye for the first time. Her eyes fixed on mine, as if trying to read into my thoughts. "I wouldn't want to slow you down," she said.

I studied her oversized brown eyes and angular face. The freckles on her nose like stars scattered about the night sky. I couldn't leave her by herself. "Of course, you will come with us. Now let's go and you can tell us about yourself."

◆ ◆ ◆

"I'm getting hungry Mama, maybe we should stop and eat," Luba offered and glanced back at Sofia who had slowed her walk to almost a stop.

"Yes, I can hardly feel my feet. We should take a break and have a quick bite to eat before we continue," I said. I took a mental note of what food we had left. It wasn't much. We did have money, but I didn't want to use any more right now unless we absolutely had to. I hoped we could make what food we had left last until Bobruisk. I unwrapped our leftover parcel of bread, meat and cheese that the old lady had given us, and gave some to Luba and Sofia, before starting myself.

"My father was an artisan baker before he was taken away by the Nazis. He owned a small bakery right underneath our house," Ester said before taking a bite of her bread.

"Oh my, I'm sorry," I answered. It must be painful to see a reminder of him every time she eats.

"Mama would help him in the mornings and I would come every day after school. They would sneak away before the sun came up and start preparing the dough for the bread and pastries. Inviting me to start my day, I would rise to the smell of baking and Mama coming back upstairs to get me ready for school," Ester began.

I watched her as she told her story, her arms moved around as she spoke, motioning through her thoughts. She paused for only a few minutes to take a bite of her stale bread and continued with her story. Was I hungrier today, I thought to myself, or was her story making my mouth water for a pastry?

As if answering my thoughts, Ester asked, "Am I making you girls hungry yet?"

Luba and Sofia nodded and I wondered where she was going with this. Did she have some pastries hidden in her bag for us?

"My father taught me something special when I was a little girl, and I will teach you. One day, I came home from school and went straight to the bakery. It was close to the holidays, so we were very busy and when I walked in, I noticed the shelves were almost empty. The cases had only a few pastries left and the line was still long. This was good I thought to myself, my parents would be happy to have such a successful day. But I was hungry. Usually when I got there, I would choose something from the case and have plenty of time to eat before I needed to help."

"What did you do?" Sofia asked

"I had to help. I stood behind the case and helped box up the pastries for the customers. Each one looked better than the last and my stomach began to rumble."

"My stomach is rumbling for one right now too," Luba exclaimed.

"After we sold everything that had been made that day and all the customers left, I turned to my father and said, 'I am starving. I can't go another minute without some food.' So, my father and I went upstairs where my mother was making dinner. Waiting for her to finish was like torture, I was so hungry, until my father came and sat beside me and began to tell me about the most elaborate pastries he had ever seen in Paris. After the first few, I thought I was going to die right there, but then slowly I started to feel full from the thoughts of food."

"Really?" I asked. I would have thought you would get hungrier.

"You see my father survived the first world war and there were times during and after the war that he had almost no food. He explained to me that during those difficult times he would think of the most wonderful food he could imagine and picture it in his mind. Sometimes his comrades would join in and go around sharing their favorites, until eventually, your mind tricks you into thinking you are full. Maybe one day you will use my father's trick. I never had to use it until now, and I am thankful for that."

"Where did the Nazis take him, Ester?" Luba asked.

"They took both my Father and Mother away at the same time. I wasn't there when it happened, but a neighbor told me that they came in the middle of the night. They trashed the apartment and took everything they could find which held value and took my parents. I was told they were transported, but I have no idea where. I haven't heard from them since,"

Ester replied. I noticed her arms were still by her side as she spoke, but her fingers trembled ever so slightly.

The hair on my arms pricked up in response and I was beginning to understand why Ester sometimes stared off into the distance. Her mother and father were possibly out there, somewhere, and she was still looking for them.

♦ ♦ ♦

We passed through village after village. We waited at each station, and wished that the next train would be ours, but it never had enough room, so we continued on foot. Hope began to dwindle, but nevertheless we continued. Often, I wondered how we would make it. How would I force the girls to keep going when I could barely move myself? I imagined how strenuous traveling this way would be for my Mama and Papa. Could they even survive it? So many thoughts raced through my mind, but I had to continue to keep myself motivated for the girls. No matter how hard it was, I still tried to keep the girls' spirits lifted. We sang songs and recited poems. Sometimes, I made up fairy tales with funny plots to keep Luba and Sofia laughing. Having Ester with us made the time fly. She started out by telling us stories of her childhood and as we began to know each other better, she was able to open up about what happened to her and how she ended up here in Russia. She was a natural storyteller with a voice that could sing with the birds. It helped the girls to have her around, but as the days trudged on, it became harder to divert their attention because they could easily see how frustrated I was with our misfortune.

♦ ♦ ♦

It had only been six days since the war on Russia was announced, but more had happened in those few days than in the past six months. This morning, we woke to the birds chirping and the air feeling slightly warmer. We had averaged five to six hours of walking a day, for the past three days and we were hoping our luck would change. Our stockpile of food was as drained as we were. With each passing hour, I worried more about Luba and Sofia, but I also started to worry about myself. Voices inside me were screaming, demanding my attention. I pushed them back, but I knew it was only a matter of time until they would take over. I missed Abraham already. I longed for his touch and his assuring eyes. I needed them to tell me we would get through this.

After we stopped at the next station and saw the overfilled trains yet again, I decided we should walk along the road in hopes that a truck would stop and give us a ride.

We walked for over an hour while cars passed us by one after another, and none of them even slowed down. "Mama, I'm tired," Sofia whimpered, "My feet hurt. Do we have to keep walking?"

"I know, dear. Maybe a car will stop and drive us the rest of the way. Try not to focus on your feet hurting. You are young; your youthful feet could carry you across the country and back." I gave her a wink, hoping it would ease her whining.

"And be thankful your shoes aren't falling apart like mine are!" Luba chimed in.

I looked down at her shoes and noticed the seam had come apart, her toe starting to stick out. She hadn't even said anything. Luba was not one to complain. My heart glowed with pride as I realized how helpful she had been in these days when I needed her the most.

"You didn't even tell me, my love. When we get to Bobruisk, I will have my Papa fix them for you."

After a while, a few trucks caught up to us, and as I looked back, I met the gaze of one of the truck drivers. Our eyes locked as he passed, and I thought for a second that maybe he would stop, but when I looked ahead, he was still moving. I lowered my head, exhausted and sad. Suddenly Luba said, "Look, the truck pulled over! Maybe he will take us." We picked up our pace and caught up with the truck.

"Hello, where are you heading?" The man asked through the window. Now up close I could see the truck was dark green, but at first glance it had looked brown from so much dust and mud.

"We are going to Bobruisk," I answered in a hopeful tone.

"I'm heading that way. Can I give you a ride?" A pair of square glasses framed his soft, green eyes and they suited his long, kind face.

"That would be wonderful," I said, "We could use a break. We have been walking for three days and need to get to my mother and father. My name is Raisa, and this is Luba, Sofia, and Ester." I stretched my hand out to meet his.

"Nice to meet you, I'm Viktor. We should be there in about an hour."

Then Viktor helped us into the truck. He had rough hands and dirty clothes, but his easygoing voice was calming. We piled into the truck happy to have a break from walking. The back was fully loaded with tools and metal barrels. We had to step over and under a few things to get to the upright barrels where we could take a seat. They were near the edge of the truck, so we held on to the side as the truck jumped over the bumps in the road. The metal was rigid and chilly, but as inflexible as it was, it was a much-needed vacation for our feet. As the truck picked up speed, the washed-out fabric on the sides flapped with rage in the wind.

As we drove, I thought back to the last time we had visited Bobruisk, the city in which Abraham and I were born. It had been nearly a year ago. We traveled there to celebrate my parents' thirty-fifth wedding anniversary. We celebrated with friends and family and it was good to see faces that I hadn't seen in years. I loved the way the room felt that night. There was so much love and happiness in the air, and I wished I could have caught it in a bottle to release in these times of desperation.

Trying to keep my mind focused, I made a plan for the rest of the day. When the truck stopped at a railroad crossing, I explained my plan to the girls, "Once we arrive, we need to help everyone pack and gather as much food as possible. We will take a short rest and then leave in the early evening."

It was comforting to know that we would have a place to sleep and get cleaned up, even if it would be for a short time. Something inside told me that it might be the last chance to get a good night's sleep for a long time.

"Look Mama, we just entered Bobruisk!" shouted Sofia when we neared our destination. It was around lunchtime when we reached the center of town.

The truck pulled over and we thanked Viktor as he helped us jump down onto the uneven pathway. As we walked through the town, the smell of fresh baked bread escaped through a cracked window of a small bakery. I froze in place, letting the smell overtake me. I wanted it all over my body, on my clothes and in my mouth. We had been rationing the remaining food to make what we had last longer, so we were hungry, and the smell made my tummy growl and my mouth water. As we looked around, it appeared that this part of town hadn't been hit by an air raid, and we were thankful that our family would likely be safe.

"Raisa, this is where we say goodbye," Ester said as she stopped on the corner of the street.

"Ester, you are welcome to join us. Please come meet my family, tell them your story," I pleaded.

The girls shuffled anxiously next to Ester. They had grown used to her company and they looked to her like they would a big sister. "I am so thankful for you three girls, but you will have to tell my story for me. Raisa, you picked me up off that bench and gave me the willpower to keep going. I don't think I would have continued if it weren't for you. I was at a dark place in my mind. Right now, I need to figure out for myself where this journey is going to take me next. I wish you and your sweet girls all the best." She motioned to Luba and Sofia to come give her a hug, while I stood back and watched them say their goodbyes.

"I hope your feet carry you to wherever you wish to go. You have escaped hell and you deserve to find happiness," I said into her ear softly as I hugged her close.

She whispered back, "I wish this as well, but nothing but sadness looms over us unlucky Jews, especially, while war ferociously takes over. Stay safe my dear friend. I will always carry you in my memories." She turned and disappeared into the alley with confidence.

Still feeling as though we were missing someone, I reluctantly led the girls through a narrow street and knocked on door number seventeen. Everything about the street, from the ornately placed cobblestones below, to the familiar signs in the butcher's shop next door, transported me back to my childhood years. Memories of my favorite moments flooded back to me as I imagined myself running through these very streets, playing with friends without a care in the world. My twin braids flipped around as my best friend Lana and I skipped along the cobblestones. Lana and I were neighbors from birth up until we married and moved away. Her name was Svetlana, but everybody called her Lana. She was much taller than me, and her long blonde hair was usually in two thick braids with ribbons tied in bows. Her blue eyes were stunning, and I sometimes wondered how they could possibly be as blue as the sky.

We were born a month apart, so our Mamas were pregnant together and became best friends through the shared experience. When school started, we met Nina, who lived a few streets away and the three of us became inseparable. Nina was the balance we didn't realize we had been missing and when she started playing with us, it was as if she had always been around. I admired her beautiful doll-like complexion, with her pale skin and smoky green eyes. I was the shortest girl in my class, but Lana and Nina never made me feel different like some of the other boys and girls did.

During the summer months, you could find us running around in the grass in front of our house. We would stay out until the fireflies lit up. We caught them into our hands and counted who had more. Sometimes we played tag with the other kids in the neighborhood, but the three of us usually stuck together, our bond as strong as our wills.

In the fall, we jumped in the leaves and played hide and seek until our Mamas called us to come home. We hugged and made plans for the next day before running inside. During the winter, we played in the snow or inside one of our homes with our dolls. Making snowmen and snow angels were our favorites, but sometimes we would go sledding with our Papas. We built the most magnificent snowman in the neighborhood. Not only was he giant, but he was also unusually detailed. We made sure to find the right items for his arms, nose, buttons and mouth. One year, we found a squirrel's stockpile of acorns and made the snowman beautiful acorn buttons. His eyes were made from two screws that we found on the street. Mama gave me a spoiled carrot for the nose, and his mouth and arms were made from sticks. That year was so cold that he stood for more than a month. We even made him a snow family when more snow fell.

These images were among so many others, but not all of them were happy ones. I can easily recall the times when we lived in fear because we were Jewish. When I was a little girl, around eight years old, the first world war started. With it came a wave of hate for the Jews and many were forced to leave their homes. If we wanted to celebrate a Jewish holiday, we had to do so in hiding and behind closed doors. Although I didn't understand why at the time, I remember running through the streets with Papa to get the matzah during Passover. We went late in the evening when the sun was already down for the night. With the path illuminated only by the light of the moon, we carefully made our way to the Rabbi's house to collect the precious flatbread. Years later, after the first war, the tension eased, but not for long, and the hatred never actually left.

My parents were not as religious as others, but we regularly celebrated the high holidays. We spoke Yiddish at home, and most of our friends were Jewish. Mama was my support, a shoulder to lean on and an ear to listen to the ups and downs of my life. Without her, our family would have surely collapsed to pieces. When I was a little girl, Mama did everything for everybody. She never stopped, devoting her life to Papa and her four girls. She was as tidy as she was clumsy, and her rough overworked hands showed every hardship she had overcome in life. Papa on the other hand, was my light, perpetually guiding me in the right direction. He was the most stubborn person I knew, but also the most interesting and passionate. He was a tailor by trade and his attention to detail and patience was something I admired even as a young girl. As the eldest daughter, I was naturally the closest to Mama and Papa, and they looked to me to help take care of my sisters. As a child, I hated the responsibility, but as a mother, I was grateful because it helped me raise my own children.

As we stood before the entryway from my past, it seemed as if nothing had changed and Bobruisk was exactly the same as it was so many years ago. Except when the door swung open, I was no longer greeted by my Papa's youthful face. I threw myself into his arms. Running my fingers through his wavy grey hair and looking into his tired brown eyes, I realized how aged he was.

"Papa, it is so good to see you are well," I said, embracing the sudden sense of security that came from being in his warm arms.

His eyes glistened with tears, and his lips turned upward. "Raisa," he said, "We have been so worried about you. Come in, come in!"

When we walked in, we were welcomed by the entire family. Everybody had gathered to listen to the radio and talk about what to do. They were so happy to see us, and everyone embraced us lovingly.

"Where is Abraham?" Mama asked, worried. She came and sat by me on the sofa and reached her hand over to mine. Her rough hand felt like home, sending a rush of warmth through my veins.

"Five days ago, Abraham hurried home when he received word from his manager that the Nazis had entered Lithuania and were killing all the Jews. We packed our bags and planned on leaving early the next morning. Instead, we were awakened by the air raid signal and rushed to the bomb shelter...," I said as all eyes rested on mine.

"We had to run and it was so loud. I was scared the bombs were going to get us," Sofia chimed in, her face flushed as the memories rushed forward.

"Minsk turned into an unrecognizable city over a few hours. After the bombs stopped, people were everywhere, running, crying, screaming or lying quiet on the ground with nobody to mourn them. Most of the homes were destroyed, including ours." I felt myself begin to sweat as tears welled up in the corners of my eyes. Mama's hand clutched mine a little tighter, but I still wasn't sure how to continue.

"Raisa, I'm so sorry. I can't imagine what you have been through these last few days. Why are you only arriving today, why didn't you come by train?" Hana, my eldest sister asked.

"We went to the train station, but all the trains were full and while we were deciding what to do, the Red Army came and rounded up all the men to go to the front." I looked down at my hands hoping it would help to keep myself together, but I could no longer keep my emotions wrapped up.

"Oh, Raisa. Don't worry, my baby. Come here to me," Mama pulled me close to her triggering the release of tears I had held back. She gently ran her hand down the length of my back, reminding me that I wasn't alone anymore.

Noticing I needed a break, Luba finished, "After Papa left, we had to walk here because there were no trains." Everyone looked uncomfortable in their seats, suddenly sensing the gravity of what was happening.

"We must leave as soon as possible," I said, regaining my voice, "everyone needs to pack up and gather all the food they can carry. We must flee. The Nazis are nearing, and we need to go before they come."

"No, no, no. We aren't going anywhere," Papa shouted.

"But, Papa. We can't sit here and wait. Have you heard anything I have said?" I snapped back.

"They probably won't even make it all the way here. Even if they do, the last time the Fascists occupied Russia, they treated us better than the Russian soldiers. We can't pick up and leave. We are too old to run. Maybe you should all go, we will stay."

"No, Papa. If we go, we will all go together," my sister, Gita, chimed in. She sat on the chair next to Papa, perfect posture as usual, she hadn't changed one bit. I may not always agree with her, but this time we were on the same page, and her input was the most important to Papa, so I was glad she stepped in.

"When we were walking here, we met a Polish refugee named Ester. She told us unimaginable stories of what happened to her. So unthinkable that she couldn't have made it up," I said.

"That is Poland. How do you know that will happen here?" Papa said defensively.

"Papa just listen to what she told us." I took a few deep breaths and wondered if Papa had already made up his mind. He was stubborn, but I knew that I had to try convince him. We couldn't leave them here, I had to do something. I gathered my strength and began to tell him Ester's story, "When the Nazis arrived, they kicked everyone out of their homes to make room for themselves. Many of them were transported to other places and they placed all the remaining Jewish families inside a ghetto. Not like the ghettos from before, Papa. Soldiers tore apart their home searching for anything of value. They yanked the ring from her finger and stomped on the silver menorah before tossing it into a bag." Hana and Mama both gasped, while the others sank in their seats. Papa's face softened, but I knew he wasn't convinced yet. "All the Jews were crammed into a tiny section of run-down buildings with barely enough food to survive. The Nazis decided they wanted to clean up the city and they used the Jews to do it. She was ordered along with many others to clean the public toilets and sweep the streets. Then signs went up restricting when Jews were allowed to come and go from their homes. If someone was caught out past curfew, they often never made it home." Everyone listened, wide-eyed as I recounted all the horrible things Ester had told me. I found it hard to keep going. My neck was stiff with stress and my head ached, but I continued, pushing it away as best as I could. "Nazis regulated the hours of operation of the Jewish businesses. The orders continued to flood in, and the conditions only worsened. People were banned from baking bread, and soon after, the ghetto was entirely closed off from the outside world." I looked around the room, searching for an ally to help me with Papa. My eyes rested on Hana.

"That sounds awful. How did they get out?" Hana asked.

"I'm not sure exactly how, but she escaped with her husband. Not long after they fled from Poland, her husband was taken to the Red Army and she was left on her own."

"Papa, Raisa is right. We need to go. We can't sit here and wait. It is better to be safe than sorry," Hana said, pleading with Papa. Her cheeks flushed to match her rusty red hair.

"Alright. We will go together," Papa finally said, defeated.

For the next hour, everyone busied themselves packing clothes, valuables, and gathering food, while I went to pay a visit to Abraham's sister, Leia. It felt strange walking through the streets alone. I hadn't had a moment to myself for the past five days. At first, I breathed a sigh of relief, relishing in the time to myself, but that vanished quickly when my head began to spin with everything that had happened in the last week. I stopped walking and turned into a narrow alley between two buildings. I hadn't been walking quickly, but yet my breath was labored and my heart tightened. I ached for Abraham. I braced myself against the building and crouched into my hands unable to control the grief that had overtaken me, and wept.

Once I was able to pick up the pieces of myself and regain some composure, I stepped back out into the street headed to

Leia's house. I felt lighter, as if I had let go of a layer of myself, like a snake sheds his skin to allow itself to grow.

◆ ◆ ◆

Leia opened the door releasing the smell of fried onions and potatoes. "Raisa. What a surprise! Come in, come in," Leia said pulling me in for a hug. The aroma covered her like a blanket as I breathed her in.

"Come sit down. I'll be right back, I need to finish preparing dinner," Leia motioned to the sofa as she turned to the kitchen. It had been years since I had been there, but everything looked the same, only worn with age. I wished she would hurry, if we were to leave tonight, I needed to get back and try to rest. Fatigue had set in hours ago, I had no more energy, but was somehow still moving.

As the church bells in the distance struck two o'clock, Leia rushed back into the room. "I'm sorry it took me a few minutes. Tell me how you are," she said sitting down into the chair next to me.

"Luba, Sofia and I arrived in Bobruisk a few hours ago. We walked most of the way here from Minsk. The trains were all full. So many people are evacuating after the bombing in Minsk. Have you heard about this?" I asked, wondering if the news had filtered through all of Bobruisk yet.

"I did hear. We have all been worried about you. I'm so glad you made it out safely. Where is Abraham?" She asked flustered, suddenly realizing that I hadn't said his name.

"He was taken into the Red Army back in Minsk." My eyes stung as I replied. They welled up and clouded my vision for a moment.

Leia fumbled with her skirt and breathed heavy. "Are you going to stay here in Bobruisk then? With your family?" She asked, leading the conversation away from Abraham. She tried to hide her shaking hands in the folds of her skirt, but it was no use.

"No. That is why I am here. Before Abraham left, he asked me to come here. He really hopes that you and your family would go to Moscow and join your father and sister."

"Leave our home? Surely, the Nazis won't come this far!" Leia raised her voice in protest and stiffened in her chair.

"I think they will. They are advancing quickly. Please don't wait, gather your family and go at once. We are leaving tonight. I have convinced my Mama, Papa and sisters to go. We will likely head south, as I heard they are sending many evacuees there," I explained.

"I will talk to everyone tonight. I will tell them everything you said and do my best to make them go. I wish you luck on your journey. I will pray for you and Abraham, and your family." We both got up and Leia bent over to kiss my cheek. "Thank you for coming, my dear."

"Of course. You are family. I will pray for you as well. Please send letters to Abraham if you can, and let him know how you and the rest of the family are doing. Send it to the military post office with his information and they will forward it to him."

"I will. Be safe," she called out after me.

The bells struck three on the walk back to my parent's house. I dragged myself through the streets afraid that if I stopped, I wouldn't be able to continue. I was emotionally drained and my feet and legs were ready to give out.

Once I got back, I took a short break and then we washed up and I helped my family finish to pack their belongings. Papa busied himself easily fixing Luba's shoe with a thick needle and thread. I wished our life could be mended with such simplicity. We took a few hours to nap and eat lunch. None of us were ready to leave and go into the unknown. We lost ourselves inside our own minds, struggling to make sense of the life unraveling before us. It wasn't so long ago that I was under my parents' roof in happier times.

CHAPTER FOUR
ANXIOUS EYES

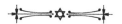

11 JANUARY 1925
Bobruisk, Belarus, USSR

It was early when I woke up in my parent's house. Darkness still scattered about the room. Butterflies began to flutter inside my stomach and my heart beat lightly with excitement.

I lay in bed for a few more minutes breathing in everything around me. Twelve days before, the stroke of midnight changed the year to nineteen twenty-five and brought a surge of optimism for the future. On the sixth of January we celebrated my nineteenth birthday, and this morning would be the last time I would wake up in this bed, in this room with my parents and sisters. That night, I would marry Abraham, the man of my dreams, and move into the room next door to start our new life.

I quietly slid out of bed and put on the warm clothes draped over the chair next to me. I tiptoed out of the room and threw on my fur-trimmed coat and hat before opening the front door. A gust of frozen air slapped my face like a sudden rush of adrenaline. The sun was just beginning to make its way up, and the blanket of snow shimmered around me. The trees looked like they were caked with pearl-white icing, and their branches were weighed down as if they carried the weight of the world. Everything looked perfectly calm and untouched. My brown boots sank into the stiff snow, and as I made my way to the outhouse, the sky burst into color.

I shut the door of the outhouse and turned to head back towards the house. Papa now stood outside in the same place I had been a few minutes earlier. It was his typical stance, arms behind his back with one hand grasping the other arm's wrist. He stared out into the winter wonderland with anxious eyes.

"Papa, I'm sorry," I said, "Did I wake you?"

"No, no, Raisa. I couldn't sleep. Why are you up so early?" asked Papa, as he wrapped his arm around my shoulder.

"I am excited for the day to begin."

"Are you nervous?" He asked me, measuring my expression.

"No, I am incredibly happy, Papa. Abraham is wonderful. I am so lucky we found each other."

"Good," Papa said, "Now let's get inside before we freeze out here. How about I make us some tea?" Snowflakes fell around us, twirling and dancing their way through the soft wind.

"Of course, Papa. I would like that." Inside, we found the rest of my family had awakened. It felt like my birthday because everybody smiled when they saw me and gave me a warm hug. It was hard to imagine that life was going to be much different than it was now. Abraham and I would stay in the small room next door, but somewhere deep inside I knew that after tonight everything would change. I would no longer be a girl; I would be a woman. I felt my face blush as I thought about it, as I thought about Abraham.

Our relationship was an unusual one. Most of my Jewish girlfriends had their husband chosen for them. They had to learn to love their husband after they married. I fell in love with Abraham the moment we locked eyes. That instance became the start of a new chapter in my life, marking the story of how it all began. We were both guests at my friend Maria's wedding. He was the only person in the room my eyes were instantly drawn to. He stood taller than any other man in the room, over two meters tall, and his gentle eyes smiled at me with such warmth that happiness radiated from within me.

It was frowned upon to spend time alone with a man that you were not married to, but from the moment we met, we became inseparable. Our parents did not know, so of course we only saw each other when no one else was around. Abraham was the kindest man I had ever met and the love that he had for me exceeded every expectation I had ever imagined.

Sometimes we secretly met in the park and walked hand in hand among the stillness of the evergreen trees. Each time his hand grazed my skin, a flutter of excitement turned my cheeks a shade warmer. We talked for hours, but it felt as if we had known each other for years. Even the cold air didn't bother me. Being near him saturated me with warm emotions. I loved it when he talked about his profession, watchmaking. His words sped up, and his eyebrows lifted in excitement as he spoke about it. It was easy to tell that he was not only passionate, but also good at his job. His dream was to own a small shop in the center of town.

A few days earlier, he described exactly how he imagined it… "It will have a large window in front with a display of watches. Next to the watches would be my favorite item in the window. I saw one of them in a store in Minsk, and ever since, I have dreamt about it. It was a miniature watchmaker automaton sitting at his table. He had an eye loupe and held tweezers in his right hand. There were tiny watch parts on his table and even little tools. When it was plugged into electricity, the watchmaker continuously moved his head and tweezers up and down, as if he was working on a watch. I know it would catch people's attention as they walked by, just as it had mine. Inside, I want a simple shop with my bench and tools off to one side and a small case with watches on the other side. I wouldn't need much, but a place of my own is something I have wished for."

"That sounds amazing," I said, "I hope that one day you get to have your own place, I think that would be incredible." I gave him a quick smile and soon our conversation floated away to another topic equally as engaging.

Each time we met, we grew closer. I longed for his soft touch and to breathe his scent as he bent over to embrace me. He was as respectful as he was romantic. I loved that he possessed a confidence that was not overwhelming; instead, it was charming. Abraham comforted me with his gentleness, which made sharing my thoughts with him second nature. We spoke of our fears, mainly about feeling like outsiders in our country, but also about our future aspirations.

After about three weeks of meeting in secret, I was home daydreaming about Abraham when there was a knock on our door. Papa answered, and I instantly knew it was him. He towered over my father and his deep voice resonated throughout the house.

"Hello, my name is Abraham Tsalkind. May I come in?"

"Yes, come in," Papa answered, unsure of himself. I glanced over at Abraham and wondered why he did not tell me his plans to come to my house.

Abraham sat down on the worn couch across from my father. He looked over at me and smiled before confidently saying, "Samuel Moiseevich, I would like to ask your permission to take your daughter, Raisa's hand in marriage. We met last month at a wedding and as soon I saw her, I knew I was madly in love with her. We have seen each other since and gotten to know each other better. Your daughter is the other half of my heart. I promise to take care of her until the day I die. If she will take me, of course."

Mama came to me and grabbed my hand. She looked me in the eye.

"Mama, I love him," I whispered. She looked briefly at Papa to give him the nod of approval.

"Tell me more about yourself and your family," Papa asked him as he shuffled nervously in his chair.

"I am a watchmaker," Abraham said, "I have two brothers and three sisters. My father is a locksmith. I was born in Bobruisk, but we moved away when I was a young child to Mogilev. We moved back about a year ago. Some friends helped me find a watchmaking job here in Bobruisk."

"Is your older sister Leia?" Papa asked suddenly perking up. "Did she marry into the Altshuler family?"

"Yes, that is correct," Abraham said, "They live nearby. They have a little girl, Riva, and they expect another baby in a few months."

Papa sat for a moment and looked back at me and my sisters, who now stood right beside me, waiting in anticipation.

"They are a good family..." he started to say, then paused for what seemed like forever. "I am usually a good judge of character, and I sense you are a good man. I can tell by the look on my daughter's face that you have clearly impressed her. I give you my blessing."

I couldn't believe it. I stood in the middle of the house for a moment relishing in the excitement, letting it become a part of me. I tried to think back to a time which made me happier, but I couldn't recall one. Mama invited Abraham to stay and have some lunch while getting to know each other a bit better. Not long after we sat down to eat, everyone was laughing and chatting away so much that it seemed as if Abraham had been a part of our family for years. Afterwards, I walked Abraham out.

I looked up at him like I had so many times these past few weeks, but this time I overflowed with pure joy. I playfully intertwined my hands inside of his.

"Why didn't you tell me you were going to ask Papa?" I asked.

"I didn't know yesterday," Abraham said. "After we parted last night, I couldn't stop thinking about you. You were in my thoughts at every moment. Everywhere I looked reminded me of you. When I closed my eyes to sleep, I imagined us married and starting a family. When I woke this morning, I knew what

I needed to do. I couldn't continue another day without knowing if you would be with me forever."

I felt so lucky and full of love in that moment, but all I could manage to say was, "When can we marry?"

"Next month you turn nineteen," Abraham said, "how about right after your birthday?"

"I would love that." I replied not knowing how I could wait that long. It all seemed so perfect, almost too perfect, but I knew deep down that Abraham was the right man for me. After the shock passed, I allowed myself to breathe and let the excitement and happiness sweep through me.

♦ ♦ ♦

The next few weeks spun in a blur of excitement as we let our friends and family know about our engagement. Abraham and I went with our parents to the *ZAGS* office, where we signed the official marriage certificate. In my eyes though, the next day was our real wedding, when our Rabbi, family, and friends were there to witness the beginning of our journey as husband and wife.

Mama and my sisters helped me get ready. I put my hair in a bun, letting a few curls frame the sides of my face, and applied my makeup. Mama helped me slip into my dress. I meandered over to the mirror and took one last look at myself. I was glowing as much on the outside as I was on the inside. I couldn't wait for Abraham to see me.

Papa came in a few minutes later. Our eyes met, and the proud look on his face made me smile. He paused for a few moments, as if replaying in his mind the highlights from the moment I was born until this very day. Suddenly, his smile grew, and his eyes moistened.

"You are a beautiful bride," he said, as he wiped a tear rolling down his cheek. "You are an incredible daughter, and today you will become an even better wife. I love you."

"I couldn't have said it any better, my dear," Mama said, swallowing her tears back. "We are so proud of the woman you have become. We better go my love. Abraham is waiting for you."

I put on my coat and we headed to his parents' house where Abraham and I were to be married. As soon as we saw each other, my heart filled with happiness. His gorgeous grey eyes assured me yet again that I was safe and that I would forever be loved. As the Rabbi concluded his blessings, he handed Abraham a glass wrapped in a blue handkerchief and explained to us that joy must always be tempered. The ceremony ended with a bang as Abraham stepped confidently on the glass, breaking it on the first try.

After our family and friends clapped for us, Abraham turned outwards. His hands held mine as he addressed the room.

"I would like to say a few words to my bride, and I have something I would like to give her," he said. He turned towards me once again, reached into his pocket, and pulled out a box. "This is for you, my love. May it forever remind you of this beautiful day."

My heartbeat quickened as I carefully untied the bow, trying to guess what could be inside. A velvet box the color of deep red wine trembled ever so slightly in the palm of my hand. The velvet was so soft and luxurious. I knew it had to contain something special. I opened it and felt my eyes widen with delight. Inside lay a small silver Star of David on a delicate silver chain.

"Abraham, this is incredibly beautiful," I said, trying to hold back my tears of happiness.

"I believe this *Mogein Dovid* is not only a symbol of our faith, but also of our unity." Abraham took the necklace from the box and gently held it between his slender fingers. "When I look into the center, I see our foundation, the start of our life together. Interwoven from the center are the six points, which play a significant role in our future as husband and wife. Starting from the bottom is love. Our foundation is rooted in our love for each other and our future children. Next, is faith, then honesty. Opposite of love is family, taking its position at the top. And lastly, but surely not least, are happiness and, most importantly, health. May this symbol remind us of who we are, and of what we are meant to become together."

Abraham motioned for me to turn around and then carefully helped me put it on. I glanced over at Mama and Papa and I was moved by how happy they looked. Their tears of joy flowed freely as they pressed together in a warm embrace.

I turned and looked up once again into his eyes. "Abraham, I promise that I will love you until death do us part. I will have faith in you no matter the hardships. I will be always truthful, for I have never met a more honest man than you. Together we will make a family that thrives on happiness. And, I hope more than anything in this world that we will grow old together, always remembering what brought us there. I love you, Abraham."

We turned to face our family, and our hands met with ease as we walked down the makeshift aisle. Each smiling face that greeted us was like a ray of sunlight, illuminating the room with warmth and happiness. When we reached the end, Abraham lifted me off my feet and twirled me around while his soft lips gently met mine.

After the ceremony, we took our places at the head of the table. A line of friendly faces extended down the room as each of our guests waited their turn to greet us.

"My dear Raisa and Abraham. Please take this gift from Papa and I and use it for your new life together." Mama handed me a small sealed envelope with our names beautifully written across it. "May the pathway to your life together be winding, with twists and turns so you continue to balance and surprise one another. But at the same time, heading forward, towards the future, never regretting the past, and loving each other with every breath." The familiar scent of her intense perfume struck me as we kissed and hugged.

Mama had a way with words, especially when it came to weddings and birthdays. For special occasions she would give my sisters and me cards with poems or stories scrawled in the neatest penmanship I had ever seen. Each letter was so elegantly formed that the words came together like intricate lace.

As the envelopes piled up in a mound on the table and the line had dwindled down to a few guests, I noticed how full the tables began to look. The food was prepared by the women in our families and everything looked as if it was made by an artist. The pickled mushrooms didn't simply sit in the bowls, they were cleverly arranged amidst the other vegetables. Radishes were cut to look like red mushrooms. The dessert table included a rainbow of fruits placed in the shape of flowers while the swan shaped pastries sat elegantly among them.

Once all of our guests found a seat, we each held up a shot glass of vodka. After a speech to our future, we drank the bitter vodka, and kissed the bitterness away, as the whole room chanted, "*Gorko, Gorko, Gorko…*" Everyone drank lightheartedly and enjoyed the food. Each toast was prepared with such thoughtfulness and included many well wishes. As the night continued, I only felt more loved and blessed to be a part of two families.

"*Hava Nagila, Hava Nagila, Hava nagila ve-nismeha…*" Suddenly, Abraham and I were lifted up on chairs above the heads of our guests. Our friends and family sang the folk song about rejoicing loudly as they formed circles around us. They held hands and whirled around us, celebrating in song and dance. Abraham and I were connected by a single white napkin that I held onto with one hand as the other gripped the chair, hoping I wouldn't fall off as we bobbed up and down to the beat of the music. My necklace bounced around reminding me of the importance of this beautiful day, and as the dusk turned to darkness, and Abraham held me tightly through the night, my thoughts drifted to our future.

CHAPTER FIVE
ENDLESS

1 JULY 1941
Bobruisk, Belarus, USSR

In the early evening of the twenty-eighth, the nine of us walked hurriedly to the Bobruisk train station. The sky filled with dark grey wispy clouds and hid the sun. A foggy mist made the air cool and refreshing as we rushed through it.

Luba, Sofia and I led the way. My sisters, Hana, Gita and Lubov followed right behind us. Oscar, Hana's little boy, trailed in the back with his grandparents. He held firmly onto Deda's hand, and it was obvious that he had taken over the role of being the father figure ever since his own father passed away two years earlier.

The first train arrived and was so full, that only five people in front of us were able to squeeze in before the doors closed and it whizzed away as fast as it came. The next train however, arrived about an hour later and the nine of us made our way on. There were no seats, and most people sat on the floor with their belongings, or simply stood. It was not a regular passenger train, but freight cars with nothing inside and only a few small windows towards the top. We sat together in one cluster holding our belongings. The cold metal floor was hard and unforgiving. The train was crammed with so many people, there was hardly any room to breathe, and because we sat in the middle, we couldn't even look out of the windows on the ends of the car. The rocking made me nauseous, and the smell of stale urine, vomit and feces didn't help. Poor Luba looked sicker than I felt. Even in the dim lighting I noticed the color had drained from her face. I could tell that she was going to be sick several times. She tried so hard not to let it come out, but the smell and the rocking were unbearable. When she could no longer contain herself, we pushed through the crowds to a bucket in the corner of the train car and she threw up. I held her and tried to make her feel better. Just when I thought there was nothing left, she inhaled another whiff of the air and heaved over the bucket.

I held her shivering body close to mine as I fashioned my scarf over her nose to filter out the foul smells. Her face looked pale and blue as we pushed our way back to the rest of our family. We were on the train for what seemed like days, but when we stopped at the next station, I caught a glimpse of the clock, and it had only been a few hours. The doors would open, and through the cracks, we saw the desperate people on the platform staring back at us, hoping to find some room on the train. No one exited our train car, so the doors closed once more, and we continued on our journey. Time seemed to drag on forever and without something to focus on, I began to think about Abraham. I wondered what he was going through and if he was doing better than we were. I tried to imagine him at the training center, well fed and making new friends. Of course, I had no idea where he was or what he was doing, but I had to hold onto that hope. I pushed away the awful images of what could be before they made me cry. I looked over at Luba and Sofia bouncing to and fro with the bumps of the train. The softness of the edges of their faces seemed to have disappeared and they suddenly looked much older. They had both been so brave. I wished I could tell Abraham, he would have been proud of our girls.

At the end of the day, part of me longed to walk outside again, even if that meant being sore all over. My belly growled with hunger, but the thought of food made my stomach turn. How could one eat anything with the stench of bile and feces all around you? When the sun started to set, I realized we had no choice but to eat before there would be no light left.

"Luba, Sofia, we must eat now. I know the smell is unbearable, but come a little closer to me, and I want you to hold your piece of cheese right under your nose while you eat your bread. Let's try," I whispered, as I handed them each a piece of cheese and bread. It did help mask the awful stench, and we were all able to eat the meager meal.

The train stopped often at junctions and small stations, but we never knew for how long. We quickly learned that these stops were our only chance for a bathroom break. There were no steps or ladders and we had to jump and help each other to get on and off safely. With no time to worry about being modest, we squatted down right next to the train cars and carefully hopped our way back through a minefield of pungent piles to get back in time.

The first overnight ride we had on the train seemed endless. In the last light of the day I noticed my parents looked pale right before the sun began to set. Gita and Lubov sat with their hands interlocked and their heads resting on one another. Hana sat nearest to me with Oscar by her side. His brown hair fell in waves, framing his round chubby face and brown eyes. Baba insisted that it was time to cut it, but Hana said she could not get herself to cut his baby curls, even if he was already five years old. His head lay in her lap and his eyes begin to close as he stared at his favorite toy snuggled tightly in his hands. It was a miniature plastic Pinocchio figurine. The doll's arms and legs moved back and forth stiffly. I could tell by the faded paint that Oscar had given the little Pinocchio a great deal of love.

Sofia, Luba and I held each other close, and I tried to close my eyes to sleep, but sleep never came. The sounds of the train, the screeching, the clacking, and the wails of the babies right next to us were a constant reminder of our dreadful surroundings. Every time I started to doze off, I was awakened again, and the night dragged on and on until the sound of nearby explosions jolted us from our sleep.

"Mama, what is happening?" Sofia asked, "What was that noise?"

Her eyes swelled with fright as the sounds grew louder. Fear ignited inside the train car like a blazing fire. "They are bombs," I said.

Shock creeped into my veins sending a rush to my head. I became nauseous from the hurricane of panic and confusion all around me. The train came to a sudden halt, the doors were flung open, and people started to jump out and run.

"Luba, Sofia, you hold onto me and don't let go. Run as quickly as you can," I said looking into their eyes for reassurance.

Luckily, we had our bags on our backs, and we ran out as quickly as the crowd in front allowed. When we escaped the train, there was no shelter to protect us. We became moving targets, like deer in a meadow. The next wave of planes roared towards us, with bombs dropping around us like thunder. I didn't know what to do so I threw the girls on the ground in front of me and I covered them both with my body. I tasted the stench of sweat from the girls' clothes. The pounding of my heart echoed underneath our bodies. I squeezed my eyes shut and braced for the worst. We lay there until there were no more sounds except the cries of people around us. We slowly picked ourselves up and looked at each other to make sure we were unharmed. We found the rest of our family and embraced them, thanking God for our safety.

I looked around and saw the carnage before us. The deceased were scattered across the field like pieces of a jigsaw puzzle, with their relatives bent over them in agony. People ran and screamed in search of someone they had lost in the commotion. There were entire train cars that had been hit with bombs, and people began to help unload the deceased. Bodies littered the side of the tracks, with no one able to properly mourn their loss and bury them. We had to keep moving, and as hard as it was, we had no choice. Mechanics checked the train cars and tracks for damage. I hoped that they were fine so we could leave, because the thought of looking at the devastation before us for much longer was unbearable. The wailing of the grieving families weighed heavily on my heart and even then, I knew their cries would forever replay in my mind. Luckily, the tracks escaped harm, so we shuffled back onto the remaining train cars.

We had plenty of space to stretch our legs. I should have been able to breathe freer, but instead I felt guilty taking up the space which was occupied by someone's loved one only hours ago. I was weak as the tingling slowly dissipated from my body. The train became quiet as people around us held their heads low to pray and take a moment of silence. I prayed for Abraham. I prayed for the girls. I prayed for the entire family. I had only one request, our lives.

Once the shock subsided, a storm began to brew inside the train. People were no longer distraught; they were angry with worry.

A woman clutched onto her frightened son. "Oy, my Papa. Papa, Papa, Papa. Why did you leave us alone? Why?" she moaned in agony, willing for a response she would never receive.

I stroked my hand over my necklace, feeling each rounded point underneath my sweaty fingers. I tried to close my eyes and disappear into a faraway memory, but instead they shifted from one dark corner to another, unable to escape the heartache. Another woman who sat across from us cried into her handkerchief. Her weeping echoed along with the others into a somber harmony.

The constant mourning of those around us became louder in my mind as the train continued forward for hours until we arrived in Kiev.

♦ ♦ ♦

I stepped out of the train still caught in a mixture of emotions, and my head hung heavy as I attempted to process them all. Fear had nearly strangled the life out of me, but luckily, I had the girls to keep me grounded. Anxiety tugged at every part of my soul as I processed our broken past and unknown future. I wondered how much more my girls would have to endure. I tried to look strong for Luba and Sofia. If I was scared, I knew they must have been too, and I wanted to help them. I wished I could erase the past few days and take away all the devastation from their pure, innocent hearts. Instead, I did all I could think of. I took Sofia by the hand and I tried to distract her by singing some of her favorite songs.

I admired the birds as they carelessly chirped away, wishing I had their freedom as we sat and waited in line with the thousands of other evacuees waiting for the same thing. A way out. The girls sang and moved about to help the time pass. In the larger stations we went in small groups to the bathroom and suffered through more long lines only to use the toilet. We tried to save our food as best as possible, but as the night drew nearer, we became hungry.

At some train stations, there were areas right outside or across from the station which were set up for refugees. Here you were able to obtain some hot food and boiled water. Often, they had little to no food left and after standing in line, you could be turned away with nothing, but nevertheless, it was worth trying. Hana, Gita, Lubov and I decided to go together to see if we could get dinner for everyone. The four of us walked with our arms intertwined, connecting us together like an unbreakable chain.

"Do you think that Mama and Papa are feeling alright? Papa is so stubborn, even if he was physically hurting, he would not admit it," Gita asked out loud what I had been pondering for a while. It wasn't surprising. She had always been the most outspoken of the four of us. She was a strong-willed investigative attorney. Her eyes reminded me of Mama's, and her neatly made bun was habitually done precisely the same way. Gita had a confidence about herself that can sometimes be pushy, but I knew she had a kind heart. She was in her own category, persistently doing everything her way. She studied hard and fought her way into her job. Although I was not particularly close to her, in many ways, I looked up to her and her ability to be such a powerful, self-sufficient woman.

"I also wondered about this. And what about Mama, she has mentioned her back pain a few times and sometimes I catch her flinch in pain. I pray every day that they will make it through this," Hana added.

We walked on for a few minutes and I tried to figure out what to say. As the oldest, it was up to me to try to keep them thinking positively. I had seen how pale my parent's faces had become, but worrying only made matters worse. "The journey has definitely taken a toll on them, so we have to work together and make sure they eat and rest as much as possible. We are fighters and we will get through this, all of us will, I promise." It seemed to be enough for now, and soon we began talking about something else. As we approached the line for food, we were thankful to see that the people walking back had bowls with hot soup.

We waited in line for about an hour until it was our turn. I rejoiced inside when I realized there would be enough food for all of us. The tall, skinny lady at the front looked at our papers and counted out our portions. Her stony expression was accompanied by her abrupt motions as she counted the ladle servings into each bowl. Thankfully, Mama had brought her aluminum pot along from home, so we poured the portions inside and carefully carried our pot of gold back to the others.

We enjoyed the warm soup, even if it was merely salted water with a few potatoes and barley. We savored the bits of potatoes and there were even some strands of carrots. Luba was generally the slowest to eat. She took the tiniest bite possible and kept it in her mouth for a while. She said it made it seem like it lasted longer, or somehow that there was more of it. Sofia couldn't wait to eat her food, and finished her portion before I could even start mine. Even though it was warm outside, it was nice to have a warm meal. It heated us up from within and filled our hungry bellies.

The trains whizzed by, and people were able to board, so the line became shorter, but very slowly. Although we knew that we would be waiting a long time, at least we were not walking by foot or smelling the foul odors like before. I hoped we wouldn't spend the entire night in the darkness again. Time seemed distorted as we switched from trains to crowded stations. Among the chaos I looked for the moments of peace.

"Luba, do you want to play cards?" Lubov asked. Their newfound friendship made me smile. It was nice that Luba had someone to talk to. Lubov, my youngest sister was nineteen, only three years older than our Luba. She was studying to be a lawyer like Gita, and although she was smart like her, she had a softer side. I frequently thought of her as a combination of Gita, Hana and myself. She had a way about her that I loved—she was a perfect balance of smart, strong and loving.

"Sure," Luba answered, "What are we playing?"

"Durak?"

"Yes, but you deal first," Luba said, handing the cards to Lubov. Lubov dealt six cards to herself and six to Luba. The next card was a queen of hearts, the trump card. Watching them play was almost as fun as playing, if not more. The world around them seemed to fade into the distance as they threw down cards. The sounds of their chatter and laughter brought a smile to my face, even when I didn't think any form of happiness was possible.

As the night closed in, my body began to scream. The lack of sleep had exhausted me. I sat next to Sofia, holding her hand, until my eyelids became too heavy to hold open anymore. A few hours later Hana woke me. We moved forward in line as another train had arrived and gone, and I hoped that we would get onto a train by the morning. For the remainder of the night, we took turns taking naps, and getting some much-needed rest.

The next time my eyes opened, the sun was beginning to rise. A train approached, sending a breeze through the crowded platform, and the people in front of us moved forward. We walked down the platform to see if there were any cars available. We were lucky. We found one close to the end that had room for our entire family.

CHAPTER SIX
FEAR ALL AROUND ME

2 JULY 1941
Kiev, Ukraine, USSR

As we boarded the train in Kiev, a sense of relief overcame us. The train station was a chaotic mess; people were everywhere, waiting and hoping to get onto a train. We once again pushed onto a freight car, this time with no room to move around. I wondered if there would be enough air to breathe for all of us. The sick feeling Luba had the first time on the train came back with vengeance. At first, she was able to keep herself together, but soon enough she was back hunched over releasing the small amount of food she had in her belly. This time, however we didn't make it to the bucket, and it ended up all over our shoes and some vomit landed on the older woman next to us.

"Look at what she did! Can't you take your child to the bucket to be sick? She made such a mess!" the woman shouted at me, her cheeks red with anger and her eyes enraged.

"What is wrong with you? She is sick! Don't be such a witch!" I snapped back at her. She shot me an evil glance and found herself a new spot, while I tried to wipe as much of the mess off our shoes and the floor, but I couldn't wipe away the smell that began to permeate throughout the hot train.

"I'm sorry Mama. I got it on both of our shoes. I feel terrible…" Before she finished, tears swelled up in her sad little eyes and as they slid down her face, my chest tightened.

"Luba, come lean over close to me and try to focus on the window up there. I know you can't see much of the outside, but you can see the sky and trees as they go by. It might help with your motion sickness. I love you honey. I am so sorry. If I could, I would take your pain away," I whispered into Luba's ear.

Luba leaned against me, while Sofia laid her head on my lap. The stench radiating through the train paired with the constant swaying motion also made me queasy. I could make out the trees and the sky whizzing by and having something to focus on helped. I tried to forget where we were, but I sensed the eyes of the other passengers peering at us with resentment, as they too had to inhale the awful stench.

"Luba, is it working for you?" I asked.

"Yes, I do feel a little better. Thank you, Mama."

Luba's soft, warm body nuzzled up against me, and Sofia's curls cascaded onto my lap. Holding the girls close gave me comfort. I wished I could capture these moments when time stood still, even if it was for barely a minute, it was my minute of peace.

As time passed, my body started to get acclimated to the train, but my mind took over. Whenever I closed my eyes, all I saw was the devastation around us. I saw our home burnt to ashes. I saw us running for shelter as the bombs whistled above us. I saw the perished bodies lying in the dirt, each of their faces ingrained in my memory forever. The images were so vivid that I could almost reach out and touch them, each vision saturated with its own smell and emotion. I tried to wipe them away, but I kept seeing them as if they were etched into my eyelids.

In order to escape from my mind, I tried to focus on something else. Sometimes, I looked at the people nearby and searched for hope in someone's eyes or the innocence of a child playing, oblivious to the turmoil around us. I loved how easy it was for children to distract themselves. I watched Oscar pick up a rock and play with it for an hour. I wished I could be so carefree. Hours passed and the stations passed by as our train headed towards Stalingrad.

As we rode further into the countryside, the warmth of the early morning sun began to heat up the train. My spirits were lifted when we soon made a stop in a small village called Izmalkovo. A tiny sign and a wooden bench, which was falling apart, marked the station. A woman who sat near the door opened it wide to take in the fresh air. As the door slid open with a screech, we were greeted by the local women and children. "Get your fresh fruits and vegetables," they chanted as they walked towards the train. Their tired sun-kissed faces flashed eager eyes as the doors opened like dominoes. The women carried large baskets of vegetables as they walked down the platform calling out their wares. The children stood closely behind them with smaller baskets of fruit. I instantly saw by their clothing that these were simple, hard-working country people. All of them wore light colors to reflect the sun while they worked on the farm, but to me they only reflected the stains of their toil. They sold the little food they had in exchange for rubles or anything valuable. Everyone pushed forward with their arms outstretched, shouting over the next person to tell them what they wanted. I hoped that we would be next, and the train wouldn't leave before we had a chance to buy.

"Four tomatoes, a bag of sour cherries, five cucumbers and four apples! How much?" I shouted to the woman nearest me. Her long blond hair rested on her shoulder in one thick braid. She wore a turquoise scarf over her head that matched her eyes. She gathered the items as I called them out.

"That will be twenty-one rubles. I also have some kielbasa. It is eight rubles per link, would you like some? It is my last bundle."

"Yes, we would like two. Here is the money. Thank you!" I couldn't help but feel lucky in a place where luck did not seem to exist. With this blessing, our family would finally fill our empty stomachs with fresh fruit and vegetables.

I hugged our bundle of fresh food wrapped in newspaper as I made my way back to the other side of the train car. I unfolded the *Pravda* newspaper and noticed it was almost two years old, dated August twenty-fourth, nineteen thirty-nine.

"Look, it's the issue with Stalin and Molotov after signing the German-Soviet nonaggression treaty," I said as I passed it to Papa.

Papa turned towards me and quietly replied, "How ironic, look what good that did."

♦ ♦ ♦

It was afternoon when we began to stir. The sounds were distant at first, but still caught our attention. Sofia shouted over the raised voices inside the train, "Mama what is that noise?"

"That sounds like gun fire!" Were they shooting at the train? At once the walls surrounding us no longer felt like protection. "Stay down, crouch on the floor." A rush went to my head as I knelt beside the girls and my family, sending me off balance. The familiar whir of the airplanes drew closer.

The train came to a jarring halt. Everybody was shoved into the person in front of them with such force, that panic rippled through the train with a wave of screams. The train was under attack, and people fled to find safety. As we ran into the forest, the terror-stricken screams and the rattle of bullets surrounded us. Sofia tripped and scraped her palms, but we couldn't stop to tend to her wounds. I quickly pulled her up, held onto her arm and helped her move forward as fast as we could. Papa led our family and we huddled together and hid behind a large tree. Nazi planes flew low and aimed at fleeing people. The swastikas on the sides of the planes would be another image carved into my mind forever.

I held Sofia and Luba underneath me. Sofia shook in fear, and although I couldn't hear her, I knew she was crying as well. I held onto them both a little tighter and closed my eyes for what seemed to be an eternity. My necklace clung to the sweat on my neck as I prayed for us to survive.

"Is everybody alright, was anyone hurt? Are we all here?" Mama shouted as she checked everyone to make sure we were whole. Tears of happiness rolled down her face as she realized we were all safe.

I looked into Sofia's puffy eyes and gave her a warm hug, wishing that it would take her fear away. I searched around for some Plantago plants, and found two leaves, about the size of her palms. I placed them onto her hands and put them together so the leaves would stay without moving. "Hold your hands together like this, my dear. These leaves will help heal the wound, as they kill the germs. My Baba taught me about this plant when I was a little girl like you."

With our ears still ringing, we cautiously joined the others as they headed back towards the train. Walking back to the train was just as difficult as running away from it. Even though we had been through this days earlier, it didn't make seeing bodies strewn across the grass like autumn leaves any easier. There was no way to tune out the wailing of the people in mourning. And there was surely no way to avoid the anguish that swelled up inside me.

I smelled fear all around me. We were running for our lives into the unknown. None of us knew when or where our final destination would be and most importantly if we would all even make it there. How could our lives have changed so much in just one week?

We sat under the melting sun, trembling like icicles with panic. We waited nearby while the train and the tracks were checked for damage and the foremen made sure the train was able to continue. As the minutes and the hours ticked by, the sobbing of the suffering may have become softer, but their sorrow only grew greater. Once the train was inspected, we boarded and started moving. It was easy to feel the loss of those left behind as I scanned over the emptiness of the train car. Looking over at my family, I tried to understand the meaning of all that had happened. Why would the Nazis shoot at unarmed families? How could a human commit such atrocities to another human? I simply couldn't understand it, and the more I thought about it, the more painful it was. We spent the remainder of the day on the train and as night fell, I watched the eyelids of the people around me begin to close like candles blown out one by one. I succumbed to sleep sometime deep into the night. I awoke early in the morning as the sunlight peeked through the bullet holes, sending beams of light flickering about.

"Did you get some sleep my love?" I asked Sofia, whispering in her ear when she awoke.

"I did, Mama."

Not long after, the rest of the family slowly started to wake up. Grief was splashed on our faces, but at least our eyes showed more life than they had the day before.

"How about some breakfast everyone?" I asked as I reached into my bag to get out the package of food that we had recently bought. We learned quickly to be careful about how much and when we ate. We tried to eat the smallest portions possible, so we always had food left, just in case. My biggest fear was to be left without any food for my girls, so sometimes I took a smaller portion for myself.

We had run out of water hours ago and couldn't continue much longer without it. Luckily, we were nearing the next station. Usually one or two of us would run out to replenish. We never knew how long the train would be stopped, so we had to hurry. Separating was a huge risk, as we witnessed families become separated far too often, but to be without water was also unhealthy. This time I offered to run and get it.

I jumped out of the train and chaos was all around me. My heart thumped so hard, it felt like it was about to burst out of my chest. My sweaty palms gripped the beat-up aluminum flask. Adrenaline raced through my veins as I made my way to the line for the boiled water. I looked back to make sure the train was still there, but the crowds of people blocked my view. The thought of being away from my girls frightened me, so I kept reminding myself that I couldn't allow us to get separated. My turn to fill up the canteen with hot water came in a few minutes. I raced back to the train fighting my way through the crowd. It was already slowly moving, and passengers started to close the doors. I screamed, "Wait, don't close the doors please!" Luba and Sofia motioned for me to hurry. I locked my eyes onto theirs and ran as fast as I could. The train accelerated slowly, but I would not have made it if I had been a minute later. A thin old man held the door and pulled me in. The girls drew me in close, their hearts beating with fear just as loudly as mine.

◆ ◆ ◆

We continued our journey eastward for the entire morning. Then the train stopped for reasons unknown and we sat on the unmoving train well into the early evening. Usually, we didn't get off because we felt safer inside. Maybe we were afraid of being left behind, or being spotted when a Nazi plane flew overhead. Sometimes, however, if we were hungry and lucky enough to have a train car with a working stove, we went in search of nettles. The plants grew in large groups, making them easy to spot. The green, slightly fuzzy leaves stung when touched, but that could be avoided if picked by the stems. Once boiled, they made quite a nutritious soup. We used every trick we could remember that had been passed down through the generations to keep our stomachs from going hungry.

This morning was a nice break from the constant bumps, swaying and confinement. When we were stopped, we were able to have the doors open. This sent a breeze through the car changing the filthy stench to fresh forest air.

We looked out at the beautiful scenery and admired the tall trees standing firmly before us. I imagined myself, Abraham, and the girls walking through the forest picking berries and collecting mushrooms. There were deer prints on the ground below us as we made our way deeper into the forest. The sounds of rustling leaves and laughter rang through my ears as my thoughts drifted from one fantasy to the next.

"What are you thinking about, my love?" Papa whispered into my ear. I told him a little about my dreams that the forest inspired me to have during the lonely hours that day. "Those dreams will be real again someday. I know it seems far away and unreachable, but I promise one day you will be happy again. Dream away my dear and we will race towards them." Papa's words sank deep into my heart and I hoped he would be right.

As the sun descended onto the horizon and the sky filled with color, the train doors closed, and we continued on through another long night. Waking up the next morning was the same as the morning before, but each day that passed, the burdens people carried began to show on their faces. Children became more and more agitated and hungry, and some started to look ill. None of us knew what was happening in our hometowns and if our friends and other relatives were safe. People sometimes spoke about what they saw while they were fleeing, and each story was just as terrifying as the next. I closed my eyes and tried to carry myself away from the present and into the past, back to the memories of being a young and eager mother.

CHAPTER SEVEN
BIG SISTER

1 JANUARY 1931
Minsk, Belarus, USSR

At first, I worried about our move from Bobruisk. We had only been married a few short months when we left our families and started our life together in a new city. When Abraham told me that he had secured a good job in Minsk and that we would need to leave soon, my stomach turned with uncertainty. Later, I realized it wasn't because I was scared to move, it was because I was pregnant with Luba. Being pregnant was hard on me at first. The first few months everything seemed to make me sick. Sometimes, a certain smell made me queasy. Other times, I felt unwell from nothing. Abraham was incredibly supportive. He held my hair back when I would get sick or bring me water after tucking me back into bed. It was during these months when we moved to Minsk that he started our little tradition. As Abraham left for work, he went through his normal routine. He would get dressed, eat breakfast, and give me a hug and kiss before heading outside to open all the shutters. One morning, after he walked around the house to the last shutter, he peeked his head in through an open window to give me another kiss. From that day, he never left for work without getting the second kiss through a window.

We lived in a medium sized one-room house with a humble kitchen and an outhouse in back in a beautiful part of Minsk. In the corner of our cozy bungalow was the brick oven with an open space for the wood and a hole with a shelf right above to cook. Since the oven was so large, there was even an area to lay on top. The oven stayed warm throughout the night long after the fire was out. Luba slept there during the colder months. Abraham and I often teased her that she must be part cat because she could curl up and lay in the sunshine or near the fire all day.

Near the oven, along the wall, was a side table that we used for preparing our meals. Right above was my favorite window. It was the only one that glowed with sunshine. The two cut crystal glasses on the shelf next to the window caught the sun and sent all the colors of the rainbow dancing through the room.

In the middle of the kitchen area stood a small wooden table with four aged chairs. Beyond that was our bed. On the other side, against the flower wallpaper was the sofa that Luba used as her bed. Above hung photos of both my family and Abraham's. The thick, dark frames accentuated their monotone expressions. On the other window hung pearl-white sheer curtains with delicately embroidered flowers. In front of it was a table with my sewing machine. Its black body was adorned by red, green and gold inlaid designs of flowers and wheat spikes. The sound of the silver wheel spinning as I turned the crank made a familiar hum; it transported me to a faraway place, away from all my worries. In the corner was a large chest with drawers. It was cherry wood and it had ornate metal handles. It was my favorite piece of furniture because it looked different than anything else in the room. It stood out, and my eye was oftentimes drawn towards it. Right outside the front door was a small patio with an aged wooden rocking chair. That was Abraham's chair. He loved to sit out there in the evening after dinner. Sometimes, Luba came out with him and sat by his feet. Abraham told her stories while they stared into the sky and gazed at the stars. I loved those moments. I stood there unnoticed and watched them as if a real-life fairy tale unfolded before me. Those brief memories were the ones that stood out most and made me realize how lucky I was.

◆　◆　◆

One of my happiest memories was a few months after Luba turned five years old. I woke her early in the morning with a full smile on my face. "Luba, wake up it's the New Year, we have something special for you and it looks like *Ded Moroz* came in the middle of the night and brought you something too."

Luba slid out from under her warm covers and slipped on her warmest sweater and slippers and joined Abraham and me over by our New Year's tree. It was beautifully decorated with ornate glass ornaments, shining with gold and silver. My favorites were the snowflake and icicle ornaments.

I loved decorating the tree, and this year Luba was old enough to do it with me. Every year near the end of December, Abraham chopped down a beautiful tree for us. Then we would get out the special box of ornaments. I carefully unwrapped each ornament from the pieces of cotton that they were nestled in and we took turns putting them up. That year I showed Luba how to place them around the tree and how to space the same ones on opposite ends. The entire room filled up with the smell of the fir tree and it was intoxicating. We made pouches out of paper to hang on the tree and we filled them with candy, nuts and small presents for the neighborhood children and friends. Luba had so much fun going from house to house to see the wonderful trees and collect the treats. She would count all the trees she visited and then she compared with her friends who saw the most.

"Here you are dear," Abraham said as he handed Luba her gift.

It was wrapped in grey paper and tied together with a red string. Her eyes widened as he handed it to her. Her sweet little face perked up as she untied the string. Inside she found a beautiful scarf that I had been knitting for her over the past few weeks. Each day, after I laid her down for a nap, I would carefully get it out and sit by the window so she couldn't see what I was doing. It was a beautiful blue, like the color of the sea reflecting the clear skies. There were vivid red roses blooming throughout with stems of green leaves connecting them together.

"Mama, Papa, it is so beautiful. I love the flowers! Mama, did you make this?"

Luba embraced me as I answered, "Of course I did, I hope you wear it in good health, my love. And this one is from *Ded Moroz*!" I said excitedly. I wondered how many more years until she no longer believed in *Ded Moroz*, but for now I couldn't help but enjoy the tradition.

This present was wrapped in a light brown waxy paper and tied together with white twine into a neat bow. It was small yet heavy and I knew she was going to love it. She quickly unraveled the bow and the paper slid back exposing a block of dark chocolate.

"I guess *Ded Moroz* wanted to get something sweet for our sugar-coated girl," said Abraham.

"It smells delicious! Can we have some with breakfast to celebrate the New Year?" Luba asked, beaming.

"Of course, we should!" Abraham answered as he brought the chocolate into the kitchen.

"Now it is your turn to open your present, Mama and Papa!"

Luba was so excited. She could hardly sit still. The gift was wrapped in old newspaper that she had brightly colored making it look more festive. Together, Abraham and I tore off the paper revealing a beautiful picture. Underneath the glass was a grand bouquet of dried flowers tied together with a yellow bow. Around the edges was a design Luba had drawn and on the back was a charming note signed by Luba and the date.

"There are no words for me to describe how much I love this, Luba!" I said.

Abraham chimed in, "What a wonderful gift! I know exactly the place for it." He stood up, walked over to the kitchen, took out a hammer and nail, and hung it right above my favorite chest of drawers. He was right, it was the perfect place.

"Luba, tell me how you made this? Did you do this all by yourself?" I asked.

"Well, I have worked on it for a while. I wanted it to be perfect. I did have some help. Remember that one day when we had a picnic at Gorky Park?"

"Of course, honey." One of her favorite hobbies was picking wildflowers. I could recall on that day she picked an entire bouquet and brought it home.

"When we got home, Papa showed me how to dry the flowers inside books, so I put all of mine into one of the heavy books on the shelf."

"I didn't even realize you had dried them," I said.

"Later, I decided to check on my dried flowers. I had forgotten about them a while ago and I wanted to know what they looked like. The flowers looked darker and faded, but I thought you would still like them."

"They are awfully nice, and they are just as beautiful, only in a new way. What made you decide to make them into an art piece? Abraham asked.

"I wanted to make you and Mama something nice with them, so I started by gluing them together onto a piece of white paper into a bouquet. Then, I colored a pretty design on the edge of the paper. I wasn't sure what to do next, so I went next door to Klara and she helped me with the writing. She even gave me a frame to put it in so the flowers would stay preserved."

"There are so many different varieties in this bouquet," said Abraham as he began to count them.

"I already counted. There are seven different flowers! There are the purple flowers over here and these bright yellow flowers with tiny petals and white centers." She pointed to each one as she described them. "The red ones with paper thin petals are one of my favorites, and these blue ones are so pretty. Then there are the white ones, some with yellow centers, and others purple and even these ones which are shaped like bells." Luba explained with excitement brimming from ear to ear.

"We are so proud of you. You are so creative and thoughtful," Abraham said proudly as he sat next to Luba with his long arms wrapped around her like a blanket.

Afterwards, I cut a sliver of chocolate from the bar and split it into three pieces. I gave Luba her portion and she could barely wait to get into her mouth. She took tiny nibbles and savored the taste on her tongue as long as she could. The rest of the chocolate we saved to eat for special occasions.

"We have one more present for you!" I said, turning to Luba, then to Abraham. The secret inside of me was about to burst out.

Nearly jumping out of his seat, Abraham excitedly said, "You are going to be a big sister this spring!"

"Really? I can't believe it! I am so excited! I want a little sister please, please, please," Luba shouted as she jumped around the room.

Her excitement brought me so much happiness. I knew she would be cheerful because she loved babies and frequently helped the neighbors with their little ones.

That night, I fell asleep with the smell of the New Year's tree all around me. My belly was full, and my heart was happy, and I knew this would be a day I would remember forever.

CHAPTER EIGHT
STALINGRAD

16 JULY 1941
Stalingrad, Russia, USSR

The trip from Kiev to Stalingrad took fourteen long nights and fifteen full days. During that time, we were shot at and bombed by Nazi planes a total of five times. Each time we did the same as the last. We fled the train, ran to find a place to hide, and huddled together for safety. So far all of us made our way to safety and made it through the shootings and bombings unharmed, but the fear that our luck would run out soon weighed me down like an anchor on a boat. The sounds of planes flying low and releasing a storm of bullets were now a dull, but constant ringing in my ears.

Much of our days were spent waiting. A few times our train was damaged by the Nazis and we had to wait for it to be fixed. The train also continued to stop several times a day for a few hours for no reason. Once we stopped for an entire day, from sunrise to sunset we sat on the train. I didn't mind the stops and it didn't seem to bother anyone else either. It was a chance to stand up and breathe some fresh air and watch the weather change around us. The sun warmed a little more each day, and although the world looked grey, everywhere I turned, the colorful flowers peeking through showed a slight glimmer of hope.

Once we arrived in Stalingrad and stepped out of the train into the brightness of the afternoon, we instantly saw the toll that the past few weeks had taken on us. Our faces were now more defined and sculpted, leaving the depths of our emotions with nowhere to hide. Our clothes fluttered in the wind, showing how loose they had become on our frail bodies. Mama and Papa looked stiff, and their movements seemed delayed and tired. I couldn't shake away how nervous I was for them. They were well into their fifties. I was twenty years younger and this trip was even hard for me. My body hurt like it had aged ten years over these past few weeks.

"Where do we go now? Are we going to stay in Stalingrad?" Sofia asked as we shuffled slowly out of the train station.

"We need to find a place where we can all rest tonight. Tomorrow we will figure out the rest," I explained to the girls as we neared a fountain directly outside the train station.

We had been surrounded by people nonstop since leaving Minsk, but now, in the shadow of this gorgeous fountain, we seemed alone, finally free from being shoved or packed into a train or overfilled station. The sounds of the fountain and the birds chirping above were the only sounds I heard. I stood, taking in the grand fountain and the gentle breeze, when I realized what the fountain was. Six boys and girls stood with their hands linked together to form a circle around a crocodile. They depicted a scene from one of my favorite poems called "Barmaley." Abraham and I told the girls the story often before bed. Before I could tell the girls, Luba shouted, "Everybody, I think this fountain is from 'Barmaley'! Look at the crocodile in the middle!" The sudden realization brought a twinkle into everyone's eyes.

A few of us started to recite, "Little children! For nothing in the world, do not go to Africa. Do not go to Africa for a walk! In Africa, there are sharks, in Africa, there are gorillas, in Africa, there are large evil crocodiles. They will bite you, beat and offend you. Don't you go, children, to Africa for a walk. In Africa, there is a bandit. In Africa, there is a villain. In Africa, there is terrible Bahr-mah-ley! He runs about Africa and eats children, nasty, vicious, greedy Barmaley!" For a moment I was transported back to our home, sitting next to the girls on their beds, reading them the story as they gazed back at us with wide eyes. I tried to push back the thoughts that I would never step into that home again, hoping to get a few moments of happiness, and as I looked around at my entire family, I realized how lucky I was.

"Papa, Mama, do you remember one of my best friends growing up, Nina? She moved from Bobruisk to Stalingrad when we were around fifteen. You must remember her. You were close with her parents. I have been in close contact with her over all these years, have you kept in touch with her parents?" I asked.

"We were close with her parents, but we lost touch with them. I had no idea you stayed in contact with Nina," Mama answered.

"I should have her address in my book if I grabbed it before we left," I said, as I nervously rummaged through my bag looking for the book. I rely on order and efficiency and am typically organized and well kept. Being on the road like this had taken me way beyond my comfort level. After a few minutes, I flashed a smile as I pulled out my book, happy with myself that I didn't forget to take it.

"I think we should go to Nina's. I don't have any close friends here other than her. Does anybody else have any other suggestions?" I asked.

No one had any better options, so with the address in hand, we headed to Nina's house to see if she could help us for the night. We stopped quickly for a map and after a twenty-five-minute walk we approached her apartment building. My head swayed as if I was still on the train as I gazed up at her building. It was a gleaming, white stone, four story building. It was on the corner of a smaller side street and the building curved around as we turned the corner to the front entryway. It was as graceful on the inside as it was on the outside. We walked up two flights of dark wood stairs wrapping around us like a snake and stood before door 3A. One soft knock on the door, and a woman emerged. She had light brown hair and kind green eyes. Her hair was pinned back neatly into a bun. Her apron was tied carefully at her waist and the once brightly colored fruits pictured on the front were now faded and at the moment hazed over with flour. As soon as she saw me, her eyes glistened with tears and her lips turned upward. She outstretched her arms towards me, "Oh Raisa, is that really you? Come in, come in!"

Once inside the apartment I could see why we had been good friends. We both had similar design styles and the same obsession for being clean and organized. Although the space wasn't large, everything was put away neatly in its place, as if Nina was expecting company. The furniture seemed newer and looked inviting. The floral wallpaper in the entryway reminded me of the wildflowers Luba picked and made into a picture for Abraham and me years ago, and somehow it brought me comfort.

"Nina, meet my girls, Luba and Sofia. You remember my Mama and Papa and my sister Hana. This is her son Oscar and my other two sisters, Gita and Lubov. We grew up together going to the same school and we lived close. It has been so many years since we saw each other last." I said to the girls, with my arm around Nina.

"Are you all healthy?" Nina asked concerned.

"I'm sorry for coming to you unannounced like this with my entire family, but we don't know anybody else here in Stalingrad, and we need a place to sleep for the night," I said, wishing I was seeing my best friend under different circumstances. We told her what we had been through the past few weeks, and without a blink of an eye, Nina escaped to the kitchen, and started to prepare some food for us. Nina told us that she and her husband Boris had two children, one boy who was recently sent into the army to fight at the front, and a girl named Tanya, who was a few years older than Luba. She had just arrived home from work for lunch, and as soon as she walked through the door, I noticed she shared the same beautiful green eyes as her mother. Luba and Tanya talked for a few minutes and formed an instant connection, as if they had always been friends.

We crammed ourselves around the dinner table and enjoyed what seemed like a feast before us. For the few hours that we sat around the table in the company of old and new friends, it seemed like we jumped into another world. We let our worries be forgotten for a short time, and instead enjoyed each other as we shared happy memories. That evening, we stayed awake until we could talk no longer and our eyelids felt heavy. Nina gave us some blankets and helped us to lay them out on the floor for our beds. I was already asleep before my head even touched the pillow.

CHAPTER NINE
MISFORTUNE BINDS US TOGETHER

26 JULY 1941
Stalingrad, Russia, USSR

The morning sun began to heat up the room like a warm fire as we woke up from our makeshift beds on Nina's floor. We had no idea where we would go next, but part of me wished we could stay in Stalingrad. I enjoyed reconnecting with Nina while Luba and Tanya were getting along so well. It would be nice to stay here for a while until the war blew over. I doubted that would happen though. We were told that we needed to register as refugees and the government would then send us where they needed us to work.

"Mama are you going this morning to find out where they will send us? Can I come with you?" Luba asked with hope in her voice.

"Sure, it will be nice to have some company. Mama, Papa will you be able to keep an eye on Sofia?"

"Yes of course, Raisa. Go, and take Luba with you." Mama answered, as Papa gave me a nod of approval.

"Go ahead and get ready so we can leave right after breakfast," I told Luba, but she started to dress even before I had finished.

We ate quickly and wrote down the directions from Nina. Soon enough we approached the registration office. The line of people snaked out the door and curled around the building. I couldn't even make out the end of line until we walked to the other side of the street. I was used to the lines already. My whole life had been spent going through them. Whether we waited for food, shoes or a train ticket, the lines were never-ending. As we took our place in the back, I looped my arm through Luba's and we leaned into each other.

"Mama, how are you doing? How are you feeling? This has been so much to take in and you have been so comforting to Sofia and me, but I haven't asked how you are."

"What can I say, my love? Yes, there has been so much to deal with these past few weeks. It is hard knowing that we will have no house to go back to, but there is one thing that is more important than that. We are safe and together. Maybe you heard the Yiddish saying, *Umglik bindt tsunoif.* It means misfortune binds us together. We will be fine no matter what, as long as we help each other and have one another to lean on."

Luba nodded, but looked into the distance, undoubtedly collecting her thoughts. A few steps closer in the line and she asked, "But what about Papa? I already miss him, and I worry for him."

"Papa will be fine, he is a survivor, and he will live for us. He easily adapts to new places, and somehow finds the positive in every situation. His outlook on life will help him keep going, even when times are tough. I know how much he loves us, and he will do anything to make it back to us." The words flowed out of me freely. I knew them well. I often repeated them to myself ever since that day at the train station.

We stood in line for the next three hours until we eventually made it inside the building. I didn't realize how strong the sun had beat down on us until we were inside. My skin felt tight and my head warm. We mostly stood without much talking so people around us wouldn't hear, or we talked about unimportant topics like the weather. Once inside, the line took another two hours, until it was our turn. Thankfully, Mama packed us a lunch in case the lines were long. It was unbelievable how many times I had said to myself, thank goodness for Mama. She remembered the little details without exception and often thought about specifics that no one else did.

As we approached the plump dark-haired woman behind the counter, I noticed the unhappiness in her tired eyes. Her stern voice matched her grim face. I gave her the information she asked for and then Luba helped me fill out the paperwork for the entire family to be registered as refugees. The woman explained that registration took about a week and we would have to come back to check and see if it was done.

"What will we do for a week? Where will we stay? Do we have enough money for a place to stay?" Luba asked me on our way back home.

"I'm not sure, dear. We will have to talk to the rest of our family, but I hope Nina will let us stay until we get our papers and we can give her some money in return."

Nina and Boris refused to let us leave and welcomed us to stay without hesitation or a second thought. The week we spent with them felt like a vacation after what we had been through. Luba enjoyed getting to know Tanya. Sometimes she took Luba and Lubov out, and they spent time with her friends. Sofia happily played with her Baba and Deda and loved the attention. It was during this week that I became somewhat relaxed. I even believed there was a possibility that the war would soon end, and we would go back to Minsk to rebuild our life.

After a week, I returned with Sofia to the registration office to check if our papers were ready, but after we spent most of the day in line, we came home with no answers. Our papers were still being processed, and they told us to come back again in a few days. The next time Luba and I went together, but we left long before anyone had woken up. As we stepped out of the front door onto the wet pavement, the light from the moon led us all the way to our destination. A short line already formed outside of the building. Drops of rain rested on the leaves and flowers from last night's soft rain shower. Luba and I watched the sunrise in the distance, and, as much as I wanted to have hope, I couldn't suppress the heaviness in my chest.

"Good morning," I said to the same plump woman who had taken our papers over a week ago. She looked up at me and without any emotion at all, she asked for our names. We gave her our information and in ten minutes she returned with a few papers for us. I glanced them over, thanked the woman and we left.

"Mama, what does it say? Where are they sending us?" Luba asked as we walked back to Nina's house.

"We will go to a small town where we will work on a kolkhoz."

"We will live on a collective farm? But we don't know how to do that type of work. How will Baba and Deda do manual labor at their age?" Luba asked the questions which were already buzzing around in my mind.

"I don't know, my love, I don't know."

CHAPTER TEN
THE SUMMER SUN

15 AUGUST 1941
Kilinchi, Russia, USSR

As we readied our bags for our next trip, I thought about the struggles we had encountered these past two months since the war began in Minsk. I never expected that we would be so far away from home, and I definitely could not have imagined that we would be sent to live and work on a farm. Looking around Nina's home gave me a bittersweet taste in my mouth. On one hand, we truly enjoyed our stay with them these past few weeks. I loved that I was able to reconnect with my old friend and meet her beautiful family. On the other hand, we could not stay any longer and impose on them. We had to go to where the government offered us jobs, we had to survive.

With our bags full of clothes and food, we spiraled our way down the same staircase we came up and stood at the entrance of the building. I did not want to say another goodbye.

"Nina, my dear, I don't even know where to begin. I can't thank you enough for everything you and your family have done for us. You have been so generous and thoughtful. I loved meeting your family and getting to know them, even in these times." I pulled Nina close to me and gave her a tight hug, sad that I had to let go of yet another person in my life.

"You are always welcome in our home Raisa. We enjoyed your company as well, and I wish you safe travels. Please be careful and write when you can." Nina knelt down to adjust Sofia's dress. She tried to keep herself from crying, but her eyes glistened anyway. After we exchanged hugs with one another, we headed back to the Stalingrad train station, ready to board the next train to our new destination.

As our stomachs began to rumble for dinner, we approached our new town. Kilinchi was located southeast of Stalingrad along the Volga River. The station was merely a single bus-stop-like booth in the middle of a field. We were about two thousand kilometers away from our home in Minsk, and as the train started to stop, I grasped exactly how far we actually were. We descended the steps of the train and jumped onto the grass. We each grabbed the hand of the next person and linked ourselves in unity to cautiously confront the unknown. We walked to the end of the narrow road where we were greeted by the local farmers. We immediately saw the vast open space around us, and it was as if we were thrown into a foreign world. The air smelled thick with manure and the dirt road sent clouds of dust billowing from underneath our feet.

"It's nice to meet you all, my name is Alexei, you can come with me and I will show you where you will live. Tomorrow we will teach you your jobs. If you have any questions, don't be shy to ask," the farmer explained as we loaded up into his horse-drawn wagon.

Alexei had warm brown eyes and a dimple on his chin. His soft expression made him seem like a kind man, but his large muscles and rough hands could make you suspect otherwise.

After a short, but bumpy ride, we arrived at his house. My eyes widened as we looked at the shack before us. Another one sat a short distance away. Beyond the houses was farmland as far as the eye could see.

"This is where my wife and our three kids live, and this house over here is where you will stay. I know it isn't much, but my wife cleaned it up as best she could. We were only able to gather six mattresses for now, but I will try to get more if I can. Also, we left you a samovar, make yourselves some tea after your journey. On the side of the house is a pile of pine cones to use to keep the fire hot." We followed Alexei over to the thatched cottage. Inside, the single-roomed cottage was bare except for the six mattresses scattered about the room.

As soon as Alexei left, I turned to Luba. "Luba, my dear," but before I finished my sentence, she chimed in, "I will sleep with Sofia, Mama."

I smiled, and with my last bit of energy tried to turn the cottage into a home. To start, I set about putting the sheets on the beds. They looked yellowed from age, but they smelled clean and were neatly folded in the closet. Mama and I quickly grabbed a side of the first sheet, while Hana and Gita grabbed another sheet and in pairs, we made each bed. We moved the mattresses so we each had our own area. My mattress was pushed up against the girls', and across from us was Hana and Oscar. Gita and Lubov were on the other side of the room and Mama and Papa had the larger mattress. We placed the samovar in the middle of the room for easier access. While Papa went out to gather pine cones to boil some water for tea, I looked through the closets to see what we could use to make the cottage feel cozy. I found two sets of curtains folded in a bag on the top shelf. They were ripped in a few places, but anything would be better than bare windows. They had dark pink on the bottom that became lighter towards the top until the pink faded to white. There were yellow and white flowers along the edges, which I found to be cheerful. I brought a chair over to the window and removed the curtain rod so I could thread it through the curtain. After I finished, we stood back and admired the subtle changes.

♦ ♦ ♦

Each morning we woke at sunrise to the sound of the roosters singing their morning tune. With our bodies still aching from yesterday's tasks, we worked in the fields until the sun set and the sky became saturated with color. First, we picked the cucumbers and tomatoes, and then the melons. We twisted the melons from their vines and placed them into the wheelbarrow. They grew exponentially heavier as we worked our way through, row after row. Farm life was much like keeping a home. They both had an endless amount of work to be done, but chores on the farm were more back-breaking than any batch of laundry I had ever encountered.

We were the only other family living on the farm, besides Alexei's. There was an additional cottage down the way from ours, but no one lived there. It was a fairly small farm and we managed, but it would have been nice to have more hands to help.

We rotated our many duties, and whether we harvested the food, sorted, or pulled weeds, we were regularly hard at work. Gita, Lubov, Hana and I pitched in to help Mama and Papa and took over the more strenuous work. We let Mama and Papa tend to the chickens, goats and cows. While we picked the fruits and vegetables, Mama and Papa sorted. Hana and I were the strongest among us, so we often fetched drinking water from the well. It was about a fifteen-minute walk to the well, and I enjoyed breathing the fresh air and having the time to think clearly, but once I arrived at the well, I often cursed under my breath, knowing what was to come. The walk back was a difficult one. I placed the pails on a shoulder pole and the pole rested on my shoulders and lower neck. As I walked slowly and carefully back, I could not help but wish I was back home. I wanted to walk faster, but I knew it would only spill the water. I wanted to rest, but the longer I took, the heavier the water felt on my shoulders.

Sometimes, when I would stare across the field, I was amazed how Hana's hair never failed to remain bright like her personality, even when she shoveled manure. Back in Bobruisk, Hana was an accountant and she and I were close, not only in age but also as sisters. One would assume that her red hair was what made Hana stand out in a crowd of people, but those who were familiar with her, knew that Hana was full of life, and her laugh was infectious. She may have been six years younger, but she stood much taller than me and was bigger all around. Everyone typically guessed that Hana was the eldest. She often tried to find the good in everything and everyone. I think that is what I love most about her.

As difficult as the work had been, I was thankful that it had brought me closer to my sisters. The long days together became a perfect place to catch up on our years apart.

As our days grew more strenuous, I regularly wished my life was different, and I longed for Abraham's touch. At the same time, I was happy we were safe, and we had food to fill our stomachs. We retired to bed early, and despite having to sleep on an uncomfortable mattress full of lumps, most nights I slept soundly knowing that we were together, and we had a roof over our heads.

Occasionally, I imagined that Abraham watched over us. When I hung the curtains, he was there, smiling at us as we turned the cottage into our new home. I had managed to keep the girls safe and survived working strenuous, long, back-breaking days on the farm. As I envisioned him watching me in wonder, he made me feel proud of what I had accomplished.

Abraham once told me that my personality reminded him of one of his complicated clocks. He took my hands and described that when they are wound, they function with precision, their gears helping one another do its job. They are looked upon for an answer, and they provide it without fail, much like I was expected to do for my family. With his hand resting on my chest, he told me how the weights carry the burden and drive the mechanism to work, precisely as my heart did. When I thought about it in that way, I was constantly wound up and ready to provide. I couldn't remember the last time I let myself wind down and turn off. I found myself routinely doing something, even when there was nothing to do. I woke up early in the mornings and lay in bed, making mental notes of my to-do list for that day. When I lay down at night, I went through the same list and made sure I checked everything off. My gears were continuously turning with worry, happiness, or excitement from the ups and downs of my life.

◆ ◆ ◆

Over the last three weeks, my skin had taken on a deep golden-brown tone from working under the summer sun. We had managed to gain some of our weight back, and we finally started to look more like ourselves again. For our hard work on the farm, each of us received one loaf of rye bread in addition to some fruits and vegetables per week. All of us learned a new appreciation for food now that we understood the amount of work required to grow it. The food that we helped to grow somehow tasted that much sweeter. We mostly had enough to eat, maybe not an abundance, and never anything extravagant, but enough for us to not be hungry.

One evening, as darkness peered into our cottage, we were startled by a quick, but loud knock on the door. It was Alexei and his wife Manya. Their three kids trailed behind their parents but stayed outside to go catch fireflies.

"Is everything alright?" Papa asked. He also must have picked up on the tension which entered the room with Alexei and Manya.

Manya nervously shifted her weight from one foot to the other while Alexei started to speak. "I received my draft notice, and I am to report for duty in forty-eight hours. I wish I had more time to show you how to work the land, but I will do my best before I leave."

I wondered what would become of us without Alexei here to do the heavy lifting and strenuous work. I imagined that our workloads would nearly double without him. Yet, my thoughts continued to be clouded by emotions for Manya. I knew what she was going through, and as I looked over at her and her glazed over eyes, I saw a familiar fear pierce through them.

I leaned over to Manya and took her hands in mine, hoping it would give her some comfort. "I wish you good luck at the front." I said, turning to Alexei. "We will do our best with the farm, and as long as we are here, we will happily help Manya and the kids in any way we can."

Alexei smiled nervously, "Thank you for your wishes, and I wish you the best as well." Alexei and his family faded into the darkness with only a jar of fireflies lighting their short walk home.

♦ ♦ ♦

"Luba, Sofia, a letter came from your Papa!" I shouted happily. I rushed inside and held the letter for them to see. We hadn't heard from him since we watched him fade away in the distance at the train station. I had been a ball of worry ever since. About three weeks before, I sent him a letter with our current address, hoping for it to reach him and he would send his reply soon.

I finally held the triangular shaped letter in my hand. Meticulously written in blue ink in Abraham's best handwriting, was our address. On the back was a smudged black postal stamp with the date. I carefully removed the folded flap from the center of the triangle and unfolded the letter. After I quickly read a few sentences to myself, I began to read from the beginning so everyone could hear,

Good day my lovely girls. Raisa, Luba and Sofia, I can write to you that I feel great and wish that you do as well. My dearest girls, I have received your letters from last week, and I cannot tell you how wonderful it was to read them. Knowing that you are all safe and doing well means everything to me. I knew that you would be traveling and on the road for a while, but I didn't expect for it to take as long as it did. I wish I could have been there with you, but know I was thinking about you each and every day. I can't even imagine how exhausting and frightening it must have been for you girls, but I knew you would get through it together. I ask you to please write me more letters as often as you can. I am in good health as they feed us well here. I know that you haven't been on the kolkhoz for too long and you probably don't want to be on the road again, but I believe another move is the best decision. I have spoken with some of my comrades and it seems like the conditions in the south are better. I would like for you, my dear Raisa, to go and request to evacuate to Tashkent. Soon it will get cold on the farm and the work will only grow harder. ▮▮▮▮▮▮▮▮▮▮▮▮▮▮▮▮▮▮▮▮▮▮▮▮▮▮▮▮▮▮▮▮. I think it would be best for you to move there as soon as possible. I think about you Raisa, and the girls, each and every day, and in the night I dream of you. Although we are far apart, I keep you girls close to my heart. Kisses to you all, Abraham

I let out a sigh of relief so deep, as though I had been holding it in for weeks. Luba came over and gave me a long hug. She too was relieved. Sofia had a huge grin on her face and

Mama suggested we celebrate with a toast from the freshly brewed tea.

Later that night, as I reclined in bed, I re-read the letter from Abraham. I was warm with happiness to hear that he was well, and that he received my letter, but my mind wandered back to his last words about Tashkent. I knew that he wanted what was best for us, but so many questions were swimming through my brain. What was written in the portion which was redacted by the government? I wished I could read underneath the layer of black marker and reveal his unfiltered words.

My mind shifted to the thought of being stuck on the train again without him, and my stomach turned with fear. On the other hand, working the farm during the winter would be hard on all of us, and I was not sure if Papa and Mama would even make it through. With Alexei gone to the front, our duties had multiplied, while our crops had begun to diminish. Would this get any better in the coming months? We had gone from our normal life in the city, to a migrant life on trains, to survival on a farm. Could we transition again? Tashkent sounded like a promising place for our family. It was after all, known as the "city of bread." Practically everyone I knew had read the book or heard the stories about how it was the land of plenty. Because it was so far away from the front, it was untouched from the devastation of the war, at least this is how it was during the famine and the first world war. How could we know what would happen there this time? What if everyone else in Russia had the same idea to flee south? Could Tashkent handle us all? As the night fell over us like a blanket, my eyes began to close with a river of thoughts still rushing through me.

CHAPTER ELEVEN

ANTICIPATION

6 OCTOBER 1941
Kilinchi, Russia, USSR

Our cottage was illuminated only by the flickering candle on the table nearby as I made my way over to where Luba was fixing her hair. "Luba, after you are done with your duties this afternoon and on your way to pick up Sofia and Oscar from school, could you go to the post office and see if any letters have arrived for us? I would like to get an early start on dinner since the days have been getting shorter," I said, as we gathered around the table.

"Of course, mama. I can do that." Luba said confidently.

We filled ourselves with warm kasha for breakfast and headed out into the cold to fulfill our chores. Fortunately, since we were living on the farm, we had plenty of fresh milk and butter to add to the cream of wheat. The weather had already changed to a fierce winter cold. We now wore our warm clothes and some nights we even kept them on under the covers to stay warm.

The weeks passed by slowly as we waited in anticipation regarding our request to move to Tashkent. We received a few more letters from Abraham and each time they calmed me, as I read his words aloud. When I was out in the fields to pick or sort the vegetables, I often thought about how his life was actually going, since he could not write details about where he was, or what he was doing.

With the change in weather came a change in crops and duties. Soon, it became my responsibility to drive the ox-drawn cart and sort the potatoes and vegetables. It was back-breaking work, but somehow I managed. I tried to focus my thoughts somewhere faraway. Sometimes, as Papa sorted nearby, I listened to his whistle sail through the air and it took me back to my childhood. They were the same tunes from when I was a little girl, and it was remarkably comforting. Whether I watched him build out back or sew a new pair of trousers as he sat by the window, the resonance fluttered through the air just the same.

◆ ◆ ◆

As Hana and Gita helped me finish dinner, Luba came home with Sofia and Oscar. She had some letters in her bag and I could hardly wait to see them. It had been a few days since we received word from Abraham. The only way I made it through the day sometimes was knowing that there was a possibility that I would receive a letter from him.

Luba took off her coat and shoes and happily declared, "Mama, I'm home and I have picked up some letters! A few are from Papa and I think this one could be about Tashkent."

"Thank you, my love! Let's read them over dinner." I suggested, as I set the table with spoons and the bowls of soup we had prepared for dinner. After a few gulps of soup, I could no longer wait, and I began to read the postcard from Abraham. As I started to read, I heard his voice jumping off the paper.

Good day my lovely girls. Raisa, Luba and Sofia, I can write to you that I feel well and wish that you do as well. My dearest girls, I have received all your letters, and I anxiously await a letter about your request to go south. I hope you hear about this soon. Please write to me as soon as you get word whether you are approved or not. It worries me that you would be on the farm when the winter begins to set in and the food will become scarce. I hope for a better and easier life for you. Tell me how are the crops doing with the cold setting in. Is there enough for everyone? ████████████████████? My feigele, my little bird, please write to me about your health, and the health of Luba and Sofia. How is the rest of the family doing? Please let me know if you need anything and I will send another parcel as soon as I can. Don't worry about me, I have everything I need. We haven't moved and I am currently doing the same work which Guriv did while in Bobruisk. Kisses to you and the girls and to the rest of the family. I love you all and miss you dearly. Abraham

His words sounded nervous and for the first time in a few weeks, it was as if I was staring down a dark alleyway forcing myself to continue unknowing of what would await me in the end. I had no idea how we would survive the winter here. The amount of food had decreased by half since our arrival. The government had rationed our portions in order to provide for the soldiers. Alexei being gone and the colder October weather had not helped either.

"Mama, who is Guriv?" Sofia wondered.

"He was an old friend of ours. He was one of the witnesses at our wedding. In Bobruisk he worked as a chef. Papa must be cooking the food for the soldiers on the front lines. This is good news. I pray this continues to be his position." I answered, reassuring them as best I could.

I took a breath and a few more spoons of soup, then continued with the next letter, which came from the evacuation office.

```
Dear Tsalkin family,
This letter is in response to your
request to be evacuated to Tashkent. We
have secured positions for you, Raisa
Tsalkina, and your two daughters, Luba
and Sofia. You will be able to board the
train for Tashkent on the 20th of
October, 1941 leaving at three o'clock
in the afternoon. Please be sure to
bring this letter and the enclosed
tickets. You must also have proper
identification for each member of your
family in order to board.
```

I looked at the last few envelopes and there was another letter from Abraham as well as a letter from friends of Mama and Papa, but there was no evacuation letter for the rest of my family. I wanted to be happy. I wanted to burst from excitement. We would go to the "city of bread," but how could I be happy when I knew the rest of my family would not come with us?

"This is wonderful news! You and the girls will go, and we will be fine here if it comes to that. Let's not worry about that until we get to it," Papa said, as he came over and put his arms around me. Then he whispered into my ear. "Your girls must be your first priority, you need to keep them safe, no matter the cost."

"Mama, let's read the other letter from Papa," Sofia requested, breaking my thoughts apart into a million pieces. I let Luba read the letter aloud to us and it quieted my nerves. He explained that he would be moving soon, so if we didn't get any post from him, to not worry. He mentioned that the move would be for the better for him and his words came across as hopeful.

All I could think about that night as I laid my head on my pillow was what we would do if the time came and the rest of my family weren't granted permission to go to Tashkent. What would we do? Was it better to go without them or stay here and risk our survival? I began fiddling with my necklace as if it would give me an answer, and in some way maybe it did. I tossed and turned the scenarios around in my mind, until I decided that Papa was right. We would have to go, with or without them. My mind was made up, but I couldn't help but feel the pain and agony inside my heart. I needed to prepare myself in case we did have to separate, but I also needed to prepare my girls. They had become accustomed to having our family around for support. I thought back to the many times Abraham and I talked about how we would conquer the next step in Luba or Sofia's life. From potty training them to getting them ready for their first days of school, and everything in-between, we went through it with them together. As I lingered into sleep, my mind dotted back to many such occasions. The times we spent preparing Luba for the arrival of Sofia stood out the most.

CHAPTER TWELVE
ICE CRYSTALS

8 MARCH 1931
Minsk, Belarus, USSR

The year nineteen thirty-one started off with a whirl of excitement, and it was still in the air, even as we jumped off into spring. This time around, I coped with the pregnancy much better. I didn't get sick the first few months nearly as often, and although I was bigger than I was with Luba, I felt well.

With the new baby coming soon, I knew it would be helpful if Luba took on some of the chores, so I showed her the ways of the house. I didn't waste any time. I started teaching her right after the new year. She was only five, but I was able to teach her the basics of how to cook and clean the house.

"Dear, please help Papa bring some water for the laundry before he heads to work. I will show you how to do the laundry. Afterwards, we will learn how to make your favorite, *pelmeni!*"

"Luba, since mama's belly has grown over the past few months, she is not supposed to carry anything heavy, so you are going to be her special helper," Abraham explained as we walked outside.

Luba nodded, and a breeze gently swayed through the trees and caught the subtle waves of her hair.

"Here are your pails, Luba. Remember to walk back slowly so you don't spill too much water," I yelled after her.

I watched her run to the well with her pails in her hands. Her arms swift and carefree, like a bird. The air was fresh and cool, but not too cold.

"There you are!" I exclaimed, when I saw Abraham and Luba walking back with full buckets. "Let's pour some of the water into the washing bowl, and I will start heating a kettle while you go for more water."

With Abraham's help, Luba poured the water into the large deep bowl which we used for washing clothes. It was metal with white enamel on top and yellow trim on the edge. The enamel had started chipping slightly in some places showing its age. By the time they came back with the second set of pails, I had the water warmed and was ready to show her how to wash the proper way.

"Thank you my dear for helping. Have a great day at work," I said to Abraham as he put his coat back on. He came over for a kiss and then hugged Luba tightly.

"First, we will add the soap to the warm water. Start by swishing your hands around like this. Then we take the washboard and scrub your clothes back and forth. We want to make sure we get off all the dirt and stains. Then you transfer it to the rinsing bowls. In the first rinsing bowl you should be sure to try to remove as much of the soap as possible. Next, put it into the third tub of water for an extra rinse. That's all, let's see you give it a try."

She grabbed the soap and swished it around in the warm water like I showed her. Next, she picked up the washing board. As she moved it, the sun caught the metal surface and it looked as though ice crystals were dancing on top of it. Luba must have noticed it too because she began to run her fingers back and forth over the crystals before she started to rub the clothes back and forth. I looked over her shoulder with approval and urged her to continue. Soon enough, she was halfway through the clothes. It was exhausting work, first carrying the pails of water, and then the rubbing. I had done it a million times, but it did not become easier over time, and I couldn't believe how well she was doing.

"It looks great, dear. I think you are about done. I'll help you with the last of them. You go ahead and start hanging them up." Hanging the clothes didn't take too long, and I could tell Luba was excited to move on to making pelmeni.

I learned from my Mama when I was about this age. I loved watching her in the kitchen. When she cooked, it was as if she were dancing. Every move she made was graceful and purposeful. It was magical to watch her hands flutter around dicing and mixing.

A few months ago, I started to teach Luba how to cook simple dishes, much like my Mama taught me. I stood right behind her and showed her how to use a knife the right way, and even how to sharpen it when it became dull. Nearly every dish we ate had potatoes in it, so she quickly became an expert in potato peeling. It was then when she realized why I always had a callus on my finger that never seemed to go away.

♦ ♦ ♦

We went inside and ate a light lunch and I started to prepare the kitchen to cook pelmeni for dinner.

"First, we need to make the dough. To start we mix the buttermilk and sour cream together. Then we add in the warm water and eggs. Lastly, a pinch of salt and then whisk." I explained carefully while I placed the ingredients on the table for her to add. She poured the ingredients into the large metal bowl. "Here is the fork, whisk away," I said happily.

"Great job Luba, now it's time to mix in the flour. Pour in the flour one cup at time."

"Mama, why can't we pour it all in at once?" Luba asked.

"Well honey, we add it little by little so that it's easier to mix and so the dough doesn't get clumpy. Also, this way we can see when it's time to stop adding flour, so we don't make the dough too tough."

She continued and did exactly as I had instructed. Again, it was hard work, to pour and mix at the same time. The more flour she added, the harder it was to mix and soon her arm begin to slow down as if it were put in slow motion, but she kept going. I knew she wanted to show me that she could do it, but what she didn't know was that I already knew she could. Soon enough, the dough was mixed, and we took it out of the bowl. I then showed her how to knead it into a ball. I handed her a piece of the soft, cold dough for her to mold and play with.

"Now that we have the dough finished, we need to cover it, so it doesn't dry out while we prepare the meat for the filling."

I brought over the pieces of beef and Luba helped me set up the meat grinder. She put the pieces in as I turned the handle round and round. Out the other side and into the bowl fell the ground meat.

Laughing, Luba turned to me, "It looks like worms, Mama!" We both laughed. It was nice to have so much fun together while we cooked.

"The garlic and onions are next. The trick to dicing the onion into tiny pieces is to first cut the onion lengthwise. Then you lay it down and slice the onion lengthwise again, but not all the way to the end, so the onion doesn't fall apart. Then cut in the opposite direction."

"Like this, Mama?" Luba asked as she tried to follow my directions.

I corrected her a little, and after a few minutes, she did it herself. Then we peeled and chopped the garlic and added it along with some oil to the frying pan to brown slightly.

"Now it's time to get our hands dirty!" I exclaimed. "First, add the garlic and onion with a pinch of salt and pepper to the meat, then use your hands to mix everything together very well."

She poured the ingredients into the meat and dug her hands in.

"It's squishy and sticky!" Luba shouted and made a funny face.

Again, we began to laugh and couldn't stop for the next few minutes.

"Now the fun part!" I said happily. "It's time to make the pelmeni. Let's start by rolling out the dough."

I handed her an old wooden rolling pin that my Mama gave me. It was nearly as long as her arm and it was heavier than you would expect. The handles were painted with red, but the paint was worn away leaving only a few traces of its color. I wondered how many batches of pelmeni it had already made.

She held the rolling pin sturdy and stepped onto the step stool to get more leverage and then started to roll out half of the dough. Once she was done, I handed her a glass and we cut circles out of the dough with it.

"Now we take about a teaspoon of meat and place it into the circle. Fold the circle over and pinch the edges tightly to make it into the dumpling," I showed her how it was done.

"It looks like a moon, Mama!"

"And now we take the two corners and pinch them to-gether," I said, smiling back as I showed her the last step. "That's it, you are all done! Now we finish the rest and then we can boil them tonight for dinner when Papa comes home. He will be so proud of you. You did a great job helping me."

My praise made her radiate with joy. For the next hour, we stood side by side and made over one hundred pelmeni. When we ran out of meat, but had some dough leftover, I brought over some raisins. "Let's put some inside and we will add these to the mix, and whoever gets them will be lucky." I said. This started a tradition, and each time we made pelmeni, we were sure to always add a few with raisin stuffing.

After we finished, I told Luba to play while I rested for a bit before Abraham came home. Lately, I was tired halfway through the day and I had to take more and more rests.

"Papa is home, Papa is home!" Luba sang happily as he walked through the door. He was smiling as usual, and as soon as he closed the door, he stretched his arms out lovingly for Luba, ready to pick her up.

"How are my favorite girls today?" Abraham asked, ready to hear about our day. She told him the details of our morning washing the laundry and our afternoon making pelmeni.

"Luba did an amazing job, she listened well and helped me so much today. Her pelmeni turned out beautifully and she even added a special surprise inside a few of them! Let's go eat, you must be hungry, my love," I said as I stood on my tippy toes to give Abraham a quick kiss on his cheek.

We sat down for dinner and we enjoyed the pelmeni with sour cream piled on top. Even though we had eaten them many times before, I knew Luba felt a sense of accomplishment because she had made them herself. I knew, because I had felt the same way many years ago after I made my first pelmeni.

As I gave Luba a kiss goodnight and tucked her in, she had a smile from ear to ear. I thanked her for being my little helper, and in return she replied, "No, Mama, thank you for showing me how to be amazing, exactly like you."

I could not have asked for a better end to a wonderful day.

CHAPTER THIRTEEN
EAT LIKE MICE

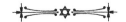

28 OCTOBER 1941
Kilinchi, Russia, USSR

In the days after we received our notice regarding Tashkent, the entire family was on edge. Hana was worried for Oscar and Mama was worried about Papa's declining health. I wrote to Abraham every day, and longed to hear some words of encouragement back, but no letter came. I knew that he was moving locations, and that he wasn't able to send mail, but I continued to have hope.

As we waited for the letters to arrive, each day lasted longer than the next, even though the days began to get shorter in reality as winter started to set in.

On October eighteenth, two days before we were set to leave for Tashkent, Luba shouted to us as she approached the house out of breath.

"Baba Khaya, everyone, come look, the letter has arrived!"

I was in the middle of gathering pine cones for the samovar when Luba shouted. I wanted to rush towards her, but a wall of fear held me back.

Papa opened the letter and read it aloud. We listened intently. The anticipation tingled through me like sparks of electricity. "… the following names have been granted passage to Tashkent, Uzbekistan on the twentieth of October, nineteen forty-one at three o'clock in the afternoon…"

We all let out a sigh of relief or of joy, maybe it was both. I suddenly began to breathe easier. They would leave with us in two days. Finally we had some great news. I couldn't help but be thrilled and relieved in that moment. At the same time, I felt guilty for being happy, knowing that others around us were not so fortunate. I knew it was still uncertain what the future would bring for us, but at least we would face it together.

The entire family buzzed with anticipation that evening as I headed to see Manya to break the news to her. A pit of guilt grew deep inside me as I thought about what I had to say to her. I felt awful for having to break my promise to Alexei, but in my mind, we didn't have any other choice. I had done the best I could to watch out for her while we were here, and that would have to be enough.

The weathered brown door creaked opened as Manya yelled for me to come inside. I found her in the kitchen, on her hands and knees, washing the floors. Her swift, distinct movements across the tiles were easy, and I wondered how she had any energy left this late in the day. Manya stopped after a few moments and said, "That should do for tonight. How are you, Raisa? Are you and the girls ready for your trip in a few days?"

"We are doing well. The girls are nervous and anxious to leave for somewhere so far away and so foreign to us. I can't blame them though, I have the same fears. I wanted to let you know that we received the letter for the rest of my family. They have been given permission to join us. So, sadly, we will all leave together."

Manya stood up straight and came over to where I stood. As she looked me in the eyes, I noticed how different she had become over the last few months. After Alexei left, her face swelled with sadness and fear, but now, pure exhaustion had taken over, and wrinkles stretched across her face like a never-ending maze. "I understand, my dear. This is good news. You will be better off. This is not your home. Although I appreciate everything you have done, and I will miss you all, I am thankful for the time you spent here with us. You were there for me when I needed you the most. I have already received notification of some new arrivals, so don't worry, we will be fine. I wish you and the rest of your family the best of luck."

"Thank you, Manya. You have been so kind to us, and I am so thankful for you as well. You made me appreciate life in a different way, and I will never forget my time here with you and your family. Please take care, and I hope we will see each other again, maybe in Minsk next time?"

"Of course. Possibly one day we will make it there." Manya held me tightly before walking me out. I listened to the sound of the door close behind me as I walked over the threshold and into the next chapter of our journey.

◆ ◆ ◆

Our last few days in Kilinchi passed by quickly as we worked in the field and prepared our bags for the long trip ahead. The morning of our departure, I woke long before the others rustled beneath their covers. My mind spun with questions. Where would we live in Tashkent? Would we be able to find work? I was nervous to be further from our home then we already were.

Ever since Abraham and I had been apart, I moved about my day as if a part of me was missing and no matter what I did, I could not make myself whole again. A tiny voice in the back of my mind made me fearful that being farther away from him would only make the hole in my heart grow larger. As I looked at the bed next to me, I tried to remind myself that I had to be strong for my two beautiful girls. I had to continue to be brave for them, even if every piece of me was falling apart inside.

The morning passed quickly, and soon we set out on foot for the train station. The air was bone chilling, but fresh. The last few weeks we saved as much food as possible in preparation for our trip, so our bags were now filled with food instead of clothes. Our clothes were layered on us to keep us warm for our trip, but they were cumbersome as we trudged through the snow. My exposed face became dry as the wind struck like a whip.

A few hours later, we arrived at the station and I never thought I would be so happy to see another train again. We boarded our train in Kilinchi and none of us looked back. Even though my mind ached with caution as we journeyed into the unknown again, I knew deep down that all of us would not have survived the winter on the farm.

◆ ◆ ◆

We were shoved into train cars overflowing with people. We huddled our bodies together as a family so we wouldn't have to be so close to the people next to us. Although we were all refugees, headed to the same place, we were still strangers, un-trusting of the unknown.

My distrust started long ago. As I looked around at the rain-bow of people that surrounded me, I noticed a girl. Something about her took me back to the memory when I learned that trust must be earned.

Before Abraham entered my life, I was a young, innocent girl on my way home from school. I noticed the woman's jew-elry first. The strands of beads hung around her neck like a cascading waterfall. The large metal earrings dangled and ech-oed the rays of sunshine as she moved. A long, pleated skirt moved freely, almost able to dance itself. Her weathered white shirt was tucked inside the skirt, the arms wide and free flow-ing. Dark curls flowed without restraint, practically bursting from underneath her blue headscarf. I saw the mystery in her brown eyes even before she approached me.

"Show me your palm and let me read your fortune." The Gypsy said, her bare feet walked closer to me.

Her face was beautiful, and her voice called me towards her, but something tugged me backwards. Since childhood, I was told many times to avoid Gypsies. "Gypsies are very talented musicians," Mama would say. "But they are also thieves. They move around from one city to the next, finding ways to get something free or someone vulnerable. Stay away from them."

"No, thank you." I said, moving away, but still feeling drawn to her.

She began to sing. Her voice rippled through me sending a tingle down my spine. I stopped, unable to peel myself away. Others on the street were drawn in as well. We stood by, like birds perched on a roof flocking together to watch. Her feet joined her voice and her skirt twirled as she danced in circles with all eyes on her.

Mesmerized, I barely noticed when a boy bumped into a gentleman who stood next to me. The man's eyes smiled at the Gypsy, entranced like the rest of us, not bothered by the intrusion. After she finished, the crowd clapped and whistled. A few started to get out their wallets or fish in their purses for loose change. When I looked up from my purse, the Gypsy was gone, and so was the wallet of the man next to me, along with wallets of a few other people in the crowd who were clearly upset. It was a setup, the Gypsy was our muse, luring our attention towards her. Meanwhile, we had let our guard down.

Talented they were. It was the first time I had witnessed their clever ways, and although I was lucky enough to not have been a victim, the vision of what they did helped shape my distrust in strangers.

Now, I tell the girls as my Baba frequently said to me, "Everyone is kneaded out of the same dough, but not baked in the same oven."

People were hungrier, dirtier, and more tired than when the war was first announced. The war had begun to take a toll on all of us, and for some, the goodness no longer showed. Instead, the resentment for this life that we were thrown into took hold and led them down a dark path.

After our first few days on the train, I realized that many people were angry, driven by hunger, and it was a dangerous place to be when you had food. We witnessed an old man open up his luggage and begin to eat that evening. Just as he pulled out the food a man jumped on him as if he was a wolf and tried to pry the piece of bread from the frail old man's hands. Others looked to see what had happened, but none of them appeared surprised and no one dared to help. The old man resisted, and attempted to hold onto the bread, but the man had already grabbed most of it and was back in the corner devouring it before we could understand what happened. The poor old man began to cry, and his body shook with fright. I glanced over at Papa. He put his finger over his mouth and motioned for us to be quiet and stay calm. I disguised my emotions on the outside, but inside I was kicking and screaming. I wanted to jump in and do something, but it was too risky. What if he jumped on us instead? I couldn't risk the safety of my own family, so as hard as it was, I kept my mouth shut.

A few hours later, after night started to creep into the train car, I could barely see Sofia hunched over herself. I leaned into her and asked, "Sofia, my baby, what's wrong?"

Barely able to hear her, she said, "I'm hungry and I'm scared. I don't want that man to attack us."

I whispered into her ear, "I know, I'm hungry too. Wait a little longer and when it's dark, we will eat." She turned and nodded. Her face was full of emotions; her eyes, lips and brows revealed her fears, anguish and hunger. My heart tightened with helplessness. I put on my strong face to cover up my emotion, wishing I could take away all her fears and worries.

Soon, the light from the full moon shined into the train car. By now, most slept and the only people up were those like us, with food. Too scared to eat during the day, we had to wait until night and quietly eat like mice by the light of the moon.

♦ ♦ ♦

We proceeded on that train for eight full days and the landscape we passed continued to be endless as if the journey might never end. My once-energetic girls had lost all trace of hope in their eyes. We were like chickens, wandering around aimlessly, and over the past few months our feathers had been plucked from us one by one. Now all that remained was bare skin, leaving us exposed and vulnerable.

A few days ago, the train stopped in the middle of the day and the doors opened to let in some light as well as fresh air. We sat in the freezing cold train and stared out into the open forest. I tried to find beauty in the vast white wilderness before us, but my mind was tired, and a shadow of darkness hovered around me. Suddenly, I caught sight of something move in Luba's hair.

"Luba, don't move. You have a little bug in your hair. Let me get it out."

The sun cast its rays directly into the train car and as I looked for the little bug in her hair, I noticed, it wasn't one bug. Her hair was infested. They crawled all throughout her hair and the sight of so many made me sick to my stomach. I gave Mama a glance to come look trying not to scare Luba and Sofia. My stomach turned in circles and I instantly became itchy all over my body.

"Sofia, dear. Come close to me. I want to look in your hair." I said as calmly as I could. Hana did the same with Oscar and Papa looked at Lubov while she looked at Gita's hair.

We checked each other and with one quick glance we knew. We were all infested with lice. Hungry, tired, and dirty, we continued on our journey with one more thing to eat away at us.

CHAPTER FOURTEEN

HOPE

10 NOVEMBER 1941
Orenburg, Russia, USSR

Hana's grey scarf was wrapped over her head and tied under her neck, but wisps of her red hair had managed to escape free and they shined like glowing flames in the sparse morning light.

"How are you doing?" My sister asked, as she took my hand into hers. Most everyone around us was still asleep. It was nice to be away from the prying eyes and interested ears.

"I'm lonely. I miss Abraham." The clacking of the train on the tracks seemed louder that morning as my mind tried to focus away from thinking about him again. Every time I attempted to push away the worry and fear, it all came back, like a weed sprouting again, days after being pulled. "His letters and photos are tucked right here inside my coat." I placed my hand over my chest. "They beat right along with my heart. Knowing they are right here close to my heart calms me. Other times, my mind wanders to dark places, and with each beat it only becomes harder to breath."

"Did I ever tell you about the first time I met Efim?" Hana asked.

"Of course, Papa invited him and his family over for dinner," I answered.

"Yes, but did I tell you about our walk after dinner?"

"No, I don't believe you ever mentioned it." I thought back and wondered why she had not shared this story before.

"Well, after dinner, he asked me to step outside with him and take a walk. I was so nervous, but I noticed he was anxious too. Knowing that we were both vulnerable somehow made me relax. We talked about our interests and the longer we talked, the more I felt at ease with him. To my surprise, I actually started to develop feelings for him. As we headed back towards the house, he asked me what I was looking for in a marriage," Hana explained.

"He did? That is unusual."

"Yes. At first, I was taken back. Most of the men I knew or talked to didn't care about my opinion or want to listen to me, but I sensed that Efim was different."

"Efim was a caring man, you were lucky that you found each other. So, what did you say Hana?" I asked.

"I told him that I wanted a marriage exactly like my older sister, Raisa. I wanted a man who would love me, all of me, for exactly the way that I was. I told him that I wanted a husband who would protect me and love our children more than anything else in the entire world. I wanted everyone to envy the love that we shared the moment we walked into a room, much like I did when you were with Abraham. After I finished, I couldn't believe that I had said all of that out loud, and I half expected for him to run away. Instead, he took my hand and said, 'I would love more than anything to try to be that person for you.' His words were genuine as his eyes met mine, and I knew he was someone special," Hana answered.

I could not stop myself from letting a tear escape as I listened to her story. I understood why she was telling it to me. Efim was the love of her life, and he was no longer with us. Abraham may be away from us, but he was still alive. Having been through a great deal over the years, she still kept her head up. She had to work hard to support both herself and her son, but managed to find time for Oscar and our family. I didn't know Oscar's father, Efim, well, but I thought he was a good man. He was good to Hana and he cared for Oscar. About three years earlier he fell ill, and he wasn't the same afterwards. The doctors said it was his heart. He was noticeably weak for a long time until he was unable to get out of bed. Hana took care of him and nursed him at his bedside until the very last breath he took. She was a good wife and also an amazing mother and sister.

"I can't believe you never told me this story. I wish I had gotten to know Efim better, it's a shame we moved from Bobruisk so quickly."

"I have time and again envied you and Abraham. That first moment I saw you together, I observed the buzz you both created from merely being together. Efim was a great man, and we loved each other very much, but sometimes fate has other plans. I know it is hard, but to worry yourself, will only make you weaker for your girls."

I was about to answer her, when the train slowed down to an abrupt stop, forcefully waking those who were asleep.

"I will run and get us some boiled water. Oscar, you stay close to our family. I will be back soon." Hana reached for the empty water container, dashed through the crowd and smiled back at us before anyone could offer to join her.

We sat waiting for her, the minutes ticked away inside my head like one of Abraham's watches. I peered through the crowd, searching for her grey scarf, but the entire station was a sea of grey as my eyes bounced from one sad face to the next.

My heart began to tick faster than the clock in my mind as the train suddenly roared to life. I continued to scan for Hana, and finally I found her. She ran quickly towards us. The whistle sounded loudly, and as the doors shut, I yelled for Hana to hurry even though I knew she was too far away. As the clanking of the wheels sped up, the realization of what happened quickly sank in. I held Oscar close as he screamed out for his mother, his tiny voice echoed through the noisy train like bolts of thunder.

All I could think of was how alone Hana must feel. We were here together, and she was by herself and with nothing but water. A flood of thoughts and questions overflowed in my head as I tried to process our next steps. How would we find her now? Did she make it onto another car on this train? Is she going to have to wait for the next one, and how long until the next one even comes? What if we don't find her?

"Oscar, my sweet boy. Please don't cry. Your mother would not want you to worry yourself sick. We will find her. Maybe she made it onto another car, and we will see her at the next stop." I tried to reassure him as best I could, but doubt shook through me like an earthquake. I had seen with my own eyes how far she was when the train started to leave, and I could not imagine how she could have made it onto the train. Even with my fears, I still wanted to have hope. Hope seemed to be the only thing we could hold onto those days. Hope the war would end soon. Hope that Abraham would live to see another day. Hope that we would end up somewhere where we would have enough food and a roof over our heads. Hope that one day everyone could live together in peace.

I turned my attention to my girls and the rest of our family. A pressure built up inside me then, like it never had before. As I stared into their tearful eyes, the weight of taking care of them felt heavier than I thought I could bear.

Sofia began to pull at my coat to get my attention. "Mama, mama."

"Sofia, stop pulling at me! Give me a minute to think," I snapped back at her. I instantly felt bad about snapping at her and could feel the tops of my ears redden with shame. I wished I could be free, if only for a few moments. I needed to clear my head and come up with a plan. Oscar had already lost one parent; he couldn't lose his mother too.

"I'm sorry, Sofia. I didn't mean to yell at you." I leaned over and gave her a quick kiss before pausing to talk to the rest of my family. "We will get off at the next stop. All of us. We will look for Hana and if she is not on this train, then we will stay at the station until she arrives." The words fell out of me like broken glass, sharp and clear, leaving my emotions bottled up inside myself.

◆ ◆ ◆

The rain struck the roof of the Orenburg train station with force, followed by clashes of thunder which grew nearer as the night dragged on. Oscar was curled up on Papa, finally asleep. Thankfully, the noises of the violent sky did not shake him from his slumber. His body could not handle any more pain and worry than it already had. Watching him shut down and find sleep was the relief that I needed.

My eyes burned, but not because I had not slept in days. Instead, they were exhausted from the constant strain of searching. Every train which passed through held thousands of people, and I was intent on finding Hana among them. When we stepped off the train into the station two days earlier, our voices united as we called out for Hana, praying for her to come back to us.

Eating didn't feel right, knowing that Hana had nothing, but I forced food down my throat for the sake of the others.

"What are we going to do?" Gita whispered into my ear. "We can't sit in this station forever. We can't leave either." The truth of her words stung, even though I had already thought them myself. They sent the hairs on my arms up and my head swirled into a tornado.

"I don't know what to do. I go back and forth. Logically, it makes the most sense to wait here longer because this is the closest to where she was the last time we saw her. There are so many plausible reasons why she hasn't arrived yet. The question is, how long do we wait? Would it make sense to try the next stop? Maybe the train she boarded didn't stop at this station for some reason." The possibilities spiraled through me endlessly as I spoke aloud to Gita. "What do you think? You have generally been the most logical, the most calculated of the four of us."

"Maybe that is so, but should we be thinking with our brains or our hearts right now?" Gita asked.

Her response caught me by surprise. I didn't think she ever thought with her heart. That was one of the reasons Hana and I felt so distant from her and Lubov. We could never see eye to eye on most subjects.

Gita continued, not waiting for a response. "I think we should stay through the night and board the next train. We can stop at the next station and see if she is there." Her voice sounded sure and steady. I listened as the sheets of rain poured down outside, wondering where my dear sister was. All I could do was trust that this was the best option, even though it felt all wrong.

The night dragged on, as the steady pounding from above continued into the wee hours of the morning, when I finally allowed myself to doze off. The regret of having to leave the station without Hana weighed on my conscience, and my heart was burdened with despair.

As I woke to the sounds of the station, my eyelids were heavy as I fought to keep them open. Everyone was already awake as I scanned from one worried face to the next. Luba handed me some bread and cheese as Gita explained what we had talked about the night before.

"We should get on the next train heading south and get off at the next stop. Maybe Hana is there. It is possible that the train she boarded didn't make a stop in this station." Gita explained her thoughts, but I knew that she would be met with resistance when I looked at Papa's face.

"What if she comes here and we miss her because we left? I don't think we should leave yet," Papa answered instantly.

"Initially I thought the same, Papa, but what if Gita is right? We have already waited two days. I agree, it's time. We should go to the next station," I said, trying to convince myself as much as I was the rest of my family.

Within a few minutes the next train came, giving us no time to contemplate or continue our debate. We rushed towards it exchanging places with those getting off. First Mama and Papa stepped on and right as Oscar was being lifted into the train car, I looked down the platform at the never-ending stream of people. My puffy, tired eyes were being drawn towards something, and then I saw her. "Hana, Hana, I shouted." She turned, and we instantly locked eyes.

We helped Oscar, Mama, and Papa back down from the train before it sped away and ran towards Hana as she weaved her way through the crowds to us. She swept Oscar into her arms and held him so tightly I thought she may never let go. Tears of every emotion flooded around us like a rising tide.

♦ ♦ ♦

We watched Hana devour some bread and cheese and huddled around her waiting to ask what had happened to her. As she swallowed her last bite, Gita asked, "Tell us, sister. What happened? Where have you been for two days?"

Hana gazed at the floor a few meters in front of her, her sunken eyes showed not only her hunger, but also her fear.

"I ran as fast as I could when the train started to leave. I tried to make it onto the last train car, but I was too far away. I instantly started to cry and shut down. Every morsel of fear that I knew Oscar was having raced through me and it tore my heart to shreds. I stood on the platform for hours, unable to move, shocked and alone. People passed back and forth, but I couldn't see them. Everything around me was a blur."

I moved closer to Hana as she paused to collect her thoughts and her body trembled with fear.

"Then a woman and her little boy, who looked like Oscar, passed by me and caught my attention. He snapped me back to reality and I knew then that I needed to get myself together and get back to you, get back to my Oscar. So, I waited for the next train going south. It didn't come until the next day. By then, hunger had creeped through me, leaving me weak, but I focused on finding my way back, and I boarded the train hopeful that I would see you soon. The train seemed colder and more unforgiving when I was alone and surrounded by strange eyes, and my mind wandered to places it had never been before. We had been going for an hour, when there was a sound of an explosion. The train stopped abruptly, and like cattle we stampeded outside to take cover."

I grabbed Hana's hand as she began to tear up. She held Oscar on one side, his arm gripped hers even as he slept.

"The sun was setting and the sky was on fire. I ran towards a tree as the bullets grazed by me. I knelt down and covered my head and prayed. When I opened my eyes, it was dark. Unfortunately, the shadows of the night did not mask the destruction that had taken place. The train was damaged, and we became stranded under the weeping sky. Those of us who were left tried to sleep in the train cars, but I was haunted by the bolts of light which illuminated the scene of destruction before me."

Listening to her detailed story put me right there next to her and I didn't only feel for her, I felt with her.

"As dawn approached, the rain subsided, but the horrors of the night did not. The rays of cold sunlight wrapped themselves around the bodies which were now arranged next to each other in a row, thanks to the group which banded together to move them into a makeshift grave. Among them, the woman and her little boy who reminded me of Oscar laid silently."

I held Hana even closer, but I knew it wouldn't take her pain away.

Hana started again, once she regained her composure. "A little while later, a new train came and here I am. I prayed that I would find you and that you would be at the next stop. Even at my lowest point, I still had hope."

CHAPTER FIFTEEN
LIFE IN COLOR

25 NOVEMBER 1941
Tashkent, Uzbekistan, USSR

Thirty-seven days we traveled to Tashkent. We were now over four thousand kilometers from Minsk and the distance from Abraham had only widened the hole in my heart. The last few weeks on the train were miserable. I looked and felt like an old rag that had been used over and over again, and then left in the cold winter sun to never fully dry.

It was hard to look at Mama and Papa. Their movements seemed strained, as though they were walking through water. Papa slept more than he was awake. I saw his eyes move beneath his eyelids, and his legs twitch with the frightening dreams that overtook his sleep. We were all cursed with nightmares, but we all dealt with them in our own ways. Mama took the opposite approach as Papa and barely closed her eyes. I sensed her fear of what awaited her in the depths of her sleep. They both spoke less, drifting further away, but we pushed them to continue.

For weeks, we had been tossed between numerous train stations, waiting for our connections and tickets to continue. Sometimes, we stayed for days in a train station for our tickets to board the next leg of our endless journey. Occasionally, we were lucky and boarded a train car with a working stove to keep warm and shelves on the sides so we could lie down and sleep. Pandemonium was the best word I could imagine to describe the state in which we lived. Nothing was in order. There was no rhyme or reason to the evacuation of the people. We were merely cattle being herded into a direction, sometimes fed, and sometimes not.

Living in a constant state of fear had drained every ounce of life and happiness out of me and exchanged it with sadness. Before we began the journey to Tashkent, I still saw my life in color but now everything had turned to shades of grey. Where I once found joy in even the smallest thing, I now felt indifferent.

◆ ◆ ◆

Two weeks ago, I lost hope in humanity. It was the moment that made me question everything I believed in. I grew up trusting that good things happened to good people, and that naturally, bad people got theirs in return. If that had been true, why were so many good people suffering at the hands of the Nazis?

The air was cold, but it became slightly warmer as we headed further south. We continued to see our breath in front of us when we spoke, and we still had on every layer of clothing we owned. Practically everyone in the train car had developed a cough from sitting on the cold floor and up against the cold walls. There wasn't much we could do about it, just as there wasn't much we could do about the lice. We scratched all the time, but it didn't help. In fact, it only made it worse. Even if we had something to get rid of them, what would be the point? In these filthy living conditions, they would come right back, so we tried to ignore them as best as we could.

The girls were leaning on each side of me as I told them a story about a prince rescuing his princess from a tower guarded by lions. A loud wailing startled us as it echoed through the train. As I looked over, I realized it was the woman in the corner of the train with her newborn baby. My pulse quickened with each scream as I fumbled to get up. Worried thoughts raced through me with adrenalin as I pushed my way through to her, fearing the worst. A few days before, I was one of a few women who helped her deliver her baby girl on this very train. The miracle of life was amazing to be a part of, no matter the circumstances, and her birth helped me to remember the bright spots in life. But now this woman named Katerina was screaming, "No, no, no, why, why, why?"

Her words sounded incomprehensible as she sobbed uncontrollably. I made my way over to her and asked, "Katerina, what happened? Tell me what I can do."

Before she answered, I looked down at the baby and noticed she didn't cry or move. Her lips had begun to turn blue and she was breathless in her mother's arms. Her mother's tears dropped down one by one, as she gazed down at her baby. "I fed her everything I had… but I didn't have enough to eat myself… and my milk never fully came in. I… I had nothing left to feed her. How could I let this happen, I am her mother. I am supposed to protect her and keep her safe… I have failed." The air strangled me as I attempted to breathe. I hurt for her, for her baby. Anger ignited in my belly and I hated the Nazis at this moment more than ever. I took the deepest breath I could manage and tried to pull myself together for her sake.

I looked into her weepy blue eyes and said, "You did the best you could. This is no place for a newborn baby. You could not have done anything more to save her. You loved her for these few days, and you will continue to love her until the day you die. You must survive for her."

I sat with Katerina and held her as she cried for the next few hours. Finally, she could no longer cry, and she fell asleep with her cold baby still cradled in her arms.

I couldn't sleep. The hate burned deep in my belly and I couldn't extinguish its flames. I kept thinking about how her innocent baby's future was taken from her before it even began. She could have grown up to be a brilliant mind, a beautiful face, or a loving soul. She didn't even get a chance to feel the warmth of the sun, breathe fresh air, or see her father's face. War took her from this world, from her loving mother, and for what? When will it stop?

It wasn't until that evening that the train stopped and a few of the men helped to dig a hole to bury the baby. She was laid to rest right next to the train tracks in the middle of nowhere with only a cross made from sticks and a few rocks to mark her grave. I stood next to Katerina and wondered how she would continue on this journey. As a mother, I could not even imagine the pain she was bearing. She was completely alone. No family to support her, her husband fighting at the front and now her only child was taken from her. I grabbed her hand and held it tightly, hoping to take some of her pain away.

◆ ◆ ◆

Days passed and I became more and more worried about Katerina. She cried day and night. The bags under her eyes grew heavier than the one she carried over her shoulder, and I hardly recognized her. I tried to feed her bits of food that she had in her bag, but she wouldn't eat anything. I begged her not to give up, to continue on for the memory of her child and for her husband. My heart ached as she sat in the corner letting herself slip away.

After a few days, we came to a train station where we needed to change trains. It looked busy and I wondered how many nights we would have to sleep in the station before we got tickets for our train. We exited onto the platform and as I looked back, I watched Katerina head the opposite way. Her long blonde hair blowing in the gentle breeze as she walked away from the station following the tracks. A pit began to rise in my belly and my heart started to pace before I even realized what was happening. I quickly grabbed the girls and put my hands over their eyes just as Katerina stepped in front of the speeding train.

People screamed and ran to see what happened, but I couldn't move. I couldn't even speak. My insides yelled, "NO, NO, NO, WHY, WHY, WHY?" Exactly as Katerina had shouted only a few days before. My body was frozen, and I didn't want to believe it. Could I have done something to stop this or should I have said something different to change her mind?

That night as we spread ourselves on the cold floor of the train station, I held onto Luba and Sofia a little tighter, thankful that I still had my family. I promised myself again that I would never give up, no matter what happened. My necklace rested against my skin as I finally surrendered to sleep and it made me remember where I came from and what I was fighting for - life, *l'chaim.*

♦ ♦ ♦

Our last day on the train was three days ago and was Luba's sixteenth birthday. When I woke up that morning, I watched Luba's face as she slept. Her long dark eyelashes and rosy cheeks reminded me of myself at her age. I remembered the day that she was born and the first moment that Abraham saw her. All of our "firsts" started to flash through my mind like a flip book, and I couldn't help but smile at our memories. The past sixteen years had flown by and my little baby girl was now a young lady, a beautiful, capable, and loving one and I couldn't have been prouder of her. As her eyes opened, I leaned over to kiss her and then I recited a birthday poem to her.

"Be always warm, self-confident, and smart.
Let your life be filled with sunshine and love.
Always trust yourself and follow your heart,
And by your family you are truly beloved.
Happy Birthday, my sweet Luba!"

She smiled up at me and gave me a warm hug. I wished I had a present to give her, but we had nothing left. We had run out of food the day before and most of our money had been spent. The best birthday gift I could give her would be to get off this train and get us some food and a place to live.

The sun began to set and the sky danced with pinks and purples when we walked out of the train station. I wanted to gaze at the sky forever, but I couldn't, the overwhelming sea of people engulfed me like a raging storm. Thousands of refugees like us saturated the train station.

When we finally made our way out and crossed the street to the square opposite the station, we found that it too swarmed with people. As we walked past, my eyes scanned their faces and each of them only looked more tired and hungry than the last. We quickly learned that these people lived there because they had nothing left, no food or money to pay for a place to sleep.

We quickly set off in search of food before the night settled around us. We soon understood why so many people were huddled on the streets, starving to death. The "city of bread" was actually a city of deprivation. We joined the others, our bellies rumbled in unison as we tried to sleep the hunger away.

CHAPTER SIXTEEN
THERE ARE STILL GOOD PEOPLE

15 DECEMBER 1941
Tashkent, Uzbekistan, USSR

We woke up that first morning in Tashkent unaware of what to expect. We were thrown into a whole new world. It was overwhelming with people here and there, and dust and dirt were everywhere. We unfolded ourselves off our belongings and untied them from each other and ourselves. We had learned by now that nothing was safe unless you secure your belongings and slept directly on top of them, or as we did, huddled together between us. We took no chances as we knew that our possessions would be the only things that would help us survive in this foreign land.

We peeled off our top layer of clothes. As the sun rose, the air warmed up slightly and at last I began to thaw from the cold we had endured on our journey. Although, it was warmer here, it was still winter, and there was a thin blanket of snow lying on the ground. At night, the gusts of cold air awoke me, and sent icy shivers down my spine.

I looked across the station and noticed that people were spread as far as my eyes could see. There were so many, and so close to one another that it was difficult to get through the people without stepping on them or getting trampled on yourself. I tried to look into the distance and avoid the suffering, but I could not. The swollen bellies of the hungry jumped out at me as if they were trying to attack me. A man who slept only a few meters from us was alive last night, and this morning he was among the hundreds if not more, that didn't make it through the night. The hairs on my arm pricked up as I let the scene before me sink in.

We walked to the market to see what we could buy with the little money we had left. The markets were filthy, noisy, and filled with thieves. We were amazed to see the abundance of food available, but the prices were extremely high. How could anyone buy any of it at a time like this? It sat there as if on display to taunt us as we walked by with our mouths watering from hunger. The fruit was beautiful, the peaches a bright fuzzy pink, and looking at them piled on the tables made my stomach growl. As tempting as the fruits were, we decided to spend the last of our money on bread and butter. We knew it would go further and we would have more food to divide between us.

The taste of the bread and sliver of butter in my mouth was unexplainable. That was the longest we had gone without eating and I couldn't imagine ever having to do it again. I finally understood what Hana had gone through those two days without food when we became separated. Truly being hungry is not a sensation that can even be explained, especially when you have to watch your children and family endure it with you. It changed my perspective in so many ways. The simple things held more value. A small morsel of bread wasn't just a crumb anymore, it was like finding a tiny diamond hiding amongst the rough. I took my time eating the delicious bread and butter and prayed that we would never have to feel hunger again.

After we finished our scraps of bread and butter, we searched for a place to live. According to the people we spoke to who lived on the streets, this would be no easy task. Only people of a higher class were given rooms to rent in nicer accommodations. Others had to live with the locals and rent a small room, but with so many refugees, finding a room was difficult.

Another problem we encountered was the language barrier. Many of the locals didn't speak Russian, and, although some of them showed no interest in helping, we did find that the locals were warm and friendly people.

We searched for hours but were unable to find any place to live, so we too joined the thousands of others who slept outside the train station. In the mornings, we would wake and go to the market to get food for the day. We started to trade our clothes for food. A shirt for a half a loaf of bread or a nicer sweater for a full loaf.

Soon after we arrived, I wrote a letter to Abraham telling him about our journey and how we lived now. I tried not to worry him, but I was sure he would notice the tear stained pen markings. I asked him to send us some money, to save us from living outside, to save us from trading every item we possessed.

One day we sat in a circle with our belongings towards the middle. We had just woken up and decided to have a bite to eat before we headed out in search of someplace better to live. Most of the people around us began to wake up and the sounds of birds chirping were soon replaced by constant chatter. Before we finished our breakfast, a wave of people stepping off the train poured through the crowds. They looked at us with the same wide eyes we had only a few days before. I took the last bite of my bread and looked over my shoulder as I sensed something near me. I didn't see anyone, but then I looked up ahead and saw a skinny, tall man holding a bag that looked exactly like mine. I looked down and quickly realized it was mine.

"Stop that man, stop him, he stole my bag!" I screamed, startling not only myself, but everyone around me, including the man who stole my bag. He started to run as I began to run after him. Lubov was right next to me making her way through the crowd. "Stop him!" I shouted. No one seemed to be

RACHEL ZOLOTOV

moving, but everything was spinning as I rushed to catch up with him. My palms started to sweat as I thought about my favorite pictures in the hands of a stranger. Right then, a woman stood up just as the man ran by and tripped him with her leg. He fell hard to the ground and I rushed over to him. Lubov and I wrestled my bag back from him. He ran off as fast as he fell, and I approached the woman who had helped us.

"You were incredibly brave to do that, thank you," I said, as I looked at her wrinkled and dirty face. She sat back down on her bag and looked up at me with tired eyes. Tiny curls of her silver hair flew in the wind underneath her colorful scarf, and they reminded me of my Baba's locks.

Her voice was unexpectedly raspy when she spoke in a tone that hovered above a whisper. "My two boys and I made it here from Poland with the help of some kind people. We must support each other where we can, otherwise, what example are we giving our children? Don't worry about thanking me, instead keep the giving alive."

"I couldn't agree more. Good luck to you and your boys."

Her kindness restored my hope that there are still good people amongst us. It also caused the guilt I had swallowed when I didn't help that poor old man on the train to resurface. I might have slipped him my food the next day to try to make up for it, but it didn't change the fact that I had not helped when the bread was being taken from his wrinkled hands. We all just sat there and turned away in fear that if we intervened, we would be next. Each family has to protect their own, but we are so much stronger if we all come together, especially, during times like this. I promised myself then, that I would think back to this moment and next time I would be braver; I will not stand by and watch.

♦ ♦ ♦

As we settled into our new surroundings, we slowly erased what we had imagined the city and its people to be like, and

124

instead immersed ourselves alongside them. The crowded one- and two-story houses that lined the streets reminded me of Minsk, but the dirt streets and the camels in the distance threw me into the pages of a storybook. Tashkent seemed to be full of variations as I walked through the streets of the old and new parts of the town. One moment, my feet led me through a large street with a square which reminded me of Belarus, but the next minute I found myself walking through steep narrow alleyways that were dark and frightening.

Each day I walked to the post office, hoping for a telegram, wishing for some word from Abraham. Seeds of worry begin to sprout up inside of me when nothing came. I didn't want to consider the worst, but thoughts of Abraham being wounded flashed before me. On December third, after eight nights of sleeping outside, I walked into the post office and came out with a money telegram and a letter. I was so relieved that Abraham was well, I couldn't contain my happiness. As I walked to the others, I caught myself smiling when I passed by a window.

"Everyone, huddle around. We have word from Abraham! Let's go find a place to read it aloud." I motioned for them to grab their bags and we searched for a place where we would not be heard. I didn't want anyone to overhear that I had received money. We found a quiet area and I began to read aloud,

Good morning my dearest girls, Raisa, Luba and Sofia. I am alive and well and miss you all very much. I received your letter yesterday and this morning I am writing you this letter. As soon as I am done, I will go to the post office and send it along with a telegram for 500 rubles. Please go and find a place to stay as soon as possible, and when I get paid next, I will send you more. I can see from your letter, Raisa that your journey was a difficult one. It hurts my

heart to know that you girls had to endure these hardships and I wish I were there with you. I promise you that we are fighting to win this war and I hope we will be reunited soon. This makes me think of a Yiddish saying, He that can't endure the bad, will not live to see the good. You my dears have endured, and now everything will be better. I will be waiting for your next letter. Please write to me as soon as you can to let me know how you are. Please write to me about your health and the health of the girls. Take care of yourselves. Hugs and kisses.
Abraham

We were saved! Knowing that tonight my family would be sheltered, my body relaxed as the tension slowly dripped away. We headed out right away in search for a place to rent. We could not afford a nice place because we had no jobs, and needed to save money to buy food, which we knew was extremely expensive. We did have our ration cards, but this only gave us four hundred grams of rye bread per person since none of us had jobs. If we had work, we would get double that amount of bread. We searched all day to find someone to rent us a room and eventually we found a place. It was much less inviting than our cottage in Kilinchi, but at least we had a roof over our heads, a place to cook, a fire pit to keep warm, and we didn't have to be as worried about our possessions getting stolen.

Our new home was an Uzbek nomad tent or what we called a *kibitka*. It was located in the old part of town along a dirt road lined with more shelters like ours. The huts were made from clay and the floors were lined with straw mats for sleeping. Towards the middle of the house was a pit where we would light a fire and cook as well as keep warm on a chilly night. When it rained, I stayed awake listening to the drops as they dripped through the roof. Sometimes I wondered, if it rained enough, would the entire roof collapse on us? The smell reminded me of the bomb shelter in Minsk, the air damp and moldy. There were no windows or doors. There was also no electricity and we had to get water from a nearby irrigation ditch. Although the conditions were slightly better than in the trains, it was still filthy everywhere and far from sanitary. We tried getting rid of the lice, but they continued to come back, with every attempt.

Living like the locals these first few weeks had been difficult on the entire family and quite a culture shock, but we tried to stay optimistic. We registered with the refugee center in hopes that they would be able to help find us jobs, so we could find a better place to live.

For now, we lived day to day, trying to navigate ourselves through the roadmap of our strange new life. We tried to get accustomed to the dust, which seemed to be everywhere. We came home sprinkled with a layer of dirt and even worse, soiled with mud when it rained. This city, like all others was filled with both bad and good. We had encountered many locals who had shown so much love and understanding of our situation. They especially loved children and while we were out walking, Sofia and Luba were often treated to a fresh fruit from the trees of the locals. The people clearly had their own struggles with food, but still shared with us as if we were their family. On the other side, our little family never had to be so careful, and although we tried to avoid the thieves and bandits which roamed the markets and streets, they were everywhere. My latest purchase of milk was one such occasion. Once we drank it, we realized it had been severely diluted with water.

I spent my time with the girls exploring the new city and writing letters to Abraham. Writing somehow gave me the illusion of being closer to him. I sometimes pretended that I was telling him how our day was as he arrived home from work. I wanted to tell him how hard this was on me and on the girls, but I knew I couldn't.

♦ ♦ ♦

It was afternoon when Papa placed the last few pieces of wood into our fire pit. We all sat around the fire to keep warm, as even the days were getting colder, and our clay hut was chilly with only straw mats underneath us.

"I'm going to go out for some more wood. We only have enough here to last until the evening," Papa said as he poked at the fire igniting the new wood.

"I'll go with you," I said. Papa nodded and after getting on our hats and coats we headed outside into the crisp afternoon. We walked along the dirt road towards the center of Tashkent. Papa walked with his hands clutched behind him as usual, and I dragged the empty cart behind us.

"Papa?"

"Yes dear," Papa answered, but he didn't look up.

"Do you think this place could ever feel like home?" I asked

"I hope we don't have to be here long enough to call it that. But I do think that you could make anywhere your home as long as you have your family. The question would be if you will ever be truly happy there or not," he answered.

"I haven't thought about it that way. I keep telling myself this is only temporary. But temporary could mean so many different things. I think the hardest part for me is not knowing where and how long we will be here."

Papa was about to answer when we were interrupted by several people speaking happily in the distance. As we neared closer to them, we could see they were looking at today's newspaper. Papa bought the Russian *Izvestiya* newspaper and I instantly noticed that something important must have happened because a large picture was on the top along with the headline in big letters. Back home, we relied on the radio for the news every day, but now we have to buy a paper to get the latest information. Lately, I haven't even wanted to read the paper. What good could it do when they have no good news to report and the pages are only filled with useless stories? Today was different, the excitement shined on Papa's face as he scanned the large font at the top.

Papa read the headline out loud, "'Honor and Glory for the Heroic Defenders of Moscow!' This is good news, my dear. The Red Army has pushed back the Nazis!" Papa smiled and continued to read further. "This article is called 'The Last Hour, the Collapse of the Nazi Plan to Occupy Moscow'. Listen to this. It says here the Nazis are complaining about the winter and arguing that the cold is hindering their plan of occupying Moscow."

We both smiled. "That's interesting. What will they do when winter actually begins?" I asked with a chuckle.

Papa nodded and continued to read, "First, the real winter has not started yet. The temperature is only negative five degrees Celsius. Second, the complaints mean that they didn't supply their army with warm clothes, even though they announced to the whole world that they were ready for the winter." Papa looked up from the paper and looked over at me. "Basically, they thought they would have occupied sooner and won the war. Their hopes did not materialize and their mistake cost them."

I felt a rush of excitement jolt through me. What could this mean? Would the war be over soon? "What else does it say?" I asked.

Papa skimmed through the rest of the article looking for any other interesting information. "Here it says that so far in the defense of Moscow the Red Army has killed eighty-five thousand fascists, and one thousand, four hundred and thirty-four of their tanks destroyed or captured as well as five thousand, four hundred and sixteen cars."

The news sounded promising and the prospect of returning home seemed closer than ever. It made me smile as we made our way to the wood distribution center. We loaded up a half a cube of wood into our cart, leaving Papa and me breathless and warm.

Our walk back was slow with the full load in tow, but it didn't seem to matter. I was excited to share the good news with my family waiting for us at our makeshift home.

How brave our fearless soldiers have been. They have been on the frontlines enduring hardships I couldn't even imagine. Tonight, we will think about them more than usual, make an extra toast in their honor, and mourn those who lost their lives for our safety. Victory was the will of the Red Army and they succeeded! Their wives, children and elders will not forget them, we must not forget what they do for us.

Later that evening, I caught Luba looking at a picture of Abraham. I had to look away when I noticed a single tear run slowly down her face. She tried to keep her worry and sadness to herself, but I knew she missed him more than ever, and so did I. Abraham, Sofia and Luba were close, so I knew it was extremely hard on the girls being away from him, especially with the holidays and spring not long after. He was always there to teach Sofia and Luba something new. There was even a morning he woke us up early to fish.

CHAPTER SEVENTEEN

DROPLETS OF WATER

2 MAY 1931
Minsk, Belarus, USSR

"Good morning Luba," Abraham whispered as he peeled back the covers to see her face. He kissed her on her forehead and said, "I know it's early for a Sunday morning, but how would you like to go to the river and learn how to fish?"

"I would like that Papa!" Luba said excitedly. She jumped out of bed quickly and dressed in her pair of black tights, a tan skirt that fell past her knees and a blue button-up sweater with a blouse underneath. Then she joined us for breakfast. She had a playful smile on her face.

Abraham often took the weekends off to do something special with us. We usually spent our time outside, even on the days that were glazed over with ice and snow crystals. I loved watching him these past five years be a father to Luba, and I couldn't wait until our second child came. After breakfast, we packed and headed out. I took my spot walking leisurely behind them. I enjoyed spying on them from afar as they walked and giggled hand in hand to Gorky Park.

It was still dark when we walked outside, and the air smelled heavy and damp. The streetlamps and colorful window signs reflected onto the wet cobblestones into streams of shimmering color. Abraham carried the fishing pole along with a net and a bucket with two hand trowels inside. I gave Luba her own bucket for the smaller fish and she loved feeling important as she carried it trying to match her Papa.

"This morning is a perfect time to go fishing. Right after the rain, the fish are typically biting. I bet we will have good luck today," Abraham said enthusiastically.

It took us about twenty minutes to walk to the river, but the time had flown by. I was entertained as I watched Abraham and Luba laugh and talk. As we approached the park, she became more excited. I was growing bigger by the hour, so I knew that this would probably be our last fun day as a family of three.

We arrived at the river as the sun was about to rise. Luba had never seen the sun rise over the water before and it was a beautiful sight. I took a seat to rest and watched as Abraham knelt down beside Luba and put his arm around her and we watched the sun make its way up into the sky. Even with the clouds, the sun beamed as it spread its orange and yellow colors throughout the sky before us. A few minutes later Abraham broke the silence, "Luba let's take our shovels and go dig up some worms!"

We headed into the forest with the buckets and shovels. Abraham showed Luba how the best places to look are under the logs and rocks. Sure enough, when she pushed a large rock over, there were a few worms wiggling around in the wet dirt. She shoveled them into the bucket and looked for more.

I watched her walk a little bit further into the forest and look down to search for worms, but suddenly she turned around calling, "Papa, Mama, look, mushrooms! Lots and lots of them. They are bright red, and some are yellow" Abraham hurried over to see, and when he knelt down to take a look his eyes lit up. We often collected mushrooms, but generally we had to travel far into the forest because any nearby were already picked. People regularly went out to look for them and once you found one, you found a jackpot because the rest would usually be nearby. Somehow Abraham knew all the different types, their names and how best to cook them.

"Luba, these are good mushrooms! These are *Syroezhki*, the most common edible mushrooms. They will taste wonderful fried with some onions! I guess the rains caused them to shoot up, and we are early this morning! You have to be extra careful with these, as they are extremely brittle," Abraham explained as he took the pocket knife out of his front pocket and carefully cut them and placed them in our sizable bucket. "It's a good thing you gave us an extra bucket, Mama, or we wouldn't have anywhere to put these gorgeous mushrooms. I will cut and you look for worms, we will need some more worms if we want to catch ourselves some fish too!"

As Abraham and Luba worked on their tasks, he told us more about the types of mushrooms. He talked about how to tell if a mushroom is poisonous. He also showed Luba how to make sure you didn't pick any that had tiny worms inside.

"The most common poisonous mushrooms are the fly agaric and the death cap. They both have what's called a skirt on the stem and that usually means the mushroom is poisonous. The amanita is bright red like these are, but they are rounder on top and have white spots all over the cap. The death cap is slightly greenish on top with a white stem and gills. If you are ever unsure of a mushroom, it's better not to pick it because it could be poisonous."

"I love to pick mushrooms with you Papa, but I think I love to eat them even more," Luba said making Abraham laugh. His bucket was filled to the top and Luba had found enough worms to last them a few hours, so we headed back to the river. I sat on the edge of the bank and watched while Abraham connected the three pieces of bamboo together to make the long fishing pole. He attached the fishing line and then showed Luba how to attach the worm on the hook and cast it into the water. He let her hold the fishing pole and she was supposed to let him know if she felt any tugs. We sat quietly for a long time and suddenly Luba jerked as something snagged her pole.

"Papa, it did it, what do I do now?" she asked frantically. He took the pole and showed her how to pull the line back in. He quickly held the line up in the air and hanging from the hook was a wet leaf and no worm.

"Hmm. That is a beautiful leaf we caught there. That smart fish grabbed our worm and swam away, didn't he?" said Abraham laughing. "That's alright. Let's try again, we will get him sooner or later."

This time she attached the worm herself. She picked him up out of the dirty bucket and he started to quickly slither to and fro. He was so slimy she dropped him three times before she could get him onto the hook. She put him through the hook multiple times so he wouldn't fall off. Then she cast the line. It didn't go far like Abraham's, but it worked. I was impressed by how well she did, and from the playful grin on her face I could tell she was having fun. Then we waited again for a bite.

That was when Abraham turned to Luba and gave her the look he does when he has something serious to say. "What is it Papa?" she asked also sensing that he had something to say.

"Luba, I want you to know that I am so excited that you will be a big sister soon. I know that you have tried so hard to help Mama lately with everything, and I am so proud of you. You are going to be a wonderful sister. Mama and I love you more than you know." His words were so thoughtful, and I couldn't have said them better myself.

"Yes, Luba. We are so proud of you. You have been a huge help to me these past few months, you are such a great helper. Thank you!" I added.

"Thank you, Papa and Mama. I love you both too and I can't wait to hold the little baby! But first, help me! I have a bite!" She stood up and Abraham helped to pull the fish in. As it was yanked in, the fish flipped and flopped all around. The scales sparkled in the sunshine and droplets of water were sent here and there. He turned towards her, smiled and didn't have to say anything for her to know that he was proud.

We fished for a few hours until our bellies rumbled, and we had no more worms left. Our buckets were full of fish and mushrooms, and I couldn't wait to get home and make a delicious dinner with them!

"Now let's hurry up and head home for lunch, I am hungry, and this baby wants to eat," I said as Luba dropped our last catch of the day into the bucket.

Abraham picked Luba up when her legs tired, and put her on his shoulders. I held the pole and shovels while Abraham took both the buckets and we dashed home.

"The view from up here is so different. I can see everything, so many buildings and the trees! I can see so far into the distance. Look Mama, I am a bird flying high up in the sky."

Neighbors walked by, smiled and waved and congratulated us on our lucky morning. We arrived home and I immediately fell into the nearest chair exhausted from the walk. Abraham came behind me and massaged my shoulders and although I wanted to take a break, I knew that we had fish and mushrooms waiting to be cooked.

"I will go and get some pails with water and we can start to clean the fish and mushrooms. How about you rest while I get started? Luba, do you want to help me carry a bucket?" Abraham asked as he continued to massage.

"Yes, Papa. Let's go. Bye Mama!"

Abraham pulled over a second chair, propped my feet up, and gave my belly a quick kiss goodbye.

It wasn't long before they came back giggling about a story that Abraham had told Luba on the way back. We washed a few of the mushrooms and Abraham cleaned some of the fish. I chopped an onion and fried them all together and we had what tasted like a feast for lunch.

It was one of those days you wished would never end but you knew when it did end, it would be a lasting memory; the kind that would be talked about at the dinner table for years to come.

CHAPTER EIGHTEEN
THANKFUL

8 JANUARY 1942
Kokand, Uzbekistan, USSR

Last month Abraham sent extra in the money telegram. I wished he had kept it for himself and bought himself something warm. The winter was fierce this year, and I worried he would freeze if he didn't have the proper clothing. But instead of getting himself a necessity, he sent the money to us, with instructions for me to get something for our girls to celebrate the New Year. I wanted to be mad at him for thinking that they needed something extra when he was fighting a war, but I knew it was no use, he loved us more than he loved himself. So, I went out and searched the market for a small tree, some ornaments, and wool to make a scarf for Abraham.

"Sofia, Luba, Oscar, come over here my dears!" I shouted as I put down the small tree and my basket with decorations and ornaments.

"Mama, you bought a New Year's tree!" Sofia gasped, "thank you, Mama!"

Hearing the excitement, the rest of my family came over to see. I noticed a smile from Hana as she watched Oscar, and even Gita looked pleased.

"Aunt Raisa, can we decorate it now?" Oscar asked.

"Of course, we can, let's all do it together," I replied, unable to say no to his adorable face.

Mama pushed aside the straw mats to make space, and motioned for us to put the tree there. It was as close to the center of the tent as it could be without being too close to the fire pit.

"I wish we had some paper and glue so we could make a paper chain," Sofia said as she came closer to me.

"Well then I guess it's a good thing I managed to get some old newspaper," I said while pulling it out from the bag. "Now, we just need to boil some potato starch in water to make glue." I motioned to Mama to start boiling the water while I went to get the starch.

Sitting on our straw beds, we folded the paper into links and glued them one by one. Once the paper chain was complete, we swirled it around the tree like a winding staircase. "Luba, could you get the cotton from the bag? Then help Oscar and Sofia with spreading it around the base of the tree."

As they stretched the cotton into a blanket of snow, I pulled out the ornaments. The old lady at the market had wrapped them for me in some newspaper so they wouldn't scratch or break.

Although the ornaments weren't our family ornaments, carrying the memories of our past, they were still beautiful nonetheless. Some shined with silver and others gold, while a few were a pinkish-purple. Many of them were plastic, depicting popular children's stories like The Firebird and *Baba Yaga*, a magical witch who lived in the forest in a hut on chicken legs.

"Look, it's Puss in Boots!" exclaimed Sofia as she picked it up from the paper. "This one is my favorite."

"I love the Little Red Riding Hood," Luba chimed in as she hung it carefully on the tree.

I watched as Oscar scanned over the ornaments carefully. Hiding under a gold one was one that I knew would catch his eye. I leaned over and picked up the golden glass globe revealing the silver one underneath.

"Mama, Mama, it's Pinocchio!" Oscar held it up for everyone to see. His smile extended from ear to ear when he hung the ornament on the tree. Watching him warmed my heart.

Taking turns, we continued to hang the rest of the ornaments, slowly filling up the tree. A few were made of glass and shaped like pine cones. They reminded me of the pine cones that dangled from the tree right outside our home in Minsk. I hung the last one and then Papa placed the star on the top to complete our New Year's tree.

◆ ◆ ◆

The holidays were supposed to be a time of celebration. It was a chance to look back at the year and acknowledge the good and the bad. I started the New Year feeling detached and alone, however, as it was the first in seventeen years that Abraham and I spent apart. I didn't want to reflect on the past year without him by my side. I thought it would only make me feel further away from him, but I knew he wanted us to celebrate and be thankful for the good. On the eve of the first, we enjoyed each other and the food we could manage to make over our fire pit. We admired our tree as it glistened and reflected from the nearby candle light.

Clink, clink, clink. The tip of Papa's spoon lightly tapped his glass of tea which was raised in the air. "I have a few words to say as we bring in the New Year. Of course, I want to wish you all health and happiness. I hope that this year we defeat the Fascists and go back home, all of us, safe and sound. I would like to bring in the New Year with a story. It's about a poor man, his family, a goat, a cow and chickens." He put his glass down and settled onto his straw mat with Mama. His eyes closed tight for moment as if he was conjuring the story from his memory, like a magician pulling a rabbit from his hat.

I loved Papa's stories. Normally shy and soft spoken, he didn't strike me as a storyteller, but once he began to spin a web of words, it was as if he transformed into another person.

"A poor man lived in a small one-room house with his wife and six children. But, with so many of them in one room, they would get in each other's way. He didn't know what he could do, but he knew he couldn't stand it anymore. His wife told him to go talk to the rabbi. With no better idea, the next day he went to talk to the rabbi," Papa recounted the story easily as if he had told it many times, although I didn't recall this one.

All eyes were fixed on my Papa as he continued, "The rabbi greeted him, but could tell that something was troubling him. 'Whatever it is, please tell me so I can help,' the rabbi told him. So, the miserable man told the rabbi about his situation at home. 'The eight of us sleep and eat in one room. I feel like I can't breathe. We have started to yell and fight with one another. I can't take it anymore,' he told the rabbi." I took a sip of tea and looked over at Mama. She was absorbed in Papa's story, nodding her head and following along with a slight smile on her face.

"The rabbi thought long and hard about his problem. He paced back and forth a few times, until finally he stopped and said, 'Do what I tell you and things will be better. Will you promise to do just as I say?' The poor man promised. Then the rabbi asked him a question, 'Do you have any animals?' The man told him he had a cow, a goat, and some chickens." Papa paused and took a drink and then asked, "Does anyone have any idea what advice the rabbi was going to give?"

Sofia blurted out first, "He told him to sell his animals and get a bigger house?"

"That is a great idea, but that wasn't it. Anyone else?" Papa asked. "No one? Well then, I will tell you. He said, 'When you get home, gather all your animals and put them inside your house to live with you,'" Papa continued with a smile.

At this everyone laughed. "Oh no, that will be even worse," Oscar cried out.

"That's exactly right, Oscar. It was much worse, but the man promised to do exactly as the rabbi said, so he did. The next day he went back to see the rabbi. He couldn't understand why the rabbi would give him such bad advice. 'Rabbi, please help me, the animals, they are all over the house. It's awful. What can I do?' he pleaded with the rabbi for help. The rabbi listened carefully and told him to go home and take the chickens back outside. So, the man went home and did just that. But of course, the next day was the same problem, so he went back to the rabbi and said, 'The chickens are gone, but the goat is eating all of our things and making a mess.' So, the rabbi gave him instructions to go home and remove the goat from his house. Any ideas what happened next?" Papa asked, looking over at Sofia and Luba.

This time Luba spoke first. "Did he come back again and complain about the cow, and the rabbi told him to take the cow back outside?"

"Precisely, my dear, and the next day the poor man came back to the rabbi and said, 'Thank you, rabbi, we have such a good life now. The animals are back outside and the house is quiet and clean. We even have extra room now! What happiness I have!'" Papa finished the story, raised his glass and motioned for us to do the same. "I wanted to tell you this story so you could see that no matter how little, or how bad you think you have it, life could always be worse. Appreciate what you have and take life as it comes at you. Happy New Year!"

"Happy New Year!" we shouted in unison and our glasses clinked together in honor of the first toast. I enjoyed Papa's story. It was a good lesson, especially in these times. It did make me appreciate that although our life right now was trying, it could have been worse.

"What a wonderful lesson, Papa. Thank you for sharing it. I think we can all take something from that into the New Year," Hana said. "Now let's eat!"

Although it was not the small feast we usually had back in Minsk, I was thankful for the bread and modest amount of food on our plates, and for the health of my family. But more than all of those I was thankful for the card from Abraham. As the minutes ticked closer to midnight, I held onto the New

Year's postcard as if I were holding on to him, unwilling to let it go for fear he wouldn't be close to me when the clock struck nineteen forty-two. On the back of the card was a beautifully written message from Abraham wishing us a happy and healthy New Year. He promised us that he was healthy, wore warm clothes, and that he was fed well. His words sounded encouraging and hopeful. They gave me the reassurance I needed to calm my nerves, at least for the moment. On the front of the postcard was a giant Russian soldier defeating a tiny Nazi soldier while running through the snowy forest in the moonlight and twinkling stars above them.

"Mama, it's almost time," Luba shook my arm, pulling me out of my trance. I looked up from the card and noticed everyone was getting ready. All the cups had been refilled with tea and ready for the countdown.

"Ten, nine, eight, seven, six, five, four, three, two, one, happy New Year!" Our cups clanked together and we passed around hugs, kisses, and wishes for the New Year.

Once we were all too tired to stay awake any longer, we laid down on our straw beds and huddled close for warmth. I pulled my star out from under my blouse, gave it kiss, and whispered, "Happy New Year Abraham, I love you."

CHAPTER NINETEEN
EVERY LAST CRUMB

2 MARCH 1942
Kokand, Uzbekistan, USSR

After more than two months of waiting for a response from the refugee center, we finally received word in early February. The entire family was directed to relocate to a city called Kokand, where there were jobs available for us. I was hopeful that this move would be better. Even though it was further away from Minsk in distance, I was ready to get out of the overcrowded city of Tashkent. Kokand was a fairly large city, located in the Fergana Valley of Uzbekistan.

We started our journey on a quiet early February morning, and traveled about two hundred kilometers east of Tashkent. The train chugged along the entire day, only stopping to load and unload surges of fatigued refugees. None of us were looking forward to another journey on the train, especially Luba. I wished she wouldn't get sick again and I hoped my parents would continue to overcome these difficult times. We did the best we could to hide our despair of being on the train again, but there was no way to disguise the pure exhaustion we all suffered from. The living conditions in Tashkent left us feeling like shells of ourselves. It wasn't just the sleeping on straw mats, or lack of clean running water, or the cold wet nights, it was everything put together, and it nearly consumed us all.

Upon arrival in Kokand, we immediately registered with the local refugee center. Then, we were sent to the bathhouse to be sanitized. All of us were crammed into a tiny crowded bathhouse to wash the filth from ourselves. They had us remove every article of clothing and place them into a giant heap with the others. Then we washed for twenty or thirty minutes. Women, children and men, showered in the same room. I felt violated. I tried to wash away the embarrassment from my naked body, but it clung to me like a few wandering eyes did. In the meantime, our clothes were steamed, and in the next room we found them in a giant heap waiting for us, smelling stale and slightly damp. Each of us dug through to find our own clothes, but the pile was so big, it was like searching for a needle in a haystack.

Even after the bath, we were still covered with sores from the lice, which ate at our scalps and left us itchy. In order to kill them, we soaked our hair in a concentrated mixture of salt water every other day, but it took us weeks to be fully rid of them. I can't even describe how relieved I was when they were gone.

In Kokand, we were able to settle into much better living conditions. Each family that had an enlisted soldier fighting was eligible to receive a certain amount of money to be sent to them monthly. The money was sent through a telegram through the post office. I filled out the necessary paperwork and each time I only needed to show my identification to be able to retrieve the money. The amount each family received was dependent on how much the soldier made according to his rank and also what amount the soldier himself cared to send home. Every month, Abraham sent us at least one thousand rubles, which before the war started would have been a large sum of money, but with so much inflation, it only stretched so far. For example, a kilogram of pork cost four hundred rubles and a kilogram of flour was two hundred rubles. A dozen eggs now cost around one hundred and seventy-five rubles, or one cabbage was typically seventy rubles. We had nine mouths to feed and an apartment to pay for, so we had to make the most of the money he sent. Once most of my family began to work, we were able to have more food on the table. We no longer had to endure the pangs of hunger that haunted us only a few months back and instead we had just enough food to keep ourselves from being hungry. We were comfortable. The money we saved that Abraham sent allowed us to afford an apartment with three small rooms and a kitchen with running water. Mama, Papa, and Lubov slept in one room while Gita, Hana and Oscar slept in the other room. Luba, Sofia and I were in the last room. We each had a bed and, although this place would never be our home, especially without Abraham, it was as close to one that we had been in for the last year. I tried to make the most of our life as it was, but most days I couldn't erase my thoughts of Abraham. The longer I went without him, the farther I felt from reality. Each day I was more scared than the last. What if this was my new forever?

♦ ♦ ♦

Sofia joined me in the kitchen earlier than normal one morning. It was a few weeks after we had settled into our apartment and the realization of how far we were from home had finally begun to sink in. I was alone when she shuffled in with hunched shoulders and a sad face.

I placed my tea cup down carefully. "Good morning, Sofia." I bent over to kiss her flawless porcelain-like cheek, wondering what worried thoughts were running through her mind today.

"Good morning, Mama." Sofia plopped herself down on the chair beside me. She may have been eleven, but her face was that of a pouting five-year-old. Her eyes darted down as I tried to meet her gaze.

"Sofia, my dear, what's wrong?"

"I miss…" Sofia's voice trailed off into tears. "I, I, I miss Papa… and our home…" She managed to get out the words between sniffles. "And… my friends. I don't even know where they are. I want to go back to my school, with my friends. When are we going back to Minsk, Mama?"

I wanted to have an answer for her, but we no longer lived in a time of knowing. Everything around us ticked like bombs ready to blow. All we could do was wake each morning and confront them. I put my arm around Sofia as she sobbed into her hands. "Oh honey, I know you are homesick. We all miss Papa, Minsk and our friends. I wish I knew when. I want to say soon, but I really don't know. What I do know, is that there are many other evacuees here feeling exactly like you are right now. We all miss the same things, and to get through this we should lean on each other. Do you understand?"

"Yes. It's just that I feel like I am forgetting. I don't want to forget." She said beginning to cry again while shaking her head no.

"Forget what, Sofia?" I asked, pulling my handkerchief out of my pocket for her.

She took a moment to wipe her nose and then she focused on me with those pouting eyes. "I can't remember Papa's voice like I once did. Even his face feels like it is fading away from my memory. I look at a picture of him to help me remember, but I don't want to have to remember. I want to see him." Embarrassed, Sofia hid her eyes once again.

My cheeks reddened and my hands trembled slightly as I listened to her. My heart was listening, and it reached out to hers. We both had the same fears, the same thoughts. "Sofia, don't be ashamed. I know what you are going through."

"You do? Really?"

"Yes. I spent many more years with your Papa than you, but I also sometimes feel like he is moving farther away from me. I struggle sometimes to remember a certain detail, but I try not focus on that. I like to remember certain memories instead. For instance, the moment when Papa first saw you after you were born, or the day you took your first steps. Did I ever tell you that story?"

"That is a funny story," Luba exclaimed as she walked into the kitchen, "I remember that day."

"You do? You were only about six years old," I asked, surprised.

"Yes. For some reason that day stuck in my head," Luba replied.

"I'm not sure if you ever told me," Sofia replied.

"You tell it to us Luba. I will make you girls some breakfast and tea," I said as I moved towards the teakettle and slowly began painting the scene of that day in my mind. I remember it was spring, and the rain hit the roof like woodpeckers in the forest. Sofia was almost one year old and she was into everything. That Sunday morning after breakfast the four of us were playing together on the rug.

"We were all together on the rug playing with you. You were crawling everywhere and pulling yourself up onto Papa. I remember walking with you as you held onto my fingers, but you wouldn't let go," Luba began.

"We knew you could walk on your own. You were very stable, just scared," I chimed in.

"Anyway, you were playing with a doll. It was your absolute favorite doll when you were a baby. It was mine before you were born. It was a little girl with her hair in pigtails. Her ribbons were blue, and her dress was pink. Or was it the other way around?" Luba laughed, "It doesn't matter, I guess. Just then, Papa had an idea. He stood you up on one end of the carpet and told us to go to the other end. We wanted to see if you would walk yourself to one of us, and if you did, which one of us would you choose. Mama, Papa and I each called your name, motioning for you to come."

Luba paused for a moment, allowing me a few words. "Your Papa thought you would go straight to him, but instead you stood there, looking at us like we were all crazy."

"And then you walked over to your doll, picked her up and started to play with her. The three of us began to laugh and clap in excitement for your first steps," Luba said smiling as she recalled the joyous moment.

Sofia smiled too as we passed around the pot of kasha and more memories of the four of us together. I was still worried even though they were now smiling. I knew that underneath her smile Sofia was still hurting. So was I, and so was Luba. How could we not be? Was I doing this right? What more could I do? I asked myself these questions hoping for an answer, but instead I continued to tread water, praying that I wouldn't drown.

♦ ♦ ♦

Mostly, we kept to ourselves, but as I explained to Sofia we needed to learn to lean on each other, so we made friends with a few other Jewish and Russian refugees. We even made friends with some of our Uzbek neighbors, who welcomed us into their neighborhood graciously. We learned that the locals were mainly Muslim and were quite traditional. They were devoted to their religion and customs. Their distinctive Mongolian features, paired with the colorful caftans and round hats, were of no resemblance to the refugees which had flooded their city. As I passed the locals in the street, my eyes were overwhelmed with the array of colors and patterns which leapt off their long robes. Even the simple striped ones the men wore were interesting to look at, but I admired the robes with intricate floral designs.

I observed how some of the locals disliked that communism was forced onto their traditional way of life, and that distaste was sometimes reflected onto the refugees. In spite of the communist propaganda, the Uzbeks maintained much of their ethnic lifestyle. Right near our apartment was a *chaikhana*, an Uzbek tea-house. Inside, the local men sat and sipped tea for hours. It was unusual in that it served not only the purpose of a tea-house or restaurant, it was also a meeting place and sometimes even a hotel. After peeking into the window, I could see it was a calm and serene place. Inside, rested low platform-like beds covered in rugs. The men sat on them with their legs crossed. In the middle was a small table usually filled with tea cups and bowls of *plov*, an Uzbek rice pilaf. I wondered why I never saw women inside, and was told by our friendly neighbor, Feruza, that it was considered indecent behavior for a woman to be there.

The locals had different customs, wardrobe, and language. There were also people from all different parts of the Soviet Union and also from different countries. The Jewish people were another faction within the various cultures, furthering our divisions, but yet, here we were living in unity, despite all of our differences. How is it that we can live as one mostly peaceful unit, but the Nazis can't get along with anyone that isn't like them? Where does hate like that come from? I thought about these questions often, too often in my lifetime. The answers seemed so far away and I wondered if I would ever reach them.

Luba, Sofia and Oscar stayed home with us until the start of school in September. Papa, Hana, Gita and Lubov worked in the same shoe factory doing odd jobs. They worked like automatons on the assembly line, going through the same motions over and over again. They must have felt a sense of accomplishment since the shoes they produced went to the soldiers who fought our war. We each played our parts and did what we needed to survive in this foreign land, but every day I continued to go in circles without Abraham.

Mama and I stayed home to cook, clean and watch the kids. We would also go into the center of Kokand to buy a newspaper or hear the latest news which would be broadcast from a loudspeaker. Many people would gather there and look at the small black plate that shouted the latest bits and pieces of what was happening across Europe. We also took turns waiting in the lines to get bread and other food items. As the family of a soldier, we were entitled to three hundred grams of bread per day per person. The earlier in the morning I left, the better chances of us receiving our rations. Sometimes, they ran out, and we couldn't get any for that day. I usually set out at six in the morning before the sun had a chance to rise. When it was my turn, the lady took my ration cards and cut out the date stamp for that day from each card. Then, I watched her measure out the bread to make sure she placed every last crumb into my bag.

CHAPTER TWENTY
COTTON FLOWERS

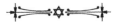

7 JULY 1942
Kokand, Uzbekistan, USSR

I opened the door to the main entrance of our apartment building. A wonderful smell drifted through the air. As I inhaled, my stomach turned with excitement. Just then, my neighbor, Feruza opened her door to check her mailbox. The smell intensified with the whoosh of her door, and my mouth began to water.

"Good morning Raisa. How are you today?" she asked in broken Russian, her brown eyes twinkled as a smile emerged.

"I'm doing well. How about you, my friend?"

"We are good too. I am doing some housework and making a special dinner. My youngest son is celebrating his birthday today."

"I was wondering where that heavenly aroma was coming from. What are you cooking?" I had missed my own kitchen back home, and part of me envied my neighbor.

"Plov. It does smell wonderful. I use my grandfather's recipe. He was considered the king of plov in my family. Typically, my husband made the plov for our special occasions. It is not a dish the women customarily take part in, but life has to continue, and it's up to us to continue our traditions." She explained, smiling.

"I want to learn how to make it. Maybe one day you can show me?"

"How about today? Are you busy? I started only a little while ago, and I would love to have some company." Feruza's voice sounded lonely and I knew how she felt. Her husband was also off fighting at the front while she took care of their three children.

"Actually, I am not busy today. I would love for you to teach me! I will go upstairs, put this bread away, and let my Mama know."

I slipped my apron on and tied it in front into a neat bow before heading back over to Feruza's place. I let myself in through her door, which she had left propped open for me. Directly inside was a simple room with an old sofa and a large intricate flower motif rug hanging directly above it. It was rich with burgundy, cream tones and deep blues. A few steps further lured me inside to her sunny and colorful kitchen. Although it was a small kitchen, everything was neatly put away on the shelves or tucked inside the cabinets and behind the curtains. A cozy, round, light wood table with five chairs sat directly under the window warming itself up from the sun streaming in. The splashes of brightly colored pots, dishes and other kitchenware were cheerful. I admired how the Uzbeks weren't afraid to use color. It made me realize that back home, most of the apartments were so grey and bleak.

"There you are. Come on in, Raisa! Let me show you what I have prepared so far."

I grabbed the pencil and paper I had in my apron pocket and wrote down the ingredients as she recited through them.

"First, you start with the meat. I have already cooked it but let me explain how you must prepare it. I usually use double the amount, but I was lucky to get my hands on any lamb at all. Anyway, you must pat the meat dry before you cube it so when you cook it, it will sear and keep the juices inside."

She opened the lid to let me peek in. The smell of onions, carrots and lamb skipped around the kitchen, tickling all my senses. I also took note of the thick, heavy pot she used, and hoped I could find one like hers for a good price at the market.

"You add oil to the pot, just enough to cover the bottom and heat until it is smoking hot. Cook the lamb until it's golden brown. Next, add two chopped onions and cook until they are golden. Shred three or four carrots and add them on top. Don't mix yet, keep layering. Add in some salt and pepper, one teaspoon coriander, and about two teaspoons each of cumin and paprika. Then, add about one and a half cups of water. It should barely cover what is inside. Cover with the lid and simmer for an hour."

"Do I mix it while it is simmering?"

"No. Do not mix it until the very end. I have been simmering this for about a half hour now. Would you like to help me with the rice while it finishes?"

"Of course."

"A long-grain rice works best for plov and the most important part is to rinse the rice before using it. Rinsing removes the extra starch, making it fluffy and less sticky. Actually, the best type of rice to use is called Devzira, and it is grown right here in the Fergana Valley. Devzira is not grown at the large farms because it is a low yield crop, but I know several of the small farms that grow it only for making plov. Here is the mesh bowl for you to rinse the rice. Add three cups of the dry rice and rinse until it is clear."

I washed my hands and rinsed the rice by swishing it around with my fingers. Each time I added more water, it became clearer, until we both agreed it was ready. While I rinsed, Feruza readied the water for boiling and put out the heads of garlic.

"Has plov been a tradition in your family for a long time?" I asked, wondering if there was a story behind this national dish.

"It has been around for a long time. Some say it dates back to the tenth century. There is a romantic legend that is well known about plov. Have you heard of it?"

"How interesting, no I haven't. Please, tell it to me."

"The story goes that the son of the Bukharian ruler fell madly in love with a beautiful woman from a poor family. Of course, since he was a prince and she was the daughter of a handcrafter, they were not allowed to be together."

Of course, I thought to myself. "Isn't it always how the story goes? There is usually something or someone that is untouchable. If only every culture allowed us to marry for love."

"Maybe someday it will be like that, but traditions are hard to break when they have been passed down for centuries. Anyway, the prince became tormented from a broken heart and began to fall ill. He stopped eating and sleeping and grew thin. When his condition continued to get worse, he was taken to an Avicenna, a Persian physician. The prince refused to disclose his heartache, knowing that there was no remedy. The physician put his finger on the prince's pulse then he began to name all the city's neighborhoods. The physician took note when the prince's pulse quickened and in that way he was able to narrow down the neighborhood, and then the family, and finally the girl whom the prince was in love with."

"That's quite a technique!" I said, still wondering how the story relates to plov.

"Yes, he was very cunning. With the mystery revealed, the physician proclaimed his treatment: The prince must eat plov once a week until he is healthy again and then marry the girl he is in love with. The young prince soon recovered, and they lived a long and happy life together."

"What a wonderful love story! I always loved to listen to my grandmother tell me about the old legends and tales passed down through the generations."

"It is a sweet story. This is why plov is customarily served at weddings and many holidays and special occasions. We still have some time until we are ready to add the rice. How about we sit and have some tea?"

"That would be lovely."

I watched her remove the blue and white ceramic teapot from the shelf. It was beautiful. I had noticed these distinctive teapots when I walked by the tea houses and at the market.

"This is a traditional Uzbek teapot with hand-painted cotton flowers." Feruza explained as she saw me admiring it. "They are usually painted blue because the color is considered calming and is meant to soothe while drinking tea."

Feruza pulled down two matching cups and motioned for me to have a seat. "This type of cup is called *piala*. They are more like small bowls, since they have no handle."

"They are beautiful. I love the pattern on them. I have seen similar cups at the market. Maybe one day I will buy a set to take home." My heart ached after I said the words. I missed Minsk. I often feel so removed here in Kokand, but yet I felt a certain closeness with Feruza. Something about her reminds me of home when I am near her, but I haven't been able to figure out what.

"Here, the tradition is to only pour a half of a *piala*. This is so you don't burn your fingers while holding the cup and also the tea cools faster," She said, as she poured the hot tea to halfway, first in my cup and then in hers.

The green tea was light in color, but surprisingly rich in flavor. I held the cup close to my nose, smelling the uniqueness of the traditional Uzbek tea.

"The tea is delicious. Thank you," I said, placing the cup down.

"Of course, my friend. I'm glad you like it," she answered. Her eyes twinkled as they caught the sunlight casting in through the window. She smiled at me from across the table and asked, "tell me, my dear. How are you doing? It must be hard to be so far away from your home and not have your husband to help. I know what it is like to not have my husband around, but I am home." Her arms stretched across the table to meet mine. Her hands were warm and smooth, like rose petals.

"It has been hard being away from home, you are right. But, being away from Abraham is tearing me apart inside, and I don't think it would matter much where I am. He would still be away from me." Feruza squeezed my hands. I knew she understood. I heard the same longing in her voice when she spoke of her husband.

"It is a lot of weight we carry around. All of us women left behind to take care of everything. It's a lot of pressure. I feel it every time I look in the mirror and notice a new grey hair, or when I walk through the streets and see a friend struggling. But mostly I feel it when I look at my boys." She released my hands and took a long sip of tea, hiding her face.

"Feruza, may ask how your boys have been dealing with their father being gone? I don't mean to pry, it's just that I'm worried about my girls," I asked.

"They miss him so much. I know they do, but they seldom say it. They don't talk much about him. I try to ask, but it only seems to make them upset. I tell myself it's because they are boys, but really, I think they are just scared. I try to keep them busy because it's the only thing that helps me through the day. Tell me, what is going on with your girls?" She asked.

"Sofia came to me the other day. She almost broke me apart," I answered. Now I tried to cover my face with the tea cup, but I knew it wouldn't hide the well of tears in my eyes. I took a deep breath and continued. "She told me that she was afraid she was going to forget Abraham. That he was beginning to fade away from her memories." I closed my eyes for a moment trying to compose myself again.

"Oh, that poor sweet girl, and poor Mama." She smiled softly at me. "That must have been hard. You suffer from having to talk to your girls and I suffer from not being able to talk to my boys. Either way we suffer. The joys of being a Mom, right?"

We both chuckled, and I felt a sense of relief just from knowing that she understood what I was going through.

"My advice would be to keep talking about him at home. Share stories, look at pictures. Embrace the smells or sounds that makes you think of him. Earlier, I said I thought the boys were too scared to talk about their father, but if I'm being honest, it's me who is scared too. I'm frightened that if I talk about him and he doesn't come home, it will only be worse. But in reality, if I don't talk about him and he doesn't come home, then what? It won't make the struggle any less real," Feruza said putting her hand over heart as if blocking it from any more hurt. "I need to try harder to get my boys to talk to me and you my friend, you need to stay strong for your girls and keep the memories alive."

I paused a moment to drink in her words and another sip of tea. "You are right. And we have each other now to make sure we hold up our ends," I said, with a smile.

A few minutes later it was time to add the rice. Feruza showed me how she poured the rice on top in an even layer, without mixing the ingredients together.

"Could you get me the hot water, Raisa? We need about four cups."

I added the hot water to the pot, one cup at a time. Then, she seasoned it with salt.

"Now we bring it to a boil without the lid and let it cook until most of the water is absorbed. That will take some time, let's sit and have some more tea."

"Were you born here in Kokand?" I asked, wanting to get to know more about my kind neighbor.

"I was born here. My husband is from Tashkent. We met there when I was studying, and we fell in love. He moved here because I wanted to be closer to my family. I am close with my parents and my brothers and sisters."

"How many do you have? Are they here in Kokand?"

"I have two sisters and three brothers. My sisters are here, and my two brothers are at the front. My youngest brother died at the front about a year ago." She said, as her voice suddenly lost all joy, like a deflating balloon.

"I'm so sorry to hear this, Feruza." I paused to think for a few moments. I sipped more of the tea, which was now at room temperature, but nevertheless tasted wonderful as it swished around in my mouth. "This war has stretched its arms farther than I could have ever imagined, affecting people from our home and beyond. The Uzbek community has been so wonderful. Your men are off fighting, while the rest of your country takes in refugees and helps them survive, even though the locals are barely surviving themselves. I hope that someday, somehow, we will be able repay you for the generosity and sacrifice you have shown."

"You are absolutely right. We have all endured our fair share of struggle, but it is for a good cause. The Nazis must be stopped and the only way to accomplish this is by banding together." Feruza paused for a moment to drink a sip of tea. She tucked her long black hair behind her right ear as she continued her thought. "My great-grandmother said to me once, 'if you have peace in your land, then you will have health in your land,' and it stayed with me. As awful as it sounds, sometimes we have to fight for that peace."

Her words resonated with me and it was as if she was inside of my mind. We sat for a while longer, sharing stories and exchanging laughs until it was time to get back to the plov.

"It looks like most of the water has absorbed. Now we add the full head of garlic on top and poke a few holes in the rice. This helps the water to boil out faster. We will cover it now with the lid and cook the rice for another fifteen minutes. Then, we remove the garlic and press it out into the rice. Finally, we get to mix everything together," she said, as she covered the pot.

"Feruza, thank you so much for showing me how to make plov. I am excited to try to make it for my family. I genuinely loved getting to know you better. We should do this more often!"

I started to gather my belongings, wondering if I might have overstayed my welcome by being there for nearly two hours, but Feruza stopped me.

"Where do you think you are going? You haven't tried the plov yet!"

"You are too kind. I don't want to impose on you any more than I already have."

"What are you talking about?! I have had a wonderful day with you. Besides, it's rude to turn down plov," she said with a wink, as she retrieved some bowls from the shelf.

I had tried plov before from a vendor at the market, but her plov was something else. I tasted her passion and expertise for cooking this national dish in every bite. After we finished, we sat and chatted a while longer, neither of us wanting to go back to cleaning our houses.

"One more thing before you leave, Raisa. Do you have one of these heavy pots?"

"We don't. I was about to ask you where to buy one."

"No need." She rushed over to a chair and pulled it over to a higher shelf to reach a large metal pot.

"Let me help you with that." I rushed to her side, grabbing the heavy pot from her.

"This is for you. It was the one we used before my grandfather died. Now we use his. I know it is much older, but it was his, and I can't part with it. Please take mine, I don't need it now, but you do."

"You are much too kind. How will I ever repay you?"

"Come by and chat. It's nice to have someone to talk to and I can brush up on my Russian."

"I promise I will. Thank you again, Feruza."

As I made my way up the few steps to our apartment, I realized I held more than just a simple pot; I carried the beginning of a new friendship.

CHAPTER TWENTY-ONE
TIDAL WAVE

9 AUGUST 1942
Kokand, Uzbekistan, USSR

Today I awoke before the rest of the family to go stand in line for bread. I gently reached over and pulled on my light summer dress. It was the one which I carried with me from Minsk. I remember how I sat in front of the kitchen window making it, but more vivid in my mind was the expression Abraham had when I wore it for the first time. His eyes danced as his smile grew. As he drew nearer to me, I inhaled his sweet scent. He told me how much he loved my dress, but I only remember his warm touch and his kisses.

I sat on the bed for a moment longer looking at the picture of Abraham and me on our wedding day, trying not to cry. I slipped out the door and walked along the dusty road to the bakery, enjoying the quiet tranquility of the morning. Reminiscing about Abraham, my mind continued to wander, until I reached a woman and her child lying in the street. Their faces were tired and laced with dirt. Her wrinkles were accentuated by the layers of dust caked inside each fold. They had nothing but newspaper to lie on, and their clothes were torn and nearly worn through. They looked familiar. I took a few steps and looked closer and realized that they were our friends and neighbors from Minsk!

"Klara, is that you?" I asked, waking them from their sleep. The little girl, Masha woke first. Her bright green eyes glowed in contrast to the dust which covered her from head to toe. She instantly recognized me and took my hand in hers.

"Raisa! I can't believe it is you. There must be a GOD. He must be looking down on us if he brought us to you. How are you, how is your family?" Klara cried happily as she stood to embrace me.

"We live nearby. Abraham is at the front. My parents and sisters are here with us. I was on my way to collect our daily bread ration, but I will go later, you girls should come with me. Let's get you cleaned up and changed into fresh clothes. Where are your things?"

Klara looked down at her feet. "Everything was stolen. Our bags, our clothes, our food, our documents. It's all gone."

My throat tightened as I held back the tears. I managed to keep them back as I hoisted Klara up on one side while Masha held her mother's hand on the other side. Klara's body was thin and frail, I wondered how she was able to walk. I couldn't even imagine what she had gone through all alone with Masha. Not ready to hear yet about their journey, we walked together in silence as the streets came alive with people and the morning sun played hide-and-seek with the clouds.

◆　◆　◆

The birds chirped loudly the next morning as they fluttered on a tree branch near the open window in our bedroom. The smell of breakfast entered the room and lured us into the kitchen, our bellies rumbling. I was still exhausted from yesterday's long day, but I awoke happy that Klara and Masha were here, safe in our home.

Sofia and Luba were already out of bed and dressed when I uncurled myself from the covers. I threw on a blue blouse and my long brown skirt, only realizing that Sofia and I were wearing the same colors after I had gotten dressed. She giggled at the sight, and together the three of us headed towards the delicious smells.

I expected to find Mama in the kitchen, making her usual breakfast, but instead I found Klara.

"Good morning! You didn't have to wake up and do this, you are too kind. You are supposed to be our guest, remember?"

"I didn't know what else to do to show my appreciation. I love cooking and I thought your Mama could use the morning off, so I sent her back to bed." A gentle smile beamed from her face, and her warmth radiated stronger than the lit stove nearby.

I glanced around the kitchen to see what she was making. Our wooden table was already set neatly with eleven mismatched plates. We had made the table from an old door that we found in the storage area of the basement. Papa made benches for each side from some old wood. Mama found a yellow tablecloth at the market and it brightened the kitchen like a full moon on a starry night.

"The blintzes are almost finished. I only have two or three left to cook. Would you gather everyone to eat?" Klara asked, as she flipped the perfectly cooked blintz over onto the stack of ready ones.

"Sure. Luba, could you get the can of apricot preserves we bought at the market and the sour cream, and put them on the table."

A few minutes later, we squeezed around our table and enjoyed the tasty blintzes until not even a trace of them were left. Together we helped to clear the table and clean up. Luba, Sofia, Masha and Oscar hurried into the other room to play together, while Papa and Lubov headed to the market. Sofia and Luba were happy to have a friendly face from back home. I hoped they would grow closer and lean on each other for support. Mama, Hana, Gita, Klara and I sat around the table drinking some more tea. We talked about Kokand and told Klara about our long journey here.

"In many ways our journey was much the same," Klara started. The look in her eyes floated far away as she started to tell us her story. "Masha and I were not in Minsk when the bombing happened. We left the day before to go to our country house for the summer. Yasha was supposed to meet us a few days later. After I heard the news of the war and that Minsk was under attack, I panicked and didn't know what to do. I tried to get in touch with Yasha, but couldn't, so I decided we needed to go back and find him. The trains were loaded with people heading further east and that alone should have stopped me from going west back to Minsk, but I had it in my head that we needed to find Yasha, so we traveled west. We caught a ride for most of the way but had to walk the remainder. That was when the man came down on top of us. He flew from the sky, like an angry crow, screeching at us with his gun."

"A Nazi airplane?" Mama asked.

"A Fascist parachuter. The parachuters rounded up people who were fleeing east. I wasn't heading east, but it didn't matter. They rounded us up like cattle and sent us back to Minsk."

Her eyes wandered for a moment and I sensed that recalling these memories was hard for her. "Klara, honey, are you sure you want to talk about this now? We can do this later if you want."

"No, I need to get it out. I have held it inside for too long. I want my story to be heard. You should know what is happening in our city." Slowly, Klara began once more. "When we arrived back in Minsk, I couldn't believe my eyes. Our city was in shambles. Where homes once stood, there were now piles of bricks. Everything looked dirty, dark and grey, even the sky. There were bodies lying on the streets in piles with no one tending to them. I was lost in my own city…" Tears dripped from Klara's face, but she continued on. "I asked around, trying to find out if anyone knew what happened to Yasha. We went back to our home, which miraculously was partially standing. The food had already been taken, but I uncovered some of our hidden valuables and I was at least happy for that. After some time, I found out that Yasha had been drafted and taken into the army. I thought about leaving, but I was afraid the Fascists would only bring us back again so we stayed, hoping we would survive. Soon, the Nazis forced us to live inside a ghetto. They gave Masha and I a space to live which was one and a half square meters. It was a partially ruined house, with no windows. Barbed wire was put up around the ghetto to keep us from escaping and the watchtowers hovered over us like giant beasts."

My heart pounded with anger as she continued her story. My eyes started to swell as I glanced at my mom and sisters, emotions around the table rose like a tidal wave.

Klara blew her nose into her handkerchief before she continued. "Soon after, they set curfew. We had to be home by ten p.m. and we were not allowed to leave until after five a.m. I watched them kill people over nothing. People were shot at gunpoint in the light of day. One time, it was a little boy. His blue hat was covered in blood as he lay quiet on the road. I still can't remove their faces from my memory, but I like to imagine that maybe this is how they get to live on, in my memory and, in others. Time continued like this, but more rules continued to be enforced. All of the Jews were forced to report for roll call every Sunday and we were made to wear a yellow star on our back and chest. We also had to wear a white patch with our house number as well. I was sent to work in a factory sewing uniforms and although we had a little bit of food to survive, I knew that we had to escape somehow."

I couldn't grasp onto all the emotions that were attacking me as she spoke. It was so much to accept and imagine all at once. I touched the six corners of my silver star, one by one, and somehow it gave me comfort as Klara continued with the details of her terrifying journey.

"I stayed up at night, looking through the open window, devising our escape route, only to talk myself out of it for fear of Masha being hurt or killed. One morning, everything changed. I arrived at work as usual, and my friend, Ida whispered to me that she had a plan and we were going to escape together. She heard about a place which was not visible from the guard towers and people had been going there each night to dig a tunnel underneath the wall. She was sure it was nearly ready, and she wanted to go that night to see it with me. I knew that if we were to ever escape, I had to take a risk, so I snuck out with her. Avoiding the flashes of light from the watchtower as we made our way through the dark, my heart pounded so loudly I worried a guard would hear it echoing through the night. There were a few others there, taking turns digging. We did our part and snuck back into our beds well before the sun rose. We made plans to return a few days later, with our girls and our bags."

Klara paused for a bit, drinking some more tea. Her story started to sink in further, and I thought about the others who were still trapped inside the ghetto. What atrocities were they suffering now?

"A few nights passed, and we met in the darkness to get to our escape route. When we arrived, oddly, there was no one there. After moving the dirt covered wood plank, we quickly realized, it was because the hole had been dug all the way through. This was our chance to escape and I tasted freedom in my mouth. We climbed through, one at a time and Ida pushed the wood plank back into place before we escaped into the thick dark forest. The first thing we did was rip off our badges. Ridding ourselves of them felt like cutting the strings which attached ourselves to the Nazis. We walked south-east through the dense woods for what seemed like months. A few times we had close calls and were almost caught or shot down by Nazi planes, but God must have been watching over us."

Relief shuttered through the room after we learned they all escaped safely. I let out the breath I had been holding. I started to boil some more water, while Klara dotted over the details of her journey.

"We found ourselves in Gomel after a great deal of walking. Sometimes we were given rides on horse carriages with room, and a few times on the back of Russian military trucks. Once we arrived, we wanted to stop, but we knew we had to leave before the Fascists came, so we continued. We boarded an open carriage train going south. One day the train stopped, and Masha and I jumped off with Ida and Leza to find a spot to relieve ourselves. Masha and I finished and quickly ran back to the train, assuming that Ida and Leza were already waiting for us. We barely made it on the train before it sped away, and as I glanced back, Ida and Leza quickly disappeared out of sight. After we were separated, the days became lonely and seemed to go on forever. We ended up on a kolkhoz doing back-breaking farm duties for a while and then we made our way further south until we landed in Tashkent. That was where all of our possessions were stolen. I wanted to get us out of there as soon as possible. I hated being surrounded by so many people dying on the streets, and thieves running about like street rats. We hopped onto a train heading further east and stepped off in Kokand for a reason I can now understand was fate."

Although much of our trip carried many similarities, it was very much her own, and as clearly as she described her experience, I couldn't begin to place myself in her shoes. I was horrified at the thought of what other Jews suffered through back home and thankful for the hope that some were able to escape like Klara and Masha.

"I am so happy that I found you and that you are here, safe with us. You were right. Your story is one that should be told, your bravery is inspiring."

CHAPTER TWENTY-TWO
SHATTERED

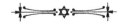

28 OCTOBER 1942
Kokand, Uzbekistan, USSR

I did not sleep last night. I tossed and turned in my bed, anxious and worried, but I didn't know why. It happens more frequently now than it used to. I often woke up sweating and nervous from a nightmare about something dreadful happening to Abraham. I only remembered parts of the dreams, but what remained in my mind was the color red. On those mornings, when grief weighed me down, it took me longer to get out of bed. I no longer felt like I was one Abraham's functioning complicated clocks. My gears were slowed by constant worry, and my heart was having trouble carrying the burdened load. I wanted to be there for my family, but some days I couldn't find the key to wind myself up, and most days, I didn't want to.

A few nights ago, I woke up shortly after falling asleep with tears streaming down my face. When I sat up, the moonlight seeped in through a nearby window, casting a soft light onto a wet stain slowly saturating my white pillow. I couldn't hush the tiny voice inside telling me something was wrong, and I hated myself for taking my nightmares seriously. I tried hard to go about my days, but I couldn't function. Mama went every day to check the mail, but nothing came from Abraham.

Today, I didn't want to get out of bed, but I forced myself so the girls wouldn't see me that way again. It was like my heart had been turned into glass and each day a tiny piece was chiseled away. I feared that one day it would be shattered into a million pieces and it would never be able to be put back together.

I offered to go to the post office wishing it would make the endless day go by faster. It was mid-afternoon as I walked through the town to the post office. People bustled through the streets. I looked for a smile from a little girl or a giggle from a baby in its stroller, but I met none. Only stern faces moved about their day, as if they carried the weight of the world on their shoulders.

"Hello, Tsalkina, please."

"One moment, I will check the back room, there are none in the front that I can see," the post lady said, as she slowly made her way to the back. A few drawn-out moments later, she came back with her arms full. "Here is a package, one letter, and two postcards for you. Is there anything else I can help you with?"

"No, thank you, this is everything," I said with relief. I hurried home with a newfound lightness in my step. By the time I made it back and finished making dinner, everyone would soon be arriving home from work and school. I waited until then to open the package and letters from Abraham. Luba read the first card addressed to her and Sofia went next with her postcard. They both had the same image of a girl and a boy walking with their school bags to their first day of school. The girl held a large bouquet of flowers and in the distance was a ruler, pen, ink, world globe and some books greeting them with a banner saying, *welcome!* On the top it said, *Happy new school year!* He wrote to them about how he was doing fine and how he wished them the best for the new school year. He told them both how proud he was of them and of course, he ended with hugs and kisses. Luba had recently begun the tenth grade, her final year, while Sofia was now in third grade.

Next, it was my turn to read the letter. I carefully opened the envelope trying not to rip the thin paper inside. It was dated over a week later than the postcards. I noticed by the hand-writing that something was different, and before I started to read it aloud, my muscles tightened with worry.

My golden sunshine, Raisa. I write to you today from my hospital bed. This is why you haven't received any letters from me the past few days. I am alive and although I am not well, I am in much better spirits today. I promise that I will survive this, and I ask of you not to worry about me. My injuries are minor. I long to hear your voice and see your gentle face. I won't worry you with the details of what happened, since they will be blacked out anyway. Please write to me as often as you can and tell me how you and the girls are. I sent you a package on the 9th of September, did you receive it yet? Sending you hugs and kisses. Love, Abraham

With the girls worried and in tears, I had to keep myself composed. Although we were worried about him, I had to divert their attention to the good in his letter. "Girls, let's not worry. Your papa is alive and doing better. He was able to write us this letter and that is a wonderful sign. The best thing we can do now for him is to write him every day no matter what. It will lift his spirits and he will get better faster. Go ahead girls, let's start writing now."

"If Papa has been injured, does that mean they will send him to stay with us, Mama?" Sofia asked. Her tears paused with a sudden realization that possibly this could have an upside.

"Honestly, I don't know Sofia. It is possible. It depends on how he was injured and how bad. If he recovers well, then most likely they will send him back to the front lines. Hopefully, Papa will let us know in his next letter," I replied. Part of me hoped that his injury would send him home to us, but the other side of me knew if they sent him home, it would mean his injuries would be severe. I didn't want to think about him in pain or suffering, I'd rather us be apart. I also didn't want to think about him being gone and what we would do without him.

The girls ran off to write to Abraham and I decided to make an excuse to get out of the house. I needed to catch my breath. I was relieved that Abraham was alive, yet still worried about his health. The nightmares from the last few nights came into my thoughts. I had felt something was wrong with Abraham. Somehow I knew, but how? I blinked away the red clouding my vision and started on my walk, without a destination in mind. The weather had been changing slowly, and now the early mornings and late evenings showed signs of the cold brisk air to come. I wrapped my favorite blue scarf tightly over my head and tied it under my chin as I walked slowly trying to clear my head. A few moments later, I bumped into Klara.

"Good evening, Raisa, how are you?" she asked, giving me a quick hug. She looked like an entirely different person than the frail being I picked up off these very streets only a few months earlier. Each time I met with her, her cheeks looked rosier in color and her figure was slowly returning to normal. After staying with us for a few weeks, they were able to register with the refugee center and get new documents. They found a cozy apartment near ours, and filed the paperwork to receive money from Yasha since he was serving in the war.

"Oh Klara, I am well. How are you? How is Masha?"

"Masha is good. She enjoys school. She says that sixth grade is much harder than last year, and she is already getting a good amount of homework. I don't think she minds, though. It keeps her mind off of everything that we went through these past few months."

"That is good. Keep her mind busy and she will have an easier time getting adjusted to this new life. She is a smart girl, I'm sure she will have a good school year," I replied. "How about Yasha? Have you heard from him?"

"Yes, more letters have come lately from Yasha and our request was finally processed, so now we can get money from his service. Also, I received a letter yesterday from the refugee center that they have a teaching job for me in the elementary school. I will start next week!" She smiled anxiously.

"Klara, that is wonderful! I am so happy you will be able to go back to teaching. Everything is falling into place. Don't be nervous, you are a wonderful teacher, they are lucky to have you," I said.

"Thank you, Raisa. I am a little nervous. It has been awhile since I taught last, but I am excited. Tell me about the girls, how are they? And you? You look worried, my friend."

"The girls are doing great in school. Luba is also busy with schoolwork and Sofia adjusted quickly and has already made new friends. I too am glad to have their attention somewhere else, so they aren't anxious about Abraham all the time. To be honest, I am a bit worried. I received a letter from Abraham today and he is in the hospital. He says he will be alright and not to worry, but of course all I can do is worry."

"Oh Raisa, I am sorry to hear this. We have to stay strong and all we can do is hope for the best. My Mama occasionally said to me in Yiddish, *Me zoll nit gepruft weren zu vos me ken geweint weren.*"

I smiled remembering Abraham's mother say these very words and we both whispered the words in Russian at the same time, "Pray that you may never have to endure all that you can learn to bear."

Her words relaxed me as we chatted a bit longer. The weight that had been pulling me down started to lift off my shoulders and my head was lighter than it had been in the past few days. We gave each other a long hug and before we turned to go our separate ways, Klara held my hands in hers and said, "I know I have thanked you before, but I really can't thank you enough for what you did for us. You saved our lives. It hurts my heart when I even think about what would have happened had you not passed by and took us into your home. You treated Masha and me like we were your family. You fed us the bread that should have been in your mouth. You, Raisa, are a wonderful person with a kind heart. Thank you again."

"A few good people helped me along the way on our journey here. I am happy I was able to help you, like they supported me." The image of the old lady who helped me in Tashkent appeared before me first and the memory of her saving my bag began to play in my mind, followed by the woman who gave us the parcel of food when we were hungry.

Her words touched my heart and filled me with happiness. They stayed with me on my walk home and even when I kissed my girls goodnight. I gazed out the window counting the stars, imagining that Abraham was doing the same thing.

CHAPTER TWENTY-THREE
MAZE OF MY OWN CONFUSED MIND

8 FEBRUARY 1943
Kokand, Uzbekistan, USSR

The flowers disappeared along with the warm summer days and dusty wind storms. The colder air had once again made its debut. Luckily, it wasn't nearly as cold as the winters in Minsk, and it even felt warmer than the last winter. The bleak weather brought a certain gloominess to the days as the sun hid behind the clouds for weeks.

Today, the sun sneaked in and out, illuminating the snow-flakes as they dropped like feathers. I watched them as they swayed through the air and fell to the ground to join the white carpet of sparkling diamonds. Everybody was gone for the day except Mama, who was sewing the holes in our clothes and mending the buttons. I sat by the fire and read over the last few letters from Abraham. Ever since he had been in the hospital, I worried more and more about him. His letters stated that he was fine and to not worry, but my heart broke being away from him and not actually knowing how he was.

Sometimes, when the mail was backed up, we didn't receive letters for ten or more days, and then all at once I would pick up a stack of over a dozen. Abraham regularly wrote two letters or postcards each day. He sent one to the apartment address and one to the post office. This was in case one didn't make it through. His devotion was endearing, and it was an example of exactly why I loved him so much.

Last month I received a letter in response to my pleas for him to tell me if he needed anything. He eventually answered and said that he could use some warm clothes and tobacco. Of course, he added that they were well taken care of and that he didn't actually need anything. I knew better than to believe this, so I made it my mission to find some nice warm clothes to send to him along with the tobacco. I started by trading some of Sofia's old clothes which didn't fit her anymore. Along with some money that I had saved, I pulled together a nice package that I knew he would appreciate.

He was so thankful for the gifts, but I was even more thankful that I could help him in some way. I found myself rereading his letter of thanks over and over again. It gave me hope. It opened a path into the future, and finally I saw some light shine through. I pulled it out of the envelope again today and started to read it to myself, mostly from memory.

Hello my dearest Raisa, Luba and Sofia. I am writing to you today the second letter. One I sent to the post office and this one to the apartment address. I hope at least one makes it to you. I can write that I am alive and well and feel great. Yesterday, I sent you two cards and today also. I am so grateful for the wonderful package you have sent to me. I am wearing the sweater now and I only wish that the smell of you on it would never fade. The wool socks are also perfect, as my old ones were beginning to get a hole in them. You ask how my health is, and I beg of you, please don't worry about me. Dearest Raisa I hope that we will soon see each other. We have defeated 70% of the Nazis and this month we will defeat the remaining 30%, and then you can return to our motherland. For now be healthy. Kisses to you Raisa, Luba and Sofia. Love, Abraham

When I read this, it didn't seem possible that we could actually return home soon. I didn't want to even consider it, but now I started to hope. Our brave men, after five long months, had finally pushed the Nazis out of Stalingrad and made their largest defeat yet. The radios blared the news from the frontlines, along with promises that the war would soon come to an end.

♦ ♦ ♦

I read a few more letters and then focused my attention outside my window. A petite woman walked with her two girls down the street. She held both of their hands and walked swiftly through the square. Her red scarf was loosely wrapped around her neck and her expression was as cold as ice. She reminded me of myself when Sofia and Luba were younger and I walked them back and forth from school each day.

I thought back to five years earlier, when the Jewish schools in Minsk were closed down as a part of a campaign against national minorities. With no other option, we sent the girls to the Russian school. Abraham and I feared for our girls being thrown into the mix, as they would be the minority. I was nervous they would suffer the same unpleasantness that we had unfortunately grown accustomed to. When they first changed schools, I didn't feel it was safe for them to be walking alone like the other kids, so I walked with them every day.

I remember one of those mornings, like it was yesterday, clear as crystal in my mind. It was a bright fall morning in Minsk. The girls had started school a few weeks before and they had handled moving to a new school surprisingly well. After I dropped them off, I walked back towards home breathing in the world around me. The trees were filled with vivid colors of reds, greens and yellows. The leaves flew carelessly with the wind, in stark contrast to our cautious life. People chatted around me, but I was not tuned in to their conversations. My mind was elsewhere, drifting into faraway thoughts about Abraham and the girls. I became more worried with every passing day. Scenarios flipped through me like the pages of a history book. Will the times repeat themselves? Will the girls be safe at school? Are other kids going to make fun of them because they are Jewish? Will they get called on by the teacher when they raise their hands? How about Abraham at work… will the comments made by some of his coworkers get worse?

Lost in the maze of my own confused mind, I didn't hear the man yelling at first. "Hey, you, KIKE! Get out of my way!" He screamed as he slammed into me with all his weight. His breath reeked of vodka. I fell backwards, landing hard on my backside. My palms felt like they had been cut by razor blades as they caught my fall to the pavement. My heart thumped like a racehorse as it jumped out of my chest and my face flushed to a fiery hot red.

"Nice necklace, you filthy Jew. You people are always causing problems aren't you?" he shouted at me while stumbling over his own feet.

I tried opening my mouth to respond, but nothing came out. Even if I could have, what would I have said? I dusted myself off and tried to stand up, but right when I thought he was done and about to walk away, it happened. It came towards my face with a whirl. A glob of spit splashed between my right eye and nose. I felt like I'd shrunk to the size of an ant. By now, people had gathered around. Everyone stared at me. Their glares bore deep holes into my soul. I sat there, paralyzed, only able to lift my arm to wipe the disgusting wetness from my face. My mind separated from my body as my head whirled with fear. Everything went black.

Suddenly, someone shook me, and a familiar voice was in my ear. "Raisa, Raisa, get up. We need to go now." When I opened my eyes, the sunlight overwhelmed me. I looked down to let my eyes adjust, and then slowly back up to see Pavel, our butcher and family friend. He gently picked me up and laced his arm through mine.

"I heard some commotion outside, but I couldn't see you, there was a crowd around you. Those disgusting people stood there and watched and not one thought to help. I'm so sorry I didn't get over to you faster. Let's get you home." My legs disappeared underneath me and it was as if I floated above the pavement.

Birds chirped loudly, as if announcing our arrival when we approached my house. I opened the front door and thanked Pavel for his help. I wanted to say more or do something to show my appreciation, but I couldn't find the words.

I walked inside and closed the door behind me, making sure to lock it. I collapsed over the sink and splashed water on my face, but as much as I scrubbed, I couldn't wash away the embarrassment. I looked into the mirror, and the entire scene replayed in my mind, like a bad song that wouldn't leave my head. Helplessness overwhelmed me and my emotions exploded. What started as tears turned into anger. My resentment towards that awful man was brimming over. Soon, I was blaming myself for forgetting to tuck my necklace under my shirt. I hate that I have to hide my necklace and disguise who I am from others. I want to feel proud of being Jewish. It's my heritage and I cherish it, but sometimes I also resent it. I am disgusted by what it has come to, what it has caused for myself, my family and all the other good people around me.

I tried to go about my day as if it were a normal one, but as the chime of the cuckoos from the hallway clock began to add up, so did my anxiety. I busied myself with preparing the vegetables for the soup I had planned for dinner, but my hands shook as I focused on dicing.

"Cuckoo, cuckoo." Another hour had passed, and I had already moved onto dusting when there was a sudden but soft knock at the door.

My heart raced and my palms sweat for a reason which I couldn't explain. It wasn't like the awful man from this morning knew me, or knew where I lived, but I still couldn't push away my fear as I neared the door.

"Who is it?" I called.

"Raisa, it's me, Abraham. I'm sorry. I forgot my keys."

I opened the door and immediately fell into his embrace. Tears instantly poured from my already swollen eyes.

"I'm so sorry, my *feigele*, my sweet little bird. Are you alright? Did you get hurt?"

"I am shaken. My hands are scraped, but they will be fine." I held my hands out, palms up, desperately trying to make them stop shaking. "How did you know?"

"A friend at work told me what happened. Pavel contacted him and asked him to relay the message to me. As soon as I could, I ran home. I was so worried."

His hands gently caressed my back as we found our way to the couch. His touch was so soft it barely grazed my skin. He must have sensed how fragile I was at that moment.

His voice was soft and gentle, but I sensed his anger as he spoke. "Tell me what happened."

At first, I found it hard to begin because I realized that speaking about it made the attack that much more real. I struggled through the details as the events from earlier unfolded.

Up until that day, besides the occasional rude comments, I hadn't experienced such hatred directed towards myself. I knew it was there; I knew it happened; but that day, it was me it happened to. I carried it around with me like a constant itch that couldn't be scratched. It made my skin a little thicker and it lit a fire inside me. Maybe one day it would be extinguished. I wished for that day for the sake of my children.

CHAPTER TWENTY-FOUR
STARK WHITE WALLS

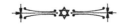

21 JULY 1943
Kokand, Uzbekistan, USSR

My hands shook as I tried to focus on my writing. Tears clouded my view and bled the ink across the page before me. I took a deep breath, but my chest felt like stretched rubber bands that were about to snap. I tried to refocus and get a new piece of paper to start over. I knew I had to write this letter to Abraham, no matter how difficult it would be. I couldn't keep this from him anymore, he needed to know, even if it would worry him. I told myself that I was doing the right thing and, with that, I started to write again.

To my sweet Abraham. I hope you are doing well. We all miss you very much and long to see you more and more each and every day. There is something I have to tell you. I am sorry that I didn't tell you earlier, but I didn't want to worry you. Our dear Luba is ill. We tried everything we could at home to cure her, but we had to take her to the hospital yesterday. Over the past few days her cough has gotten so bad that I couldn't bear to listen to her suffer any longer. Her temperature was at 40 degrees Celsius and we couldn't get it to go down. They haven't told us yet what is wrong, but they are taking good care of her. As soon as I know anything, I will write to you. I love you and I hope you are doing well. Always, Raisa

As I signed my name on the bottom, I scanned the letter and could see my anxiety clearly scratched across the paper. I folded the letter and quickly put it inside the envelope addressed to Abraham before heading out to the post office on my way to the hospital.

It was early morning, and the drops of dew from the previous night's sprinkle hadn't had a chance to dry. The air was fresher than it had been in weeks. The rain had settled the dust down. The hospital was on the outskirts of town, and as I walked towards it, it looked as if the nearby cotton field stretched on for forever. The workers were already picking, bending over like trees in a storm.

I was immersed in my thoughts about Luba as the entrance to the hospital became visible. Yesterday I begged the nurse to let me stay with her overnight, but I was refused. I tried to stay longer. I held her hand and talked to her, but they repeatedly told me I must leave. I wondered if today would be different.

When I walked through the front door, I was immediately greeted with stark white walls and the stale smell of sickness. I made my way towards her bed amongst a sea of sick patients, and leaned over to give her a kiss, pushing my mask away to graze her soft cheek with my lips.

"How are you today, my dear?"

Luba had a faint smile when she saw me, but as I scanned her listless face, I saw her condition was no better.

"I feel tired and I wish I could go home, but don't worry Mama, I will get better soon."

"I know, but first we must get you better. I made soup for lunch and some kasha for breakfast. Would you try to eat a little?" I asked with an encouraging smile, willing the answer to be different than yesterday and the day before. Her body was thin and frail. I wondered how she would recover if she didn't eat anything.

Sensing I wouldn't take no for answer, she mumbled, "I will try, Mama."

I held her hand and tried to feed her little by little, praying she would keep most of it down. When she started to cough it sent needles into the depths of my heart and I wished I could have traded places with her.

"How's Sofia?" Luba asked between a spoonful of soup. "I miss her."

"She misses you very much. She begs me every morning to come visit you even though she knows it's not allowed. She drew something for you, here it is," I answered, pulling out the card from my bag. Sofia had drawn Luba's favorite flowers on the front with the words, *feel better Luba*, scrawled across the top. Inside, she wrote her a sweet note. I watched Luba as she read it to herself. Her smile grew with each word and it made my heart flutter. The way they cared for each other reminded me of my own bond with my sisters, especially Hana.

It was late afternoon when the doctor came by to talk to us. His grey hair was slicked to one side and his wire rimmed spectacles sat perfectly on the middle of his nose. His white coat was too big for his lean stature, and he looked as if he could disappear inside it. His deep voice, however, brought him forward. His hands moved like a conductor as he spoke, and his confidence left you no choice but to believe his every word.

"Hello, I'm Doctor Levin and I would like to talk to you about Luba. We ran some tests on your daughter, and I believe she has a severe case of pneumonia. She needs to start antibiotics right away. Because of the severity of her case, the symptoms will take longer to clear up. She needs to stay in the hospital for a few more days and maybe even a week longer. I don't want to take any chances. If she stays here, she will be closely monitored. Do you have any questions for me?"

"Will she fully recover, and are there side effects from this medication?"

"Pneumonia is incredibly serious. It can be survivable, but it mostly depends on the strength of the patient. If the medicine works and her body is strong enough to fight the pneumonia, then I do believe that she will recover fully. She will need to take it easy once she leaves, and she will need to stay home and rest for another week. There are side effects with this medicine, but none of them are common. Mostly, it can cause upset stomach and headaches."

"I understand, Doctor. Thank you for taking care of her, I am confident she will recover, she is a fighter."

I quickly shook his hand before he was handed a new chart to attend to the next patient. The warmth from his smile was comforting in a place that was so harrowing. I liked Dr. Levin, but his vagueness worried me. I knew Luba was strong, but he said things like, "can be survivable" and "severe case of pneumonia." Those words were the ones rolling around in the front of my thoughts, clouding my ability to calm down. If only Abraham were here. Luba needed her Papa. I needed him too. I wished I could stare into the safety of his gray eyes.

◆ ◆ ◆

The next few days blurred together in my mind as I continued to spend them with Luba in the hospital. I usually returned home after sunset and spent my nights lying awake with worry and fear. I rose from bed early every morning and wrote to Abraham to let him know how Luba was progressing. Mama took over all the duties at home so I could be with Luba all day. After a long day in the hospital, Mama and my sisters would greet me with a hot plate of food and open arms to comfort me.

Papa, Sofia and Oscar were already in bed that night, so it was just Mama, Hana, Gita and Lubov sitting around the table. As I finished my dinner and we sipped our tea, I felt their support, just by being there.

"How is she today?" Gita asked first. "We miss our dear Luba so much."

"She is a little better. She slept most of the day, but it was restless sleep. Her cough won't let her body relax."

"Did she eat any of the soup I made for her?" Mama asked, bringing the tea to the table.

"I fed it to her throughout the day. She doesn't want much at once, but I was happy she drank it all by the end of the day. She asked me to thank you, Mama."

Mama smiled, "That's good, because I made her more for tomorrow."

"Did any mail come today from Abraham?" I asked, swallowing hard.

Lubov looked down, trying to hide her eyes. She knew I could read her face easier than anyone's. "We stopped at the post office after work today and there was nothing from Abraham," Gita answered.

"But that doesn't mean anything. Remember last time the mail was held up for weeks. Or maybe he is moving to a different city. There are so many possibilities," Hana said as she reached over and touched my arm. Her cool touch sent a shiver through my overheated body. I let it pass through me as I took a deep breath.

"You're right, it could be many things keeping the letters from coming. Maybe tomorrow one will come. Tell me, how was your day?" I asked, changing the subject before I became more emotional.

"Our days are filled with boots. They come down the production line in a never-ending stream. It really puts into perspective how many soldiers we have fighting at the front lines," Hana replied.

"Or are there so many because they have to replace their boots with new ones due to the lower quality. Now the *kirza* boots are made with a synthetic leather. I would bet they don't last as long," Gita said.

"They seem pretty sturdy. At least the soles are. I would be happy to not smell another rubber shoe sole for the rest of my life," Lubov laughed and pinched her nose with her fingers making us all laugh with her.

We each had our own daily battles we struggled with, but at the end of the day we were able to be us again, and we could laugh, cry or scream and it didn't matter. I was thankful to have them, they kept me alive in these tough times.

◆ ◆ ◆

After eight long days, Luba's health slowly began to improve, and the doctor was hopeful that she would be discharged soon. Although she started to gain strength, her cough still shook her body as if she were a wisp of grass in the wind.

Not only did I have Luba on my mind these last few days, but Abraham also had my pulse quickened with concern. I received one letter about a week ago, but it was dated prior to Luba going into the hospital and I had not received anything since. I hoped I hadn't worried him into sickness with the news about Luba.

Last night I left the hospital hopeful that Luba would come home soon. Her color had improved, her breathing was better, and she kept all her food down. Sofia missed her so much and this morning she begged me again to visit her.

"Mama, can I please go with you? I want to see Luba. When is she coming home?" Sofia's eyes were sad and pleading and I had to glance away to regain my composure so I wouldn't cry.

"Oh, my dear, remember what I told you? Hospitals are no place for children. They are for sick people. I cannot risk you getting sick too. Luba looked much better last night, maybe she will come home in the next day or two. I should leave now so I can make sure to talk to the doctor."

"Alright. I know, and I'll be good and help Baba." Sofia turned away and dragged her feet over to the kitchen draped in a blanket of sadness.

I knew the doctor wouldn't be in until the afternoon, so I decided to take my time. Usually, I was on the go, rushing from one place to the next, never stopping for a moment to pause and take in the life encompassing me.

The morning was calm and peaceful as I approached the center of town. However, in a matter of minutes, it seemed as if someone flipped a switch and the entire square came to life with people. I sat down in the center square on a wooden bench. The street was lined with cafes and shops and as I gazed into the distance, one man caught my attention right away. He was an Uzbek man with wrinkles so deep, I saw the wisdom in them from across the street. His hat looked like a sheet that had been twisted and formed to his head and his long grey beard hung low. His long *yakhtak* robe was brightly colored and his powerful eyes were mesmerizing. I couldn't look away, even when he caught my stare.

However, my attention was diverted to two little kids playing soccer off to the side. Their mother stood nearby watching them, smiling as the older child helped his little sister kick the ball. I admired their innocence. The boy reminded me of Luba at that age and how protective she was of Sofia.

I looked back to the old man again, but he wasn't there anymore. Disappointment rushed through me. Something about him made me feel connected to him, but of course the reason was unexplainable.

Suddenly, I realized that I had been sitting for too long. I stood up from the warmed bench and was face to face with the old man. His eyes gleamed like crystal balls as he looked into mine. His Russian was shaky, but understandable as he spoke with intention. "I can see you are hurting. Fear is splashed across your face, like a cold winter storm. Don't worry, *she* will be alright. You'll see."

Before I even had the chance to ask him how he could possibly know this, he was gone. As fast as he approached, he vanished into the crowd of people walking by, as if he had never been there. I stood for a few more minutes uncertain what I should do. I quickly decided that I would accept his words as a gift, and I walked towards the hospital with a little bit more hope.

The fresh air was soon replaced with the stuffy dryness of the hospital surroundings. Luba was in much better spirits when I arrived, and she was even walking around with the help of a nurse. Her timid smile lit up the room and made me truly hopeful for the first time in days. Luba and I chatted as we waited for the doctor to make his rounds. After lunch, Dr. Levin made it to her bedside.

"Hello again. It looks like you have progressed well. How are you today, Luba?"

"I feel much better today, Doctor. My cough wasn't as bad as yesterday. I have been sitting up most of the day and not getting dizzy. I even walked around earlier," Luba told the doctor happily.

"That is wonderful. I am glad to see your symptoms are subsiding. I think it is time you go home and sleep in your own bed. Would you like that?"

Luba's eyes twinkled with excitement as she sat up straighter in bed. "Yes, doctor, I would really like to go home!"

"Of course, you would. We have a few documents your mother needs to sign, and then we will get you back home. There are a few details you need to remember. You must stay in bed for a few more days. Also, you need to continue this medicine until you are done. Please rest and do not do any physical activities for at least two weeks."

"Thank you so much Doctor, for everything," I said as I shook his hand one last time.

When we arrived home, everyone was ecstatic to see Luba. The look on Sofia's face when she saw her big sister walk through the door was an image I will happily never forget. I continued to push aside my fears about Abraham and instead we sat together and talked about our day until the moon started to peek in through the windows and the stillness of the night begged for us to shut our eyes.

CHAPTER TWENTY-FIVE
WHOLE AGAIN

2 AUGUST 1943
Kokand, Uzbekistan, USSR

The milk bubbled gently. I slowly poured the kasha in and stirred, silently and systematically. I must have made it too often. It became second nature as I shifted through the motions without even concentrating on them, like brushing my teeth or getting dressed. My thoughts drifted this morning, shuffling from one concern to the next.

Luba was doing better these last few days and the color in her cheeks was returning to a rosy blush. I believe partly because she was home in her own bed and partly because she had missed Sofia terribly. She still needed help getting around, and her cough kept us awake at night, but she was eating better and drinking more water. I planned to keep her home for a few more days and if she continued to improve, maybe we could venture outside for a short walk next week.

I still had not received any letters from Abraham, and I was fearful if I did receive one, what terrible news it would contain. I tried to tell myself that they were probably traveling to a new location, or maybe the mail was held up. All of the scenarios were possible, but of course my mind continued to wander to the worst ones that I could imagine.

"Good morning, my love. Breakfast is ready," I whispered as Luba started to stir in her bed.

"Good morning, Mama. Where is everyone?" Luba asked, as she looked around the room and out the doorway to see that they had already gone.

"It's already after nine. They have already gone to work and school. Baba left early for food and should be back any time now. You slept so well this morning; I didn't want to wake you. Don't rush to get up, I can bring the kasha to your bed."

"Thank you, Mama, but I think I'd like to sit at the table since I can sit up."

I helped Luba over to the kitchen table and placed the bowl of hot kasha before her. I started to clean up the dishes when there was a soft knock at the front door.

"That must be Baba home from the market. I wonder what she will bring today?"

I rushed to open the door to help her with the bags, but as I opened it, it wasn't Baba with the groceries at all.

As I looked up, I froze for a split second, trying to make sure that I wasn't dreaming.

"Abraham, is that really you?"

"It is me, my *feigele*. I told you we would meet again," he said with a smile as he caught me while I nearly fell in shock. His touch electrified me, and his kiss sent waves of happiness throughout my body. It had been so long since I had felt his embrace, I had almost lost hope that I would ever be back in the safety of his arms again.

"Papa, is that you?" screamed Luba from inside once she heard his voice. Luba rushed from the table and ran into his arms. Abraham picked her up and spun her around. Tears of joy rolled down her face as she held onto him tightly. "How are you here?" she asked, her words muffled as her face disappeared into Abraham's embrace.

Abraham moved inside and sat down on the nearest chair. "My dear Luba, let me look at you for a moment. I had your face memorized in my mind, but I can see that you are not a little girl anymore. These two years have turned you into a beautiful young woman."

"Can you believe she will be almost eighteen?" I asked, wondering myself how it was possible that my little baby was all grown up.

Abraham shifted his gaze back and forth, taking in our faces, examining every changed detail and allowing us to do the same. His hair was shorter, and it matched a roughness that I could see in his movements. His cheekbones were more defined as was his slender body, but his eyes remained the same.

Abraham blew into his handkerchief breaking our silence. "I received the letter from your mother about you being in the hospital. That day I met with my commanding officer and asked him for a leave from duty to see you. I had no time to write you a letter as I was busy getting the paperwork together for the journey here. They found a space on the next train available, and here I am. How are you feeling, my love? When did you come home from the hospital?"

"I still can't believe you are here Papa! I have missed you so much. I am much better. I came home a few days ago from the hospital. I was there for nine days. How long can you stay with us?" Luba blurted out all at once.

"I am so glad you are better. You had me worried. I can stay for two weeks and then I have to report back to my squad. Did the doctor give any more information about her condition?" Abraham asked, looking over at me.

It took me a moment to respond. I was still thinking about the two weeks. That was all? He had been gone for two years and we only get him back for two weeks? I should be happy to see him at all, but I knew how fast two weeks would go by. It was no more than a blink of an eye, I thought. "She had a severe case of pneumonia. The doctor treated her with antibiotics and kept her in the hospital to monitor her breathing. She needs to rest for another few days and can go back to her normal routine next week. Are you hungry or thirsty? Let me make you something."

Before he had time to answer, I started to prepare some kasha and tea. I watched Luba finish her tea, her eyes shimmering as she chatted with Abraham. As she told him about her new life here, her cheeks glowed like a beautiful pink sunset and I knew that having her Papa be here would be better than any medicine available.

A few minutes later, Mama came home from the market and almost dropped her bags when she saw Abraham. I tried to peel my eyes away from him, but I couldn't. His presence mesmerized me. I still couldn't believe he was right in front of me. I sat next to him while he finished his breakfast, savoring his every movement. Afterwards, our fingers easily tangled together under the table. We studied each other's faces for another quiet moment, our dreams finally reality.

Soon enough it was time to pick up Sofia from music school. She decided that although it was summer break, she wanted to go to music school twice a week with her friends. I was glad she did, because those two days a week, her mind was busy with thoughts other than of Luba being sick, her father's absence and the war.

At last, it was just me and Abraham walking hand in hand through the dusty streets. The sun had nowhere to hide as the endless blue sky enveloped us. His touch made my heart skip like a young girl again. It brought me back to our secret meetings together before our engagement. The hairs on my arms stood up as nervousness and excitement pumped through my body at the same time. My husband seemed different, but yet the same. Emotions raced through me like a stampede of horses, until Abraham pulled me aside.

"Are you alright, have you heard anything I have said my love?" I looked up into his reassuring eyes. He bent over and kissed me, sending another tingle through every part of my body.

"For the first time since you have left, I feel safe. I am better than alright. I feel whole again." We continued to walk, and I watched Abraham take in the details of the new land I now called home.

"The market is over here. Let's walk through it since we have some time."

Abraham's eyes widened as he looked at the shelves of beautiful fruits. He was like a child in a toy store and his eyes darted from table to table unsure how to choose which to buy.

"Good afternoon. Two pears, please," I called to the large man behind the stand of fruit before us. His tanned forehead was wet from the beating sun and his long caftan was no longer white, but instead stained with dirt and sweat. I watched him as he quickly tossed the pears into a bag with his large, dirty hands and handed them to Abraham in one swift motion.

"I can't remember the last time I ate fresh fruit like this. The only thing I can think of to make this day better is to see Sofia. I can't wait to hold her in my arms."

"Let's go then. We aren't far from her school."

I led the way, pointing out places as we walked. It did not take long for us to fall back into our natural patterns as our steps synchronized and we finished one another's sentences.

The large stone building before us was grey and uninviting, but the sounds from the inside poured into the street in an explosion of notes. We arrived a few minutes early, so we stood nearby, under the shade of a mulberry tree. Abraham turned towards me and gently folded his arms around me as we waited. His smell was intoxicating, and my mind was finally relaxed and free from worry.

"That's the signal for the end of school. She will come out any moment now," I said, as I tore away from Abraham's embrace so we could walk closer to the school.

A few moments later, I spotted Sofia walking beside her two best friends. Her jet-black hair was fashionably pinned back, and her long blue skirt flowed as she walked with her friends. As usual, when I looked at her, I could see the parts of her that were from Abraham, her dark hair, the way she carried herself with confidence, and her smile. I watched Abraham as he looked through the crowd. His eyes scanning in the direction I was pointing. As soon as he locked his eyes on her, I watched his face light up with excitement. It reminded me of his expression when she was born. Sofia was so fully immersed in her conversation with her friends that she had not even begun to look around for me, so we admired her from afar.

"I can't believe how much she has grown over these past two years. I barely recognize her. She isn't the same little girl anymore," Abraham said, his eyes still fixed on Sofia, unable to look away.

Suddenly, Sofia begin to look around for me, but her eyes settled on Abraham first. "Papa!" She screamed as she ran over to him, jumping straight into his arms. They stood holding onto each other letting the world around them disappear. Sofia's face emerged from within the safety of Abraham's embrace with a smile as bright as the glowing sun.

"I can't believe you are here. Mama, did you know he was coming home? Were you hurt? Are you here to stay Papa?" Questions flowed from Sofia like a river in the springtime.

"No, no, Mama didn't know. I received her letter about Luba being in the hospital and right away I asked for permission to be with you. As soon as the paperwork went through, I boarded the next train to Uzbekistan. I wish I had been able to tell you, but I didn't have time to write a letter."

Sofia held Abraham's hand on one side and my arm slipped through his on the other side, and we walked together back home. I knew the rest of our family would be eagerly awaiting his arrival and Mama was probably cooking everything we had in the kitchen for a celebration.

"How do you like the music school? Are you happy there? I can see you have made some friends... although I wasn't worried."

"Yes Papa, I do like the music school. Actually, more than I thought I would. I don't think I am particularly good, but I enjoy playing anyway. In the beginning, we tried several instruments to see which we liked best and I chose piano. It has made the summer go by so fast, and I have made many friends here. Most of them are also evacuees from Russia. Some are Polish. Many of them are Jewish."

"Should we take the short detour home so we can show Papa the Palace?" I asked Sofia, knowing that she would love that. "It is our favorite building. Nothing like anything we have in Russia, it is known as the 'Pearl of Kokand,' and it is impressive."

"Yes! We must pass by!"

"We seem to be drawn towards it. Each time we walk by, we spot something new that we hadn't noticed before," I explained to Abraham as we headed towards the palace.

"There it is up ahead. Do you see the four blue minarets?"

"Yes, I can see them. How beautiful."

We stopped for a few moments taking in the countless details. It was full of color, each tile glistened as the rays of sunshine bounced around. There were rich ornaments with geometric patterns, arabesques, and floral motifs. "The designs are made from ceramic tiles and based on the tales of the Orient. The writing along the top is in Arabic," I explained to Abraham as I pointed out the different scenes.

"This was a great detour. Although this building is beautiful, it is not nearly as stunning as my three girls!"

We both flashed smiles up at Abraham and my cheeks began to feel sore from being so happy. It made me realize how long it had been since I had smiled so much. "We can come back and look again, let's head home so I can help Mama with dinner," I said.

♦ ♦ ♦

Sitting around the kitchen table, I felt a surge of hope, a glimpse into the window of our future. Suddenly, the prospect of the war ending soon and us being able to return to our old life seemed within reach. The stars gleamed and the moon cast its shadow through the window when we eventually headed to our rooms. Abraham helped me roll Luba's bed into Mama and Papa's room and Sofia slept on Oscar's bed. Oscar crawled into bed with Hana and then we pushed Sofia's bed up against mine for Abraham.

"Mama why do we need to move our bed's around? Why can't we sleep in here like we always do?" Sofia begged.

"Because then neither of you would sleep. Don't you remember how loud your Papa snores?"

Abraham whisked Sofia off her feet and carried her to the other room while she giggled with glee. He laid her down and tucked her in, exactly like he did before the war. Then he crouched over Luba and gave her a kiss. He took my hand and we walked together into our room.

I ambled over to the dresser to get my nightgown to change when I sensed Abraham's eyes from behind. My body thumped with longing for him. I removed my blouse and skirt without turning around, and just as I removed my brassiere, his hands began to help me. His fingers were warm and as they caressed me, my entire body quivered. He spun me around and looked into my eyes as he carried me over to the bed. I couldn't wait a moment longer. He continued to explore every inch of my body with his lips, making me want him even more than ever. When our lips finally met, I was overwhelmed with desire. He gently pressed himself against me and our breath quickened as we fell into each other.

"I love you," he whispered into my ear as we collapsed from exhaustion. Holding me tightly, we both closed our eyes and gave in to the darkness.

CHAPTER TWENTY-SIX
TEARS OF JOY

27 MAY 1931
Minsk, Belarus, USSR

I woke up in the middle of the night curled up next to Abraham's warm body. For the first time in years it wasn't from a nightmare, instead I was dreaming about the week that we brought Sofia into the world...

Mama came into town from Bobruisk. I felt as though I was ready to burst, and when I looked down at my growing belly, I knew I must look like it as well. The days ticked by slowly in anticipation for the new arrival, and it had been difficult keeping up with the chores around the house. Luba tried hard to be helpful, but at five years old, she was not able to do too much by herself. When Mama arrived, she took over, and I was able to sit back in bed watching as she and Luba cooked and cleaned the house together. My favorite part of the past few days was when Luba came to snuggle with me while Mama read us fairy tales from our favorite book, the Brothers Grimm.

As I grew older, I noticed myself starting to look more like my Mama than I had ever before. With her here, I watched her from afar and noticed how we both shared the same smile and wavy hair. Even the wrinkles forming near my eyes reminded me of her. Mama had never failed to show her devotion for me, and although she never admitted it, I knew that we had a connection which was beyond the bond she shared with my sisters. Having her around to help with the arrival of the new baby made me happy and excited to share that special time with her. It also gave me comfort to know that Luba would be taken care of when I had to be in the hospital for a week.

◆ ◆ ◆

"Good morning my love," Mama said as she knelt over Luba to kiss her nose. "I can see you are dressed and ready to go this Wednesday morning. I made kasha for breakfast, let's sit down to eat before it gets cold."

"Yummy, kasha!" Luba shouted with excitement.

She loved the way Mama cooked it. I suspect it was because she snuck in a little extra butter and sugar. I watched as she skipped over to her chair, ready to eat breakfast and hear about what Mama planned for the day.

"Luba, after we eat, let's give your Mama and Papa some time to relax while we go to the market and get some groceries. Do you think you can show me the way, and help me find everything we need?"

"Sure Baba. I can help you. Can we play outside afterwards? It looks so beautiful out today."

"That sounds like a great idea!" Mama smiled and cleaned up after breakfast while Luba rushed over to Papa and me. Abraham took her on his lap, and they started to play her favorite game. He held his hands out, palms up while Luba placed her tiny hands, palms down, on top of his oversized hands. She was supposed to take her hands away quickly or else he flipped his hands over onto hers and he would win that round. It was a silly game and they usually ended up laughing so hard they could not continue.

"I'm ready. Let's go," Mama called loudly over our laughter. Luba gave us both a warm hug and ran out the door.

It certainly was a beautiful day. As I peeked out the window, the sun shined and not a cloud could be seen in the sky. The breeze was not too hot or too cold, and the flowers bloomed in a beautiful array of pastel colors on the trees nearby.

"I see you staring outside, maybe we should go for a walk in a bit? It might be nice for you to move around a little and get your blood flowing," Abraham whispered as he gently kissed my neck, and made his way down to my giant belly. As his lips landed near my belly button, he felt a sudden kick which made him smile with delight.

"Hello my little prince or princess in there. I am your Papa and I can't wait to meet you. Mama informed me that you are going to be a lively little one with all the moving you have been doing in there. Let me tell you, you are going to love life out here. You will have a great big sister who will teach you everything, and a beautiful Mama that will love you unconditionally."

"And an amazing Papa!" I exclaimed. "I can't believe how fast these last nine months have gone. It can be any day now and although I am still nervous like I was with Luba, I am more excited."

I grabbed Abraham's hand and intertwined my fingers with his and held it up to my lips for a quick kiss. We sat together on the sofa soaking in the stillness of the moment.

I started to doze off, when Abraham leapt off the couch with his arms outstretched and ready to peel me away from falling asleep.

"Let's go for a walk, my *feigele*. As much as I enjoy the peace and quiet with you, the weather is too beautiful to miss out on. My boss allowed me to come in a few hours later today, but I will have to stay later into the evening to make up the time, so we should go before I have to leave."

I couldn't refuse him, no matter how much I tried. I weaved my way over to the dresser and changed into the only shirt I had left which fit over my giant belly. Then, hand in hand, Abraham and I headed out into the fresh air. As we walked further, the sounds of the city started to come alive. It wasn't only the clicking of the heels on the cobblestone or the haggling Baba with wrinkles like spider webs, shouting at the produce stand. It was the cooing of the baby in the stroller going past us and the singing group of children walking with their teacher to the playground nearby. Life buzzed all around us, and that day as we walked leisurely, I soaked it in like a sponge.

As we looped back around, Abraham asked, "How are you, my *feigele*? Are you tired? Should we sit down for a few minutes?"

"I am exhausted, but I think I can make it home, we aren't too far away now." I said, wondering if I actually meant it. My body was tiring, and a dull pain had appeared in my side. I didn't want to worry though. I talked myself into believing that it was probably from the walking, but soon my steps felt heavier and all I wanted was to get back to the house. I could almost hear the sofa calling my name as we approached.

Suddenly, about three steps from the front door, a warm trickle made its way down my legs and onto the stone below. I stopped and looked down at the wet rocks glistening underneath me. My heart thumped loudly with every emotion pumping through my veins. At once I shifted from excitement to nervousness. The baby was now officially on its way and all I could think was: thank goodness Abraham decided to take the morning off from work.

Abraham opened the door as I gazed down at my feet. When I looked up, he took my hand to lead me inside. "Abraham, my water broke," I blurted out in a shaky voice.

His eyes darted down and then back up. Caught off guard, he stood for a few long moments trying to find his voice. "Let's get you inside so you can sit down. Are you in pain? Have the contractions started yet?"

"I had some pain in my side, like a cramp, when we were walking. That must have been a small contraction," I explained, as I rested my weight onto him while he walked me slowly into the house. "It could be hours until the baby comes. Let's wait here until Mama and Luba get back."

Abraham quickly phoned into work and notified them that he wouldn't be coming in. Then, he paced around the house, trying to cover up his anxiety and worry by making himself seem busy.

I wondered where Mama and Luba could be when I heard the church clock strike eleven times. After the last bell chimed, music danced through the wind like twirling ballerinas and with it, more contractions took over my body. Abraham was right by my side, holding my hand when Mama and Luba came through the door.

"Khaya Berkovna, her water broke a little over an hour ago. Her contractions just started to come faster. We need to get a taxi now and get her to the hospital," Abraham said swiftly, sounding frantic. His face was scrunched up with worry and balls of sweat had formed on his forehead.

"Slow down, she is going to be alright. Remember, you have done this once before. Let me stay with her and you prepare her bag with a change of clothes and her personal items," Mama said calmly.

Luba and Mama sat next to me. Mama stroked the wisps of hair away from my face and held onto my hand while Luba sat unsure of what to do. I sensed how frightened she was by the look on her sweet innocent face.

"Luba, my love. I know you are scared because you see me hurting, but that is normal when you are having a baby. It's not an easy job, but I already had practice with you, so don't worry about me!" I said trying to put her mind at ease. Not long after, another contraction came.

"Luba, honey. How about you go and put away those groceries so they don't spoil," Mama asked her right as I squeezed her hand tightly. Luba looked relieved and so was I. I didn't want her to be so close to my pain. She stumbled into the kitchen to put everything away, but I noticed that she kept an eye on me the whole time.

When another wave of pain came and went, Mama held my hand and afterwards she whispered to Abraham to get a taxi to come to the front of the house. Luba came over to me and gave me a hug and a kiss and held my hand until it was time to leave.

Luba and Mama stood outside and watched us get into the taxi and drive away. Instead of being excited about the little baby on the way, I was scared and worried about how frightened Luba must have been.

♦ ♦ ♦

As I waited in the hospital bed for the doctor to come and examine me, a rush of emotions overtook me, until my mind went blank and I could not absorb anymore. I stared at the tiny white dots on the ceiling above me and let the sounds of the frantic hospital fade into the distance. When the doctor arrived, I wished Abraham had been the one to join him instead of the nurse. Abraham had to wait outside the hospital or in a waiting room with the other visitors. The nurse said she would notify him once the baby was born, but he wasn't allowed to hold or see the baby until we left the hospital. I was also not allowed any visitors during my time in the hospital. When Luba was born, I remembered feeling so alone even though I was surrounded by women in the exact same situation.

"Good afternoon, Raisa. Let me take a look and see how far you are. You are dilated about six centimeters, so we still have some time to go. I will come back and check on you in a little while," The doctor muttered as he snapped off his gloves.

I tried to pass the time by sitting in the chair near the window. The colors outside looked brighter than usual in contrast to the dullness inside the hospital. The bare white walls made the room cold and isolated. The screams of the women in labor nearby became hard to filter out. There were five women in my room, each in different stages of labor. Unfortunately for me, I was going to be the last to deliver, so I had to endure the screams for the next few hours.

The cries and pleas of the women echoed through the room into the hall. Just when I thought I couldn't take it anymore, it was my turn. With nothing substantial to ease the pain but the nurse's hand to squeeze, I breathed deeply and pushed until I could no longer.

◆ ◆ ◆

As I carefully nuzzled her in my arms, tears of joy ran down my face. I gazed into her sleepy newborn eyes and I longed for Abraham to share that moment with us. Instead, I sang to her and told her all about her Papa and big sister who could not wait to meet her.

That evening, I made my way to an area with nine other mothers. It became our room for the next week. The nurses wheeled our babies into the room every three hours during the day so we could nurse them. They arrived wrapped like mummies and packed like sardines on the cart. After I fed her, I walked with her to the window. Abraham stood outside, waiting in the place we agreed. I held up our sweet little bundle so he could see her from afar. He blew her kisses with one hand as he held the other to his chest, and even from a distance, I knew tears were streaming down his face.

◆ ◆ ◆

The week could not go by fast enough. I wished to go home and see Luba, Abraham and Mama so much. I wanted our little baby girl to meet the most important people in the world. She was wonderful, and as each day passed by she looked more and more like Abraham. I on the other hand, missed Luba more than I imagined I would, and I desperately wanted to go home. Finally, after seven days of being away, we were going home!

Walking out of the hospital and placing our little girl into Abraham's arms made everything I had gone through even more worth it. Watching him melt with love as he kissed her tiny nose made me feel like the luckiest person alive.

"She is beautiful," He said fighting back tears. "What should we name her? Luba has mentioned that she likes the name Sofia. What do you think?"

"I agree, Sofia is perfect."

Mama and Luba waited outside when the taxi pulled up to the house. Luba's smile widened as we came to a stop in front. She rushed over and gave me her best hug. I had missed her incredibly and I knew she had missed me just as much.

"Can I hold her Mama, please, please?" She begged once we went inside.

"Of course, go wash your hands and sit on the couch," I said

Luba waited patiently on the couch while I brought the baby over. I placed her gently in her lap and Luba held her close. She was in love from the moment they touched.

"Sofia, meet your big sister, Luba."

"Sofia? Really? That is the name I wanted. It's perfect. She is like a doll. She has a cute button nose and her hands and feet are so tiny. I am so happy I have a baby sister. I love her," Luba said quietly as she rocked Sofia gently.

"And she loves you."

CHAPTER TWENTY-SEVEN
A GIFT

29 SEPTEMBER 1943
Kokand, Uzbekistan, USSR

The trees had already lost most of their leaves, leaving them exposed and vulnerable, much like my emotions. Without Abraham by my side, I felt stripped. It was endlessly hard to be without him, but somehow over the years, I had learned to accept to live with our distance. Seeing him again was one of the best moments in my life. He made me see my life in color again. He showed us in every way, how much he loved and missed us. But that only made it much harder to say goodbye again.

Our two weeks together were like a dream, and I wished it would never end. When the sun began to light up the room each morning, I would wake to watch him sleep. The steady rise and fall of his chest calmed my nerves and brought me back to our days in Minsk. Although on the surface Abraham seemed to be the same father and husband he had been before the war, I knew that deep down he had changed. Whatever he encountered and endured on the front lines had made him a different person.

Unfortunately, it was not only the wrinkles which stemmed from his eyes like whiskers, or the silver strands which now took over his brown hair, that showed the toll the war had on him. Each night he woke, shaken from the depths of his sleep, sweating from the visions that haunted him.

At first, he didn't want to talk about his nightmares. I sensed that he thought sharing them would upset or scare me, but as the nights progressed, I continued to insist that he open up to me.

"Abraham, you're alright, you're safe. I'm here," I whispered, as I held him close after he had awoken sweating only a few hours after we fell asleep.

"I'm sorry to wake you again," Abraham mumbled, holding his head low.

I stroked his hair and ran my hands over his back, instantly aware of his tense muscles. "We have always been able to share everything with each other, without exception. I know you think I can't handle whatever it is that you have been through on the front lines, and maybe you are right, but you have to get it out. Please talk to me."

His hesitation was clear as his arms twisted around me, his fingers busy twirling my hair. Abraham was silent for a while and his eyes darted around as if he was trying to find the right words scrolled across the walls.

Slowly, he started to unravel the web of destruction which had become his life for the last two years.

"You are right. You should know what haunts me in my dreams. I also want you to know that if it weren't for you and the girls, I wouldn't be able to get through the nights. The only thing which helps me back to sleep, is envisioning you, and the girls in my mind. You bring me back to a happy place, and I thank you for this."

He grabbed the extra pillow resting near the bed and propped it behind us. His hand reached for mine as he began.

"I guess I should start from the beginning. When the train steamed away from you girls, I never thought that I would have been away from you for so long. Then the days turned into weeks, and then months and then years, and I went from living day to day to hopefully surviving them. The first few months we were sent to training where we learned how to use the tanks and guns. They supplied us with uniforms and boots. Although we were fed, I would hardly say it was enough to keep us moving through the long days of drills. I was then assigned to the 54th light artillery regiment. We were tasked with covering Leningrad from the east so the Nazis wouldn't break through Ladoga Lake and go further east. My first battle was one that we didn't win, and the Nazis closed the ring of the blockade. Instead of the Fascists occupying Leningrad, they closed it off from the rest of Russia and then heavily bombed it, leaving the people left inside to starve."

His fingers moved around anxiously over my hand. I watched him struggle as he gathered his thoughts to continue his story.

"We did everything we could to push the Fascists back, but from our trenches, we watched the sky glow with fire, night after night. After those first few days on the front, I quickly became accustomed to the constant sound of Nazi planes buzzing by, and bombs dropping nearly on top of us, but nevertheless, they left me in a perpetual state of fear. Our barracks were inside an old factory which had been shut down. There was no heat and our thin blankets didn't do much to keep us warm, but we were so tired that somehow, we managed to fall asleep. The men in my unit became my brothers. The longer the war continued, the harder it became for us all. The more we knew each other and suffered through hell together, the more difficult it was to have to say goodbye to the fallen."

I nestled myself closer to Abraham, sensing his rising emotions. "I meant to ask why you didn't write too much about the other soldiers in your unit. I thought maybe you weren't close with them, or possibly you kept your distance because you were singled out for being Jewish."

"I can see why you would think so, but it was not any of those reasons at all. Our unit is made up of many nationalities and I wasn't the only Jew. We are all soldiers, fighting for one cause and on the battlefield, we are brothers, no matter what language we speak, or religion we are. I didn't write about them because I knew what would happen if one of them were to be killed. I would be forced to not only see it happen, and then live with the nightmares, but I would also have to write it down and make it even more real. Do you understand?"

"Yes, I do. Your heart can only take on so much. Writing something down is like etching it in stone, and the words bouncing off the paper carry more than simply letters, they bear emotions and burdens and they can hold you back like an anchor." Abraham nodded in agreement and then leaned over for a kiss. His soft lips caressed mine as his dry, but strong hands found my back to pull me in tighter. We sat together, silent for a while until I looked up and asked, "Will you tell me about some of them?"

Abraham breathed a heavy sigh and repositioned himself before starting again, "Alexander and I met on the train leaving Minsk. We call him Sasha. He lived in Minsk not far from us, with his wife and two boys, about the same age as Luba and Sofia. He was an engineer and is also Jewish, so we connected instantly and often had something to talk about. We trained together and transferred together to the same unit in Leningrad. He has been my one constant, the only comrade that has been with me from the beginning. Do you remember the time that I was in the hospital?"

"Of course, I thought my heart was going to stop after I read you had been injured."

"It was Sasha who saved me. We were ambushed by the Nazis. They had come from out of nowhere, surprising us. Bullets flew left and right, and explosions shot off like fireworks. An explosion went off right next to where I was positioned. The soldiers closer to the blast were killed instantly. A piece of shrapnel hit my helmet and it knocked me out cold. The next thing I remember is waking up in the infirmary. It was Sasha who saw I was down, but still alive, so he dragged me to safety and carried me to the field hospital. I had suffered a severe concussion, but luckily no permanent damage. I would have died out there if it weren't for him."

I would have died if it weren't for him too, I thought to myself. Hearing him talk about the war made me want to lock him inside and never let him go back. The idea of him returning to bombs and bullets sent a shiver down my spine. Trying not to let my emotions show, I answered him with smile, "I am forever grateful to Sasha, and I hope to meet him and his family one day."

"I hope so too. When Sasha and I arrived in Leningrad, we were thrown into battle and you figure out who your friends are incredibly fast that way. Sasha, Sergei, Victor, Borya and I became bunkmates and brothers right away. Sergei was the prankster, regularly lifting our spirits with a laugh. Victor, being the eldest, was like a father figure to us all. He was always there to listen when we were down and would somehow find the right words to ease our pain. Borya, the shortest of the five of us, and likely the shortest in the entire regiment, was constantly the center of attention. He tells stories like a spider spins its webs, endlessly intricate and beautiful. His attention to detail carried out onto the field, and he became one of the best marksmen in our unit. We have helped each other and saved one another more times than I can count, but at war, luck only goes so far, and I have lost more friends than I have had time to make."

Tears dripped slowly and then faster as Abraham thought about his fallen brothers. Abraham reached over and played with my silver star. He focused on it as he touched it gently between his fingers. I looked into his torn soul and wished I had a way to mend it, but I knew that only time had the ability to heal those wounds.

Holding back his tears once again, Abraham slowly painted a picture of his nightmares. "Sergei departed us first. A grenade took his life. I will never forget his face as he suffered on the blood-stained dirt ground next to me. His arm and leg blown into pieces like slivers of shattered glass. Some nights when I close my eyes, all I see is red, an endless stream of crimson."

My body shuddered with his last words, as I replayed the images from my own nightmares full of the color red. Abraham's hand trembled alongside my own. We sat silent for a few minutes, giving each other a moment.

"Victor was next. His death was only a few months ago, and it was extremely hard on us all. He had so much to live for and so much more to give. He was a Jew from Poland, but spoke Russian well, and of course Yiddish. He had a wife and six children, and not a day escaped by that he didn't talk about them. He kept them alive in his mind by keeping them alive amongst us. They stopped writing back a few months before his death and one can only guess what happened to them. They were sent north to Siberia to work in a factory. He begged them to leave to move south, but she was afraid to leave and endure another long trip alone with the six children."

"I can understand where she was coming from. The trip was hard enough with two children. I can't imagine six. Especially without the help of family. How did Victor die?" I asked, unsure if I really wanted to know. I was beginning to understand the amount of weight my husband now carried around. I felt helpless and scared for him.

"He took a bullet straight through the heart. The shot might have killed him, but his heart was already broken weeks before. He never admitted that his family had likely perished, but he knew deep down something had happened. Victor was a good, kind man. Watching him die, broke off a little piece of us, but it also made the three of us stronger and more ready to fight. Besides watching friends die, we saw innocent civilians perish under the Nazis, and even our own soldiers from the hands of Russians."

"What do you mean?"

"One day our commander lined up two soldiers in front of us. I didn't know them, but I had seen them in passing a few times. The commander explained that they had been caught trying to desert, fleeing from the front lines. Nearby, I watched some soldiers digging their graves and the two men were told to strip. Then they shot them right in front of us, to be used as examples, so others wouldn't follow their lead."

"Well, there goes that thought." I laughed at myself for even thinking about it. I knew what happened to deserters, and I knew Abraham would never do it, but I selfishly wished he would stay with us and not go back.

Abraham continued slowly, "The war brings out the best and the worst in people. While most of us cope with loss and fear by focusing our thoughts on our loved ones and helping our brothers through the tough moments, others turn belligerent. Many of the men, mostly the younger ones, act as if the world owes them something for their service, and I hear many stories of them going to nearby towns to take advantage of the girls. They aren't the only ones, sadly. Many lieutenants and commanders have mistresses in one or more cities."

His voice began to trail off, and I knew he was getting tired. "I am thankful that you shared with me some of your experiences. I hope that by speaking about them to me, it helps you move on. Let's get some rest." I was exhausted with lack of sleep and more so with worry. I hoped it had helped him to let it out, but knowing more about what went on at the frontlines only made my nightmares seem more real.

He leaned over and embraced me. His warmth surrounded me, "I am lighter already. I love you, my *feigele*. Stay my little bird forever." His breath slowed as it grazed my neck and we both fell into slumber.

♦ ♦ ♦

With every passing day, Luba grew stronger and her cough completely disappeared a few days before Abraham's departure. We ventured out every day together for long walks, only the four of us. The girls soaked in every minute of the precious time we had with him. Luba talked to him about history and the latest books she had read, while Sofia chatted about her friends and what she learned in music school. Abraham even surprised us one day with something special to do.

"Good morning my girls. Wake up!" He said to our sleeping angels as we rustled them from their beds. "I have something special planned for us today. Let's eat some breakfast and then we will need to get dressed in our best clothes."

"I have the perfect dress!" Sofia said getting out of bed faster than normal.

After breakfast, we dressed in our finest clothes unsure of why or where we were headed. Excitement was in the air that morning, and it mostly made me forget that Abraham was set to leave in four days.

Sofia was the first to come running over in her dress. It looked beautiful on her. Her black hair curled at her shoulders in perfect balance with her black shoes. Her summer dress fell gracefully to her knees. The crinkled linen fabric and brightly colored design reminded me of a field filled with endless poppy flowers.

"You look stunning. What a young lady you have become. And this dress of yours... you look very fashionable," Abraham said, knowing exactly what she wanted him to say.

I had finished sewing the dress right before Abraham had arrived. I wanted her to have something special to wear for her music concert. I traded one silver spoon for five types of fabric. It was enough to make a new article of clothing for everyone in my family. Each girl got a new dress or skirt with a top. For Papa and Oscar, Mama and I made matching beige linen shirts. There was even enough left to make a tie for Abraham.

I slipped on my new dress and turned to Abraham for his approval. "What do you think?" As I waited for an answer, my hands tried to soften out the wrinkles over the curves of my body. The simple black buttons ran down the length of the pale blue dress, falling right past my knees. I carefully tied the matching belt around my waist and let the ends hang amongst the pleated bottom of the dress.

His hands cupped my face while he smiled down towards me. "You look just as beautiful, if not more beautiful than the day I met you." He kissed the tip of my nose and I felt myself blush.

Luba showed herself last. Although she looked amazing, I sensed she was unsure of herself. Her blouse was the same pale blue fabric as my dress. The buttons ran down the back of the shirt and the collar sat close to her neck. It was tucked into a long flowing skirt that fell past her knees, but not quite to her ankles. The skirt was dark blue with small white polka dots.

Abraham looked up when he heard Luba come into the room and as his face changed, so did hers. I watched as her insecurities floated away and her smile matched his.

"You girls look amazing! Let's go so we aren't late to our appointment," Papa said as he held the door open for us.

We walked for about ten minutes following Abraham's direction, surprised by how acclimated he was to the area after only being there for a little over a week. Soon after, we walked through the black iron gates of the park. Standing near a fountain up ahead, stood a short, older man with wide eyebrows. Strapped around his neck was a camera and near him sat a pile of camera gear.

"Abraham, are we getting our pictures taken?" Before he answered, the man came towards us with his arm outstretched towards Abraham.

"It's good to see you again Abraham. This must be the beautiful family you told me about. You were right, they are exactly as you described. You chose a perfect day. The sun has been hiding between the clouds, so we won't have to fight it in our eyes."

"Thank you. We appreciate you doing this for us on such short notice. Where should we stand?" Abraham asked as he turned to see how surprised we were. The girls beamed with excitement. New pictures of us as a family including Abraham was a gift that meant more than words could describe. Our old photos had become worn and tattered from holding them every day to remember one another in happier times. They were the most valuable things we owned.

We positioned ourselves facing the old man. His lens stared back at us, while he instructed us in a thin voice that was barely audible. As I stood next to Abraham and our two beautiful girls, I scanned through some of my memories. Each memory was like a bubble floating through air. Some continued to soar in all their glory into the unknown, while others had burst with the struggles of life. No matter what we endured, our mere presence in this life was beautiful, and I was thankful that our journey had brought us to this moment together.

◆ ◆ ◆

I sat in my bed and glanced over to the empty spot next to me. I still sensed him, but his soft touch and gentle breath faded slowly from my memory once again. On the table nearby sat the stack of photos from a few weeks ago. I had flipped through them so many times that I had memorized each and every detail. The photographer captured us perfectly. Each of our personalities leapt off the paper, making an array of artful images. Beneath our smiles, I saw a hint of sadness and fear, but there was also hope and happiness. They brought me happy tears as I realized what a meaningful thing Abraham had done for me and his girls.

I reminded myself that life had to continue, with or without Abraham here. We slowly reverted to our normal routines. Mama and my sisters kept me under their watchful eye for a while, sensing I needed the extra support to fill the emptiness I had after Abraham left for the frontlines. Sofia started school again. Not long after Abraham left, Luba came home excited that she had found a job. After weeks of waiting and applying at the refugee center, she was placed into a position. She officially started working last week at the local bathhouse. She cleaned most of the day and came home exhausted, but she enjoyed being in the warm steamy rooms.

We waited for word from Abraham about his safe arrival back in Russia, but so far, we had not received any cards or letters, only a money telegram and a package from when he was in Tashkent.

"Mama, I am leaving now to go to the post office to check for mail. Do you need me to stop and get anything else on the way?" I asked

"No, my dear, I think we have what we need. Do you want me to come with you? Otherwise, I will start making dinner."

"I'll be fine on my own. I will be back soon, and I can help you finish cooking. Thanks Mama."

The bright sun flooded my vision as I stepped out into the clear autumn afternoon. A patch of birds flew in a v shape overhead. Their presence was the only one in the sky, as the clouds were nowhere to be found. I envied their freedom, wishing that I too could fly away from this foreign life we lived.

The post office was in the same direction as the park where Abraham took us for photos, and as I walked down the well-known path, I couldn't help but recall that wonderful day. I turned the corner on the next street and a familiar voice snapped me back to the present.

"Raisa, is that you?"

I spun around to find a pair of blazing blue eyes staring at me in amazement. "Lana, oh my, is it really you? How are you my dear?" I began to tear up as we hugged tightly.

Her long blond hair no longer framed her face in two braids, instead it was shorter and curled in the back. I still pictured us as little girls playing with our dolls and building snowmen together. I tried to recall the last time I saw her, and it must have been at her wedding, which was over ten years ago. Growing up, I thought Lana, Nina and I would be friends forever, but as we grew older life changed. Nina moved to Stalingrad and it was Lana and me again. Nina and I wrote to each other often, and never stopped, even after we married. Lana and I grew up, married, and somehow, I didn't keep up with our letters as much as I had hoped.

"And the odds of finding each other here in Kokand. It must be *beshert.*"

"It is meant to be!" I exclaimed.

"We are doing fine for ourselves. My husband is at the front and so is our son. I came here with our daughter and my in-laws. How about you?"

"My husband, Abraham is also fighting on the front. I came with our two daughters and my side of the family. Mama and Papa are here and so are my three sisters and nephew. They will be so happy to see you again, as am I. How long have you been here?" I asked.

"We arrived a few months ago. We fled east first and ended up in the Urals, but the cold winter and lack of food pushed us to go south. I was hesitant to leave, but we had no choice at the end. I am glad we made it here. That was a journey I wouldn't wish on my worst enemy."

Standing there with Lana gave me a little boost. It freed some of my sadness and made me realize that my life would be fuller with more friends nearby. I felt lucky that I had reconnected with another one of my oldest friends, especially when we needed each other the most.

"I am glad too. I have been so busy with my girls and keeping the house straight, that I haven't had much time to make friends or visit. It would be nice if we could meet for tea one day and get to know each other once again," I said, smiling both inside and out. "I am on my way to the post office, where are you headed?"

"I would like that! I agree it has been hard to get away from life's worries, but we need to take care of each other too. I was also going to the post office. I am hoping for some mail from my boys."

As we walked together to the post office, I told her about our stay with Nina and a summary of our long trip here. Our stories intertwined as we realized the many similarities our journeys had in common. The more we talked and shared about our lives, the more I wished we had never lost touch.

♦ ♦ ♦

By the time we parted ways and I arrived home, Mama already had dinner prepared. I draped my shawl over the chair in the kitchen and emptied the stack of mail from my bag onto the table before I made my way to Mama and Papa's room.

"Mama, I'm sorry I am a bit later than expected. It smells delicious in here."

"That's alright, Raisa. Is everything alright? I started to worry."

"Yes, you won't believe who I met while I was walking to the post office! Lana… Lana Kaganskya! It was so nice to talk with her. We picked up right where we left off so many years ago."

"That is wonderful. I am glad to hear she is safe. Did you bring home any letters?"

"I did. There was one from Abraham and also a few for you and the others."

♦ ♦ ♦

Later that evening we sat around the dinner table enjoying the *borscht* soup that Mama made for us. I fished out the last chunks of pink potatoes and beets onto my spoon and then I began to read the letter from Abraham out loud.

23 September 1943

Hello my dearest girls. I am well and wish to hear the same from you. On the road I sent you four cards. I wrote to you about the hardships I had in the ticketing station in Tashkent. I finally left

Tashkent last night at 8pm and arrived in Moscow at 8pm tonight. It turned out to be a fairly enjoyable ride, as I was seated in the same car with other officers and they made good company. I sent you a telegram before I left Tashkent, and also please let me know if you collected the package as well. My train leaves from Moscow in three days. I ████████████████████████████████████ ████████████████████████████████████. Let me know how you are and if Luba is feeling better. Was she able to find a job? If so, where and is she feeling better? I worry about her doing too much after being sick. I put together an envelope of my copies of the photos, and somehow, I must have left it on the table. I can't believe I forgot them! Could you please send them to me? The images of your faces are fresh in my mind, but I like to look at your photos each morning when I wake and each evening before bed. Your beautiful faces make me the happiest man in the world. In one week, I will be receiving my next payment and I will send more money then. Did you ████████████████████████████████ you? My Papa and Manya send their regards. They enjoyed the pears I brought very much. I love you all so much, and I can't describe how much I enjoyed seeing you and holding you in my arms. Your love and

support will keep me going until the end of this war.
Sending all my love to the whole family, Abraham

"...Your beautiful faces make me the happiest man in the world." My eyes continued to scan his words. I imagined his hands on my face, his breath near my ear when he whispered words similar to those each night as he held me in his tight embrace. I tried not to let my cheeks flush from the thought of him. I rose from my seat to clear the dinner table instead.

That evening in the silence of the night, I ran my fingers over my necklace and thought about a life with Abraham and the girls, far away from here, dreaming of a future I hoped would one day become reality.

CHAPTER TWENTY-EIGHT
SHARDS OF GLASS

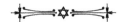

10 NOVEMBER 1943
Kokand, Uzbekistan, USSR

My hands gripped the ornate, tusk-shaped letter opener as I peered at the message from Abraham's father with anguish. Usually, Abraham sent letters back and forth to his family and he would fill me on their well-being. They had not sent many to me directly, and the pit in the bottom of my stomach told me that somehow this letter was going to be different. The words flew off the page as I read them quickly hoping to prove myself wrong.

> Dear Raisa, Luba and Sofia. I hear from Abraham that you are doing well in Kokand. I am happy to hear this and I can also relay that so far, we are still living and are fairly healthy. Right now, Manya, Freyda, her girls and I are staying with friends in Moscow, but we cannot find any jobs here and can no longer impose on them. We are fearful that winter will come, and life will only get harder

for us if we don't move now. We have already applied and been given tickets to journey to Kokand to stay with you. We will be leaving in two weeks from today, October 27th. We are hopeful that our journey will be a pleasant one, and we look forward to seeing you soon. Sincerely, Lev, Manya and Freyda

My eyes scanned over the words again, and I wished they weren't staring back at me. Over the last fifteen years, we had grown more distant with his relatives and I never genuinely had a chance to get to know them. Since Abraham and I moved from Bobruisk shortly after getting married, we did not see them often. We only returned to visit a few times and they rarely came to Minsk to see us, or the girls. My parents and my sisters came to Minsk several times a year and my family always made it a priority to keep in contact. Our families were obviously different, and I learned to accept them for who they were, but the thought of them here, without Abraham made me tense in every muscle of my body.

Abraham had two older sisters. Leia was the eldest and Freyda was next. He also had one older brother, Isaac, who passed away about six years ago. Then he had a younger brother, Sander, and the youngest of them all was his sister, Malka. He had a pleasant relationship with his entire family, except for Freyda. She persistently made trouble and caused a stir within his family. When Abraham and I first met, he warned me to stay away from her and after being near her only a few times, he did not need to explain why.

My favorite person in his family was his mother. Her name was Sara. She passed away only a few years after we married, and I wished that I had known her for longer. I admired her strength and her thoughtfulness. She was like a stone you found near the edge of the water: rough and tumbled with the struggles of life, but yet so shiny and polished on the outside.

Sometimes I caught a glimpse of her when I looked at Abraham.

A few years after Sara passed away, Lev met Manya and they had been together since. We were happy that he found a companion, but she would never fill the void that was left behind when Sara died.

The thought of having the three of them here and Freyda's three girls made me uneasy. Of course, I wanted to help his family in any way possible, but that meant less food for my own family and more pressure on me. I knew that Abraham would be unhappy about the arrival of Freyda and her children, but I quickly set my pen to paper to let him know of this news.

Hello my dearest Abraham. How are you doing? We are doing well here. Sofia has been thriving in school and is still attending her music school one evening a week. Luba is continuing to work at the bathhouse. She has fully recovered and is back to her normal self again. In your last letter you told me to go ahead and buy a sewing machine, so I found a good one at the market and it has proved itself very useful. I have found some work mending clothes and it has been keeping my mind focused. You also mentioned that you were being invited to go see a movie and instead you decided to stay and write to me. My love, you never fail to amaze me. Even with so many miles separating us, you find a way to warm my heart. I wanted to know if you are still working by yourself and traveling as much as before? Before, you had a group of three doing what you now do alone. This must be keeping you busy, so I understand why your letters have been less frequent. Nevertheless, try to write as often as you can so I don't worry too much. I am pleased that you received the photos I sent. I was worried they weren't going to come. I am also happy to say that I received the latest telegram from you. I do have some news and I am unsure what to make of it. I received a letter from your father. Have you received one as well? Your father, Manya, Freyda and her girls have decided they want to come live here with us. They are set to travel on the 27th of October. What should I do to prepare for their arrival? Should I make room for them in our apartment or look for a place for them? I hope to hear from you soon. We all love you and send you hugs and kisses. Always, Raisa

The next letter I received back from Abraham was splattered with his distaste for Freyda. He asked me to write to them and tell them that we would be leaving Kokand. He wanted them to cancel the trip and stay in Moscow. Truthfully, so did I, but I knew that by the time I wrote to them, they would have already left. It was of no use and I had to accept that they would be here soon.

◆ ◆ ◆

With only a few days left of freedom before our guests arrived, I tried to make the most of them.

"Mama, you remember that later today, Sofia, Luba and Oscar will be home with you and Papa, while Hana and I meet with Lana and Klara for the afternoon?" I asked.

"Yes, of course I remember. You reminded me yesterday, and the day before. I'm not so forgetful yet, am I? Mama smiled and put a hand on my shoulder. "You girls will have fun. It will be nice to get away from the normal routine of things."

I smiled too, thinking that although Mama was getting older, she wasn't forgetful. Her mind was still as sharp as it was when I was a child. "You're right, Mama, I'm only excited. I think it will be nice. Thank you for watching the kids."

"Of course, my dear."

The morning sped by as Mama and I prepared lunch. The anticipation for the afternoon was building slowly as the hours went by. Lana and I had planned the afternoon when I told her about the arrival of Freyda, her girls, and my in-laws. We should have some girl time before she comes and brings trouble, Lana had said. We decided an afternoon at the Yiddish Theater was just what we needed. The theater had been relocated from Kiev during the evacuation and we had talked about going, but it never seemed to be the right time. This month they were doing a classic from Sholem Aleichem called *Blondzhende Stern,* or *Wandering Stars.* I had read the novel years ago, but never managed to see it in the theater. I had only seen his *Tevye the Milkman* in the theater and loved it.

I pulled my stockings on carefully, noticing the holes that I had been meaning to stitch up, and then slipped into my long black skirt. It looked worn from so much use these last few years, but it was the only one I had. I wore every piece of clothing I had taken with me from Minsk, no matter how drab they were. I spent any extra we had making something new for Luba and Sofia. They were growing after all, and needed them more than I did. But deep down, I wished I had something new to wear for our special outing.

I pushed my head through my sweater and smoothed it over my skirt. It was the color of deep red wine. I was glad I packed it as it hides almost every stain like camouflage.

I ran a comb through my hair, noticing more silver than dark, and fashioned a bun in a matter of moments. I glanced in the mirror. My eyes were drawn to my star. It was striking against the burgundy. I moved the lock on the chain to the back and pulled the star up to my lips. I gave it a kiss and tucked it inside my sweater, safe from prying eyes.

"Raisa," Mama called from outside the door, "may I come in?"

"Yes, come in."

Mama opened the door and revealed a shawl hanging over her arm. It was white around the edges with a decorative design fanning out from the middle in colors of gold, burgundy, orange, pinks and blues. I had never seen it before. "This is for you dear. I thought you should have something new."

I waved her away. "No, no, Mama, I don't need anything."

"I know. You never need anything. When was the last time you got something for yourself? Every last *kapeika* you have, you spend on everyone else. This is for you," she said, pulling me closer to her. "Bend over, I'll put it on you."

She laid it around my back, over my shoulders, and neatly tied it together in the front. It was beautiful. The edges of the wool fabric were finished with a decorative layer of white fringe. The pattern was ornate and full of colors, and it was exactly what my tired sweater needed.

"Mama, this is beautiful! It's too much. I can't accept such a nice gift." I said.

She came closer and took both my hands inside hers. "It looks very good on you. Of course, you will accept it. I know how much you suffer with Abraham being away, but that doesn't mean you have to punish yourself as well. You have to treat yourself if you can. Since you won't do it, then at least let me."

"Thank you, Mama. I really love it. You knew just what I needed, when I needed it," I answered, and gave her a hug.

Another knock at the door came a few moments later. "Are you ready, Raisa?" Hana asked from the doorway. "You look great. Is that a new shawl?" she smiled then winked.

"You were in on this too?"

"I might have helped to pick it out," she answered playfully. "Come, sister, it's time to go."

I went to the kitchen and gave Luba and Sofia a kiss while Hana hugged Oscar. "Good bye," we both called out as I closed the door behind us.

"It feels strange being all dressed up and going out in times like this," I said as I fought back the guilt of doing something fun when I knew Abraham was fighting for his life and ours.

"It does. I won't disagree, but I do believe that we have to enjoy life, even in hard times. There is no sense in sitting around crying all day. We deserve one afternoon of theater."

"Well, when you put it that way," I teased back.

We walked along the road towards the theater. Klara and Lana were up the street waiting for us where we had agreed to meet. "Hello girls. I'm so glad you could both come," I exclaimed.

"Are you kidding me? A day away from the apartment, cooking, cleaning and looking after my family? This is exactly what I needed, what we all needed," Lana said, tucking a strand of blonde hair away from her blue eyes.

"I have seen a few of Sholem Aleichem's plays, but never this one. I haven't read the novel either. I am looking forward to it," said Klara.

"That's good, none of us have seen it. I have read it. It is a good one, a romance and a comedy. I read up a few years ago about Sholem. He was an interesting man. Do you girls know much about him?" I asked.

They all shook their heads no in unison, so I began to share the fun facts that I had remembered. "He had a mortal fear of the number thirteen. His manuscripts never had a page thirteen. Instead, he numbered it as twelve-a. He actually died on the thirteenth, and his headstone was even inscribed with twelve-a."

"I guess he had reason to be afraid of that number," Hana chuckled, making us all laugh with her.

"I also remember reading in one of his other stories a line which stuck with me. It was, 'What eyes can tell you in a minute, a mouth will never say in a day.'"

"What a beautiful quote. I love it," Klara said. "I remember one as well. It is my favorite saying. 'Life is a dream for the wise, a game for the fool, a comedy for the rich, a tragedy for the poor.' Have you heard this one?" she asked.

We all nodded in unison as we approached the theater. We found seats and made ourselves comfortable as the show began. The show took us into the lives of Liebel, a rich man's son, and Reizel, the poor cantor's daughter. They fall in love, but are forbidden to be together. They run away, leaving behind the cramped shtetl for a new exciting world. Both are passionate about Yiddish theater and join the traveling theater. She is a singer and he is an actor. Soon, they become world famous, but their success separates them for ten years as they travel across Europe and to America. They long for each other and dream of a reunion. Eventually, they find each other again in New York.

"What a wonderful story!" Hana exclaimed when we started our walk back home. "It had me laughing and crying all at the same time!"

"Me too!" Lana said.

"I loved it," Klara spoke up next. "It was beautiful. Especially the line, 'Stars do not fall, they wander.' So perfect."

"Here we are separated from our lives and our husbands, searching for something to hold onto and longing to be reunited. They were torn apart because of love, and us from war, but in the end they found each other. We have to hope that will be our fate too," I said as we neared our apartment.

"It will be," Klara answered looking into the distance. I saw her swallow hard, pushing back the thoughts we all had in our minds.

Hana reached over and grabbed my hand, giving it a squeeze. "So, what are we going to do about Freyda?" Hana smiled.

"What do you mean? What can I do?" I answered.

"Well, for one, you cannot wait on her and be her maid," Klara answered quickly. "I was your guest not too long ago, and I know how you are."

"What does that mean?" I asked, knowing exactly what she meant.

"You will bend over backwards and forwards to make sure everything is perfect for your guests. You are an incredible host, my friend, but please remember this is Freyda, she won't appreciate it," Klara said.

"She is right," Lana agreed. "Even Abraham doesn't want her here. Do what you have to and no more."

"And don't feel guilty about that," Hana added.

It was nice to have them to talk to, to support me. They knew me, my strengths and my weaknesses, but most of all, they were upfront with me when I needed them the most. "Thank you, friends. I am dreading her arrival, but hopefully it will be short term. I should start looking for a place for her right away."

The late afternoon ended with hugs and kisses before Hana and I separated for our apartment. I enjoyed the last moments of our day, and although the pending arrival loomed over me, it no longer pinched at my pressure points. I tackled the evening with a lightness in my step and a smile on my face.

♦ ♦ ♦

Mondays tended to be the hardest morning to wake up. The weather was becoming colder and the mornings darker. As we tried to make our way out of our warm beds, the weight of the week lured me back under the covers. This Monday was not only the start of a new week and a new month, it was also the beginning of a new chapter and a story that I had no desire to unfold.

Mama and I walked together to the train station. My nerves buzzed inside me like a swarm of bees. The wind was especially sharp, and it stung me like shards of glass, making me wonder if this cold bitter weather was the wrath of Freyda's personality headed towards us.

"Don't worry Raisa. I know you are burdened with a great deal of pressure, but you have to remember that your kids must come first. They are adults and they will figure things out much like we had to."

"I know Mama. I want to do what I can for Abraham's sake. I owe him that."

"I can understand. You have a generous and kind heart, Raisa. Abraham is lucky to have you."

I wanted to say, no, I am lucky to have Abraham, but the doors to the train rattled open. A sea of tired people made their descent into the Kokand station. Their eyes looking just as lost as ours had been only a few years before. It wasn't long before I spotted Freyda and the rest of her family. Her angular face bore a pointed nose and thin lips which always seemed to be frowning. Her green cat eyes had no life, yet they looked as if they could attack at any moment. She approached me first, sending a shudder down my spine as she kissed my cheek coldly.

"Welcome to Kokand. We are happy to have you here," I said, trying to make myself believe it as well. "Our place is only a twenty-minute walk from here, shall we get going?"

♦ ♦ ♦

After less than a week of living with our unwelcome guests, I realized that my fears were not misplaced. It was as if I was walking barefoot across a rocky beach on a hot sunny day every time I had to see Freyda. Home was no longer my safe place. Freyda's attitude and outlook on life left a bad taste in my mouth and I worried that I may never be rid of it.

"Good morning, Freyda. How did you sleep last night?" I asked as I walked into the kitchen. She sat at the table reading the paper.

Her eyes barely looked up as she barked her response. "Ugh, I didn't sleep but for a few hours. The mattress is so uncomfortable, and it has a smell that I can't quite name."

"I'm sorry. I have slept on that mattress for the past few years and I find it quite comfortable. Especially after the places I slept before it." I didn't even respond to her statement about the smell. I knew it was her way of being mean for the sake of it.

"Well, maybe I will get accustomed to it then. I'm sure we will be staying here for a while. Can you take us to the market today to get us some food? Maybe we can cook something different for dinner tonight?"

"Sure. I can take you. I'm sure my Mama would like that. She could use a night off of her feet," I said, making sure she knew that if she wanted something different, then she would have to cook it herself.

◆ ◆ ◆

In order to survive, I focused on the people and aspects of my life which made me happy. I tried to go about my days as usual. I continued to stand in line for our rations and I went to the post office to check for new mail every day. Ever since the day I reunited with Lana, we made it a point to walk together to the post office. On the way, I talked about Freyda and the rest of my family and she shared her problems with her in-laws or other news. We walked back either excited for ourselves or for each other when a letter or package arrived. Quickly, Lana became my rock, and I became hers.

As I approached our house after coming back from the post office, I looked down at the letter from Abraham. A single piece of light brown paper folded into a perfect triangle. Instead of going inside, I turned around and searched for a lonely bench. I sat, looking up at the sun illuminating the silver lined clouds. I took the note from my pocket, pulled the flap out from the inside and started to read his letter. I imagined he spoke the words himself.

Good evening my girls. I only today received your letter from the 2nd of November, saying that you have company. It would have been much better if she had not come, but now all you can do is move forward. Do not, by any means leave Freyda and her kids in your place. Find them a room and get them out. Don't pay for anything for her. She has the money from her husband and can use that to find her family a place. Leave Papa and Manya in your apartment if you can. I'm sorry that you have to carry this burden for me. I only wish I could be alongside you. In other news, you can congratulate me in receiving a medal for the defense of Leningrad. You asked in your last letter if I was keeping warm. I am warm, as they have given us warm coats, hats and gloves. Please do not worry if I don't write as often, I am busy now. I left yesterday morning at 5am. I just arrived home and am writing this letter to you at 3am. I am very tired, so I will go eat and have tea and go to bed. I don't forget about you or the girls for one second. You are always in my thoughts and I love you all. Kisses to my girls and please say hello to the rest of the family. All the best from ████████████. *Love, Abraham*

I glanced at my watch. I already knew it was time for me to start heading home before I even read the time, but I sat for a while longer wishing for the world to spin faster, daydreaming of a future I knew only existed in my imagination.

I folded the letter back into a triangle, tracing over the creases with my finger. I pushed aside my worry for Abraham being overworked and focused on devising a plan to get Freyda out of our home. When I was a little girl, I remember my grandmother saying, *ven dos harts iz bitter, helft nit kain tsuker* or "when the heart is bitter, sugar won't help". She was right, I had hoped that if I treated her and her girls as I did my own family that she would reply with kindness, but I was wrong. It was time to be firm and take care of my own family.

My mind filled with determination as I walked quickly back to the house. I feared if I slowed down, the fury growing inside me would dwindle before I reached Freyda. I barely noticed the changing sky or the rumbles of far-away thunder as I approached our door, almost out of breath.

CHAPTER TWENTY-NINE
SNAKE

24 DECEMBER 1943
Kokand, Uzbekistan, USSR

The candlelight flickered in the darkness, illuminating only the small frame with the picture of Abraham and me resting beside it. The flame swayed like two people dancing into the night. It was the first time today that my headache had drifted away, leaving me clear-headed and able to read the last letter from Abraham. I shifted closer to the candle beside my bed and read his letter to myself, not wanting to disturb Sofia or Luba as they dozed off into sleep.

My dearest feigele, I am happy to hear that you are finally rid of Freyda and her kids from your home. I am not surprised that she gave you a hard time and didn't want to pay the 100 rubles for the apartment. Did she really expect to pay half that in these times? She is such a rude and noisy person and to even know her and be related to her is embarrassing. The further you can stay away from her, the better. Try not to engage with her because if you do something to help her 100 times and you don't help one time, she will be angry with you, and you will be bad in her mind no matter what. You wrote to me about having bad headaches. I can tell you my dear Raisa, that this is related to your stress and worry. Don't take everything so close to your heart, you have only one. I have hope that the war will end soon, and we will be together once again. You also mentioned that you were thinking of finding work. I recommend you stay home if you can. I will continue to send money and I would prefer if you focused on the children and keeping the house. I could also sense that you were bothered by my father smoking inside the house. Please do not hesitate to speak up. He has joined your home and you have every right to ask him to go outside. You, my love, took in my Papa and Manya into your home and have treated them better than his favorite daughters, Leia and Malka. Let my Papa know that you, Raisa are better than them and you will be rewarded by God for taking them in. I appreciate you and everything you have done, and I think about you and the girls every second, even as I sleep. Please send word about your health and the health of the rest of the family. I love you all. Abraham

The truth was that Abraham had no idea how awful Freyda actually was. I only relayed the version which would not worry him. He was right, however. No matter what I did for her, it would never be enough. I came home that stormy afternoon, ready to tell her that it was time for her to leave and find a new home for herself and her daughters, but instead I opened the door to hear Sofia screaming in agony. My heart instantly dropped as I ran into the kitchen faster than a speeding bullet. Mama rushed into the kitchen from her bedroom at the same moment, and we practically collided as we entered to find Freyda and her girls sulking nearby as Sofia bent over her leg screaming. My eyes quickly scanned the room and settled on the glass of hot tea, flipped over on the table next to Sofia. I knelt beside her to get a look at the burn and as I tried to pull Sofia away, I began to shake with fear.

"One of you go pee in a cup. Now!" I shouted, not even looking up at them. How could they have been so near, and not helped, not even to offer a helping hand? What if I had been ten minutes later? "Sofia, my dear. We are going to make the burn feel better. Mama is here with you." Sofia continued to cry, her eyes red and puffy as she wiped them with her sleeve.

Mama brought over the urine and some handkerchiefs. Her hands trembled as she handed it over. I soaked the handkerchiefs in the urine and applied them to her burn. She flinched at first, but then calmed down slowly. We continued to apply the urine until her pain subsided. Freyda and her girls slowly disappeared after Sofia calmed down, but the look on their faces screamed with guilt, not shame.

"How about we go into the bedroom and rest, Sofia?" I gave her a wink, and she knew it meant that I wanted to talk to her in private, because she promptly replied, and I helped her to our room.

I shut the door and turned around motioning to Sofia to be quiet. Freyda was the type of person to listen in on a conversation. "Here you are honey. Settle down and try to close your eyes for a little bit. Let me know if you are in any pain." I said in a louder than normal voice.

"Yes, Mama. Thank you."

I sat as close to Sofia as I could and whispered in her ear. "Now, tell me, in a whisper. What happened?"

"Baba and I had just come home. We walked into the kitchen to make some tea and Freyda was already there with Maria, Riva and Lara. Baba and I made some tea and I sat down to drink, while Baba went to get changed. They started to talk about my clothes and ask if I wore such bright colors so I could blend in with the Uzbeks, or if I had been here too long and they had rubbed off on me. I told them that I liked the colors and that you had knit me this sweater, and it was beautiful. I started to sip my tea and Freyda walked over and bumped the table, making me spill. It all happened so fast, but then she simply walked towards the other side of the room and the girls followed. That was when I began to scream with pain."

As I listened to her account of what happened, I knew that my instincts had been right. Freyda had spilled the tea on purpose.

◆ ◆ ◆

The next morning, Sofia sat up in her bed, her eyes still swollen from crying the day before. I helped her carefully pull down her long underwear so I could look at her burn. As I studied her leg, I thought about how thankful I was that I had come at that moment. I knew Mama would have helped, but she may not have done the dressing as quickly. Sofia wasn't in much pain anymore and it looked like it was beginning to heal already. I, however, was not healing. My mind was like an open sore, festering and oozing with anger.

I made my way into the kitchen wishing that Freyda had disappeared, but instead she sat reading the paper and sipping tea, while her girls made breakfast like nothing had happened. I imagined myself racing in and bumping into her, just as she had done to Sofia, and watching the hot tea spill onto her colorless brown blouse. I painted a delightful picture in my mind of her running out of the house screaming and never turning back, but it faded from my vision when she looked up from her paper and opened her mouth.

"The girls are making fried eggs for us, but they were the last ones. I could have them start kasha for you, if you like?" Her words hissed in my ears like a snake attempting to scare off its predator.

"No, I will make breakfast for myself and the rest of my family as well. After we are finished eating, get ready to go. You are going to choose an apartment, today. It is time for you and your girls to find your own place. Our apartment is simply not large enough for everyone."

"But…" She shouted. An excuse trying to make its way heard.

"But, nothing. You have stayed long enough. Today you will choose an apartment and you will move out as soon as possible." The words flew off my tongue faster than I had expected, and they came out harsher too. I didn't intend to sound so severe, but I was happy I did because for the first time since I had known her, she had no response.

Freyda and her girls sat around the table eating the last of the eggs, while the rest of my family had kasha. We ate in awkward silence for what seemed to be ages, my pounding headache the only noise I heard.

♦ ♦ ♦

By the time Hanukkah started, Freyda and her girls had reluctantly moved out and were living in their own apartment. I was happy to be free of her and her ungrateful girls. Lev and Manya were still staying with us, but Manya was helpful with the cleaning and laundry, and Lev found work in an ammunition factory.

I quickly descended the steps and gave Feruza's door a swift knock. "Feruza, it's me, Raisa," I called.

"Hello friend! How are you?" she answered as she pulled me inside.

"I am doing well. Much better now."

"Did she finally find a place?" Feruza asked.

"She did. I found her a small apartment, for a good price. Too bad it is on the other side of Kokand," I said with a sly grin.

"The farther, the better. I could sense something not right about her the moment I met her." Feruza said.

"You have good sense of character... I came to ask if you and your boys would join us this Friday for dinner? Lev and Manya will be going to Freyda's for dinner and it will be nice to have you celebrate with us. Hanukkah started last night, and I would love to share one of our traditions with your family."

"We would love to join you! I am honored you would think to include us. Please tell me what can I bring?" Feruza asked, excitement showing in the edges of her lips.

"Just bring yourselves." I said, giving her a wink.

◆ ◆ ◆

Friday was the fourth night of Hanukkah, and although we didn't have a menorah to light the candles, we still wanted to celebrate the holiday in some way. Mama spent the morning doing laundry, while I went to the market to get the groceries for tonight's dinner.

That afternoon, Mama and I sat across from each other, a trash pail in-between us, and a sack of potatoes ready to be peeled. After the peeling came the shredding. Mama and I took turns, working in sync, like two ice skaters floating around the kitchen, until the potatoes were shredded and the starch carefully drained for later use.

The remaining ingredients were added and the oil heated. The familiar sizzle rang in my ears as I flipped the potato latkes to a golden brown. The smell of Hanukkah wandered through the air, transporting me back to my kitchen in Minsk. Imprints of memories hung in my mind like pictures on a museum wall, masterpieces of our life.

Soon, the latkes were piled high, the table set, and my family gathered in the kitchen, drawn to the intoxicating smell. I almost didn't hear the knock at the door with all the excitement.

"Feruza, come in!" I waved her inside and gave her a hug. Her three boys stood behind her, in order of shortest to tallest. "Perfect timing. We just finished preparing dinner. Come sit down."

"It smells delicious in here!" Feruza said, her hands reached to her stomach. "My stomach is turning in circles."

"These are potato latkes. We make them every year for Hanukkah!" I said, putting a few on her plate. "Here, give some to your boys. And here is the sour cream."

"Mama, Baba, these are perfect!" Luba said after her first bite. Everyone around the table nodded in unison, and the only sounds after were from our chewing.

My Papa was the first to finish. He wiped the corners of his mouth with his napkin and placed it on his plate next to his fork and knife. It was his signal that he was finished. "Feruza, do you know the story of Hanukkah?" he asked.

"I don't," Feruza answered shyly, "but I would love to hear it."

"That's good. I tell it every year after dinner, and it is one of my favorites." Papa smiled, and continued, "Hanukkah honors the struggle of the ancient Jews who restored the Temple of Jerusalem. A long time ago, the land of Israel was ruled by a wicked king named Antiochus Epiphanes."

I noticed Feruza and her boys listened intently as Papa spoke. It was refreshing to be able to share our customs and traditions with each other, despite being different.

"Well, this King Antiochus, like so many other rulers throughout history, decided that he wanted to rule one nation with one religion and culture. All of his people were to live and pray according to the Greek customs. So, what did he do?"

"He didn't allow the practice of Judaism anymore," Sofia answered.

"That is correct. He forbade the Jews from observing the Jewish holidays and studying the Torah. But what was the worst thing he did?" Papa asked.

"He wouldn't allow them to worship in the Temple," Luba spoke up.

"Yes. Many were scared and obeyed the King's orders, but a group of brave men named the Maccabees were determined to take back their Temple. Although they were outnumbered to the King's army, they fought hard, and against all odds, they won." Papa paused to take a sip of tea and I took a moment to think about how many times the Jews have suffered in history. The pain and loss were a continuous struggle. But the Jews seem to find a way to fight back and make it through. We are survivors. But why must we continue to defend ourselves? Will it ever stop?

"What happened next?" Feruza's little one asked.

"The Maccabees took back the Temple from the King, but they were heartbroken to find that the King had not taken care of the holy space. So, they set to cleaning and restoring it back to its original state. On the twenty-fifth day of the month they held a rededication ceremony," Papa continued.

"The word 'Hanukkah' actually means dedication," Gita chimed in.

"The story finishes when the Maccabees only found enough oil to light the menorah for one day, but miraculously that small amount of oil lasted for eight days. And this is why we have eight nights of Hanukkah." Papa finished.

"And with each candle of Hanukkah, we illuminate an important message; we have to work to find light in the darkness, and we must keep the light of religious freedom burning for all people, forever," I added.

"And we spin dreidels!" Hana said, surprising the kids with two small wooden tops. "This one is for you three boys to play with, and here is one for you three," she said as she handed the other one to Luba, Sofia and Oscar. "Go play, and show the boys."

"Thank you so much for this wonderful night," Feruza exclaimed. "The latkes were amazing! I hope you will share a recipe with me."

"Of course. Let me write it down for you now before I forget," Mama answered.

"Thank you! I loved getting to know you all better and learning about this special holiday. If only history would learn from its mistakes. Instead, we are back again, repeating them," Feruza said frowning.

I looked at the kids playing with the dreidel. They came from different backgrounds, but yet they played so freely, their innocence oblivious to the hate which surrounded our lives. I was thankful that I could witness it and be a part of it. If it was happening here, then it had to be happening elsewhere. We were the Maccabees in our own way, fighting back by showing others our true selves and loving everyone equally.

CHAPTER THIRTY
DOVES

✦

5 JANUARY 1944
Kokand, Uzbekistan, USSR

Lately, the letters from Abraham had been scattered. He wrote that they were moving around and that they were busy, so not to worry. But, how could I not suffer from a constant heartache? When he did write, his letters carried a gloominess that he could not conceal, even with his talent for words. Normally, I read through his letters and felt closer to him, as if he were uttering the words directly to me, but now he seemed further away than ever.

I held onto his latest letter for a few hours, unsure if I was ready to read it yet. Finally, I grabbed it, and opened it anyway, its contents burning a hole into my pocket deeper than I could bear.

My dearest girls, I am sorry that I have not been able to write as much as I would like. I am alive and well, and I hope to hear from you the same. I have received fewer letters from you lately. We have moved again, and I am extremely busy. Perhaps the letters are taking longer to get to me because we are moving so quickly. Thankfully, I have a moment to write to you. We have to hope that God is watching over me and I will be able to live through this. We will be rid of the Nazis soon. We are beating them, and they are running away so fast, they don't even have time to take their clothes. I will continue to await your letters, as they are the beats which keep my heart pumping. I can't tell you how much your words encourage me to keep fighting for our country, you and the girls. You three mean more to me than words can describe, and I am counting down the days until I can hold you in my arms and never have to let go. All my love from the front, Abraham

The same knot appeared in my stomach after reading this letter, much as it had for the last few. His words were rushed and desperate, making the light at the end of the tunnel seem unreachable. I quickly grabbed my pen and a few sheets of paper and sat down to write to Abraham, hoping it would lift us both into better spirits.

I wrote to him in detail about our special New Year's celebration. We had a few friends over, including Klara and Masha, and Lana with her family. Everyone made a special dish and brought it to share. Our small table was filled with some traditional dishes for the yearly celebration. Lana had made one of my favorites, Olivier salad. She managed to get her hands on all the ingredients, but it must have been for a cost. The peas, potatoes, pickles, carrots, onions, and eggs all made their way into the mayonnaise salad. I even tasted a few pieces of bologna, which was how I usually made it for Abraham. Klara made pies, filled with cabbage. The dough so flaky and wonderful, for a moment it made us forget where we were, and who we were missing. We were even able to get some champagne, and as the clock struck midnight and our glasses clinked together, I acknowledged our third New Year apart by letting myself daydream of the next year, when we would surely be all together, back home.

I captured the essence of Sofia's holiday concert by sharing the songs that she played and how her face lit up as she performed. I told him about her dress and how our Sofia was a natural-born performer.

I painted in words how different Kokand looked in the winter months. I described the snow-capped palace and how the beautiful trees shimmered with the first sprinkle of snow. I did my best to help Abraham imagine he was here with us, celebrating the New Year, joining us at Sofia's concert, or even taking a walk through the frosty streets. I hoped it would take him away from the hell he was living through and bring him to a happier place.

After signing the letter and sealing it with a kiss, I placed it in my bag to take to the post office the next morning, and then realized the time. I would be late to meet with Lana if I didn't hurry. I dressed in my warmest clothes and met the cold air as if it was a friendly neighbor. The familiarity of the chilly breeze danced under my breath as I made my way to Lana's apartment to catch up and have some tea.

"Come in, come in!" Lana shouted as I approached her doorway.

After stepping into the warmth of her embrace, we made our way to the kitchen to sit by the wood burning stove. Her kitchen, as usual, smelled like fresh squeezed lemons. It was obvious that Lana took great pride in keeping the small apartment clean and tidy, and I spotted her efforts in every corner.

"I'm so glad you made it today. Everybody is out right now, so we have the place to ourselves. I'll start some tea for us. Are you hungry?"

"Perfect. No, I'm not hungry right now. Let's start with tea," I said, as she readied the water and measured the tea leaves out. Once the tea was brewed, I helped her carry the cups over to the table. As I made myself comfortable on the cushioned chair, I noticed her golden hair was luminous from the candle flickering in the middle of the round table.

"I'm sorry I was a little late. I got lost in a letter I was writing to Abraham. How are you my friend? You look good."

"Thank you, but I feel old and tired. I picked up letters yesterday from Ivan and Lev. They both say they are healthy and hopeful that the war will end soon. I have read this so many times over the years though, I wonder if this war will ever end. How are you? Have you heard from the front?"

"Same here. I read a letter from Abraham this morning, and although he says the Fascists are running away and that he thinks they are close to victory, I don't want to get my hopes up anymore." There was a pause as I sipped the hot black tea. I watched the steam twirl away from my breath, continuously fighting back.

"I want to believe that everything will be over soon, that we will go back home, and life will resume as it was three years ago, but that won't happen. Even if we win this war and we go back home to our men, we have our homes and cities to rebuild, let alone our lives."

"You are right, Lana, but right now all we can do is have faith that our men will survive the front. We will have to get through the rest later. There is no sense in worrying about the future now."

I took her hand in mine, hoping it would calm her. I smiled as best as I could, as we moved on to another subject, but I sensed her mind was wandering.

"Do you remember that one time we met Nina at the pond to go ice skating? We must have been eight years old," Lana asked.

"Of course. It was early in the morning and no one else was there. It was just the three of us. That was such a fun morning, wasn't it?" I said, as I thought back to a time which seemed like a lifetime ago.

"It was. It is probably one of my favorite memories of the three of us. I remember how after we laced up our skates we headed out onto the lake, hand in hand. We were giggling as usual, but I do recall being careful as we held on to each other as we slowly acclimated to the slick ice beneath us."

"We skated round and round laughing and falling. Snow started to fall as we etched circles into the ice. I remember thinking how beautiful the snow was. It was cold that morning, and the snow was more like crystals instead of puffs, and as the sun shone down, it looked like glitter was falling all around us." As I thought about that day, my memories started to rush forward.

"Yes, you are right. I can picture us there so clearly, as if it was yesterday." Lana smiled

"I also remember Nina suggested we pretend to fly like beautiful white doves. We gracefully slid across the ice, our arms spread open and flapping elegantly."

Lana's eyes lit up as the memory came back to her. "Yes! I do remember. At that moment we were the most exquisite doves in the world. I'm pretty sure I wished that day wouldn't end so we could fly forever."

"What made you remember all that, Lana?"

"I'm not sure what triggered the thought, but it made me reminisce about how wonderful those times were. We were so carefree, so young and innocent, oblivious to the world. Then life changed that summer, the first world war began, and we had to grow up fast. I wish that our kids weren't experiencing a war like we did."

"Those were fun times, especially when it was only the three of us. You are right, this war has been much harder. Our babies have had to grow up faster than they should have. We turned out alright, so will they. We have gotten this far, haven't we?" I said with a chuckle.

"I don't know what I would do without you, Raisa. I am such a pessimist sometimes. I need someone like you to keep me thinking positively."

"I am so thankful we found each other. Somehow, we lost touch before, but fate brought us back together." We raised our tea cups and clinked them together. The memories of our years as giggling girls lingered in my mind as we continued to enjoy each other's company.

♦ ♦ ♦

Later that afternoon as I walked back home, I thought about my conversation with Lana. I did everything I could to ease her heartache and try to be a strong friend for her, but inside I knew she was right. What mess would we come home to? Who would be there and when would this war ever end? Those were all questions that I had thought about from time to time, but I had pushed them aside, letting them live deep inside me. Instead, I kept myself busy living the life that we had created in our temporary home in Kokand. As I neared our door, I realized that she unleashed so many questions that had now started a storm of worry in my mind. Would the answers ever come, I asked myself, and more importantly, did I want them to? What I did know was that I needed Abraham to be here for us when this war finally ended. I prayed for the day when I would get to fall asleep to the rhythm of his breathing and wake up to his smile each and every day. I dreamt about celebrating twenty years of marriage, and for it to be perfect, just like our fifteen-year anniversary had been only four years ago.

CHAPTER THIRTY-ONE
SOULMATE

11 JANUARY 1940
Minsk, Belarus, USSR

Abraham fingered the necklace around my neck as we lay in the early morning stillness. The corners of the star now rounded slightly as the years had worn them down. As he moved it around, I watched flashes of its reflection scatter onto the ceiling, as the sun pushed its way into the room.

I peeked up from the bed to see if Luba and Sofia had begun to stir, but they were sound asleep. Luba was curled under her duvet with only her nose peeking out. Sofia was sprawled to one side of her mattress with her duvet scrunched up on the other side.

Abraham smiled as our eyes met, his face playful, like a puppy. It had been a long time since we had all slept in. Usually, the girls served as our alarm clocks.

Abraham kissed my neck delicately, his lips barely grazing my skin. "I love you, my *feigele*, such a lovable little bird you are. Happy anniversary," he whispered into my ear.

"Happy anniversary. I can't believe it has been fifteen years already. You have made me the happiest woman in the world. As the days turn into years, I am more thankful for you than I have ever been. I love you for everything you do for us, and for the man you have become."

As I gazed up lovingly into his eyes, I wondered how I had been so lucky. I knew the moment we started dating that he was my soulmate. I could not have imagined a better husband and father for the girls.

"I can't believe how fast time has gone by. Now we have a fourteen and eight-year-old and it seems like only yesterday was our wedding day and I gave you this necklace." His attention drawn back to playing with the silver star which dangled down as I leaned onto my side. "Do you remember that day I came to your parents' home to ask for your hand in marriage?"

"Like it was yesterday. I was both stunned and not surprised at the same time. I knew that I wanted nothing more than to marry you. My mind was made up before you even asked."

Abraham laughed. "You usually know what you want, and you get it. That's one of the reasons why I love you. Did I ever tell you where I went right after I left your house that day?"

"Hmm. No, I can't recall."

"I planned on going home to my parents to tell them about you and our plans to marry. On my way there I decided to stop at the bakery and get something special for Papa and Mama. I was nearly there when I bumped into Khaim Issakovitch. Did you know him?"

"He died a few years after our wedding, I believe. He had a sweet little jewelry store before he was forced to close it. Am I right?"

"Yes, that was him. He was such a quiet old man with amazing skills. I loved going to his home to watch him work. He let me come behind his bench to observe. Some of the tricks he showed me over the years I have used many times while working on watches. It was sad when his store was taken away from him, it was all he had left." Abraham shook his head in disapproval as he recalled the thought. "Anyway, he invited me to come to his home. I hadn't seen him in a while, so I wanted to catch up and see how he was doing. As we were talking, something caught my eye on his bench. Before he even handed it to me, I knew it was meant to be yours."

"My silver star necklace?"

"Yes. As soon as I held it in my hands, I envisioned it around your neck. Khaim engraved our wedding date and initials on the back while I waited. It was incredible to see him form each tiny letter and number with precision."

"I'm so glad you met him that day. I love it very much." Right as I leaned over to give him a kiss, the girls came running over to our bed.

"Mama, Papa, happy anniversary!" They shouted in unison, as they crawled into our already overcrowded bed.

"Thank you, girls! Let's not get too cozy. It's time for Papa to get ready for work and you will be late for school if we don't get dressed soon. I have quite a bit of work to do over the next few days while you girls are at school. Remember, our family is coming from Bobruisk on Sunday to celebrate our anniversary, and I have plenty of cooking and cleaning to do."

◆ ◆ ◆

Sunday came faster than I expected. I had exhausted myself getting everything ready for the arrival of our family, but I was excited to see Mama and Papa and my sisters. Some of Abraham's family was coming as well, including his father, Manya, his sister Leia and her family.

Our small house was busting with family and close friends, just as the glasses were overflowing with spirits. The tables were filled with the food I had spent days preparing, and we all sat down at the extra borrowed tables and chairs, ready to celebrate.

"Everybody, raise your glasses. I have a toast for Abraham and Raisa." Papa carefully tapped a fork against his shot glass to get everyone's attention.

He cleared his throat and started his speech, moving closer to Abraham and me while he talked. "When Abraham knocked on our door fifteen years ago, I had no idea who he was. After I invited this remarkably tall man into our home and listened to what he had to say, I was sure my heart was about to explode. I knew it was time to let my oldest daughter get married and start her own family, but when I looked at her, she still looked like my little girl. I wasn't ready to give her away yet, but I saw the look in Abraham's eyes when he glanced at Raisa. The love that he had for her was unmistakable. Then the morning they were to marry, Raisa was so happy, and excited. She wasn't nervous, only sure that she was doing exactly the right thing."

Pausing for a moment, Papa put his arm around my shoulder, the sleeve of his brown sweater felt like a scarf around the back of my neck. After collecting his thoughts, he began once more. "They have given us two beautiful granddaughters, Luba and Sofia, whom we adore, and they have shown them what true love is supposed to look like. I am eternally thankful to you Abraham for making our Raisa so happy. The traditional symbol for fifteen years of marriage is crystal. It represents clarity and transparency. Knowing each other better than one knows themselves is what gives a clear and sparkling love between a husband and wife."

Mama came over and handed us a royal blue box. Abraham held the box out while I ran my hands over the smooth satin top. Carefully, I unhinged the two beautifully ornate brass clasps and anxiously opened the top. Inside were two etched crystal goblets. I instantly recognized the sticker inside with the name, Dyatkovo Crystal. I had often admired the famous crystal while passing by shop windows. They were special and perfect in every way. As we each removed one from its carved place in the box, they sent rainbow colors fluttering around the room as the light shined through them.

"Thank you, Mama, Papa. These are gorgeous. We will cherish them," I exclaimed as I gave them both a hug and kiss.

"On that note, let's raise our glasses, and drink to many more years together and to good health for these two incredible people. *Na zdorovie.*"

The clanking of the glasses resonated around the table like a symphony of bells, celebrating a night filled with laughter and love.

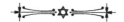
The years passed and the war continued. I read the paper as often as I could, but I learned to filter out most of the news. If I actually believed everything in the papers, then the war would have long since been over. Most of the pages were filled with propaganda meant to keep the people of Russia united and hopeful that our men were fighting for a just cause. That was nice for the wishful thinkers, but instead, I looked for the stories that talked about the places and events impacting Abraham. That was the news that gave me something to hold onto.

Last month, I found a story on the front page that revived all of us with a newfound optimism and it became all anyone could talk about. On January twenty-seventh, nineteen forty-four the siege was finally over in Leningrad and the people were free after eight hundred and seventy-two days.

As I read through the details, I pictured Abraham there. The newspaper wrote, "a roaring echo swept over the streets and squares, over the majestic buildings of the city. The rockets fluttered, blossoming the evening sky with thousands of colorful lights, illuminating the steeple of the Admiralty, the dome of St. Isaac, the palaces, the embankments, the bridges on the Neva. Bright beams of searchlights crossed in the clouds. The Leningraders, who gathered in the streets, squares, embankments of the Neva, who had recently been subjected to artillery fire, joyfully greeted their liberators, the soldiers of the Leningrad Front…"

When Abraham was in Kokand a few months ago, he told me about the blockade and the bombings. The initial failure of losing the city to the Nazis was a hard blow to him and his men, but what they saw in the aftermath was nothing in comparison. The roads to the city had been severed, cutting the people left in the city off from access to food. In turn, they suffered a gruesome and difficult life. In January the Red Army managed to open a narrow corridor to the city. Abraham said it was called the road of life and although it was an extremely dangerous route, it saved the lives of many. I met a man who was considered lucky to have escaped through this very road. He evacuated south to be with a distant family member and ended up right here in Kokand. When I was introduced to him for the first time, it was as if I could see through him. He was as thin as paper, and I wondered how he was still moving.

It wasn't long ago that Abraham had earned a medal of honor for his bravery during the defense of Leningrad, but when he spoke about it, it was as though he thought it wasn't justified. He suffered inside knowing there were so many people stranded and starving inside the city. I hoped that now he would allow himself to feel a sense of accomplishment.

♦ ♦ ♦

Days turned into weeks and the letters from Abraham came even less frequently. Even with the newfound optimism brewing that the war would be over soon, Abraham's letters didn't paint the same picture.

I tried to keep myself busy with my daily routine and this Monday was the same as any other. It was the start of a new week, but the ending of another month, and I longed for March to bring good news. I drew the curtains back and the chilly morning air blew in through the cracks of the old windows. I glanced back at the sleeping girls. Luba's arm curled over her face, and Sofia turned to avoid the light cascading into her eyes.

"Good morning girls. Time to wake up!"

"It's too early, Mama," grumbled Sofia as she pulled the covers over her head.

"Good morning, Mama." Luba smiled, as she propped herself up to a half sitting position on her bed.

Luba's sandy brown hair fell swiftly past her shoulders as she took out her ribbon to brush it. I couldn't help but notice what a beautiful woman she had become. She had always tended to look more like me, and even her character matched my own, but sometimes for a brief moment, I caught a glimpse of Abraham.

I tore my eyes away from Luba and focused on getting Sofia out of bed. Maybe it was because she would be a teenager in a few months, but Sofia had become more difficult, and on mornings like this one, I missed Abraham and his effortless approach with them.

With the girls dressed, fed and ready to begin their days, they headed out the door with Oscar in between them. Mama and I watched them skip down the street, hand in hand, a sight I never could get bored of.

"Raisa, I am going to the market this morning to pick up a few things for dinner. Do you want to go with me, or are you going to the post office today?"

"I will go to the post office, I think. I haven't gotten any letters in a while, maybe today will be my lucky day. Is that fine with you, Mama?"

"Of course, dear. I'll see you in a little while then."

I traced my steps back to the bedroom after Mama left, leaving me alone to wrestle with my thoughts. I sat down on my bed and pulled out the last letter from Abraham. I had already read over his words so many times these past few weeks that I knew every sentence by heart, but I read them again wishing that the meaning would be different. I stared at the folded brown paper in front of me. It was standard stationary given to the soldiers. It had a place for the address on the front and on the bottom was a red banner with a soldier below it. I opened it to see Abraham's words scribbled across the page. Even his handwriting appeared changed in this letter. His thoughts were stained with heartache, as they spilled onto the paper with an unusual darkness.

February 10th, 1944 - Hello, my dearest. I am not feeling well. From you, I hope to hear better. We need to get rid of the fascists and I hope that God watches over us, as the days and nights are only becoming harder. I read three more cards from you from the 24th of January, and I am so grateful for them. Let me know if you received the packages I sent to you on the apartment address. I'm sorry for not writing as often, we have been moving around so much lately. It feels like there is nothing to hold onto. Please keep writing to me. I must go now. Kisses to you, Sofia and Luba. I am yours until death. Love, Abraham

"I am yours until death..." I uttered his last five words willing them to disappear. The weight that they carried scared me, shaking free the pockets of concern that I had hidden deep inside me for all these years. I wished I could hold him close and protect him, like he had always done for me.

I wiped away my tears, once again willing myself to move through the day and continue to be strong. I grabbed the letters for Abraham from the table. Sofia had drawn a vine of flowers on the outside of the envelope. Luba's was beautifully written in her immaculate handwriting that was a piece of art on its own. I put them both in my purse along with my letter and retraced the familiar steps to the post office.

◆ ◆ ◆

I did not open the letter until I got back home. I noticed the return address was from a Boris Grigorievich as the lady handed it to me over the counter. I dropped it in my purse and hurried back. By the time I had opened the front door, the weightless letter had turned into a pile of bricks. Somehow, without even opening the envelope's contents, I sensed the burden it held.

Mama was in the kitchen as usual when I arrived. Her face was a blur before I wiped away my tears.

Mama hurried over to me. "Raisa, my dear. What's wrong?"

I reached into my purse searching for the letter inside. "I picked this up from the post office. My intuition is telling me that something is wrong. I don't know if I can open this Mama."

Mama shuffled from one foot to another, something she does whenever she is nervous. Her eyes darted to the letter and back to me several times before she spoke. "You need to open it. It may be scary, but I am right here with you. Go on, open it."

My hands trembled as my heart raced out of my chest. Slowly, I slid the letter opener through the top of the envelope. I pulled out the familiar paper and grazed over its texture with my fingers as I unfolded it. My voice sounded shaky as I read the cursive scrawled across the page.

Dear Raisa, my name is Boris Grigorievich. I am particularly sorry that I have to write you this letter instead of telling you this in person. Unfortunately, on the 17th of February, we stepped onto the Nazis very quickly and in doing so Abraham died instantly...

Mama grabbed my hand as my legs buckled beneath me. I tried to breathe, I gasped for air, but there was none to be found. I became lightheaded, the color drained from my face and my mind switched off.

When I opened my eyes, I hoped it had all been a miserable nightmare, but Mama was next to me, her hand still tightly gripping mine as she sat next to me on the kitchen floor.

"I'm so sorry, my love," Mama whispered. Her words hung heavy in the air, floating above me as I pushed them away. "Should I finish reading you the letter? I think you should hear it."

I didn't want to, but Mama began before I had a chance to refuse.

...The bomb shrapnel hit him in the head. I buried him myself in the village of Medved in the Novgorod region. I fought alongside your husband for many years. I grew to know him well. I respected and appreciated Abraham for the incredible husband and father I knew he was. He talked about you and your girls every day. I know that you already must know this, but I have never witnessed a man love as much he did. I am so lucky to have known him

and his memory will forever be carried in my heart.

Sincerely, Borya

A waterfall of emotions rushed through me, overtaking any restraint I had left to remain calm. Tears flowed out like a powerful rainstorm, as Mama held me tight. Her arms encircled my body trying to keep me together, but as the minutes ticked by, giant icebergs of my heart and soul broke off and floated away in the sea, as lost as I was now.

EPILOGUE

ALMOST THREE YEARS LATER
Minsk, Belarus, USSR

Luba stole my breath away as I entered her dressing room. It was the moment I had dreamed about ever since she was a baby. I wondered if every mother thought about what her daughter would look like on her wedding day, or what kind of man she would marry. Today was that day, the happiest moment of her life. She looked exactly how I had imagined her, she was perfect. I only wished Abraham could have seen how exquisite she looked.

"Luba, you look magnificent," I exclaimed as I hugged her, careful not to wrinkle her dress or muss her hair. Warmth radiated from her like a hot sunny day.

"Thank you, Mama. You look beautiful too! Are you ready to walk me down the aisle?"

The muscles around my heart tightened as I swallowed back the sudden urge to cry. Abraham should have been the one to walk her down the aisle. He would have been so proud of the woman she had grown into. I couldn't believe it had been almost three years since Abraham was killed. So many things had happened since then, some of them I still can't believe myself. I pushed away my tears, fighting to keep my emotions from boiling over. Even though I shared in her joy, the emptiness in my heart weighed heavier upon me today. "I would love nothing more, but first I have something I want to give you." I said as I reached into my purse and revealed a box. "Go ahead, open it."

Luba gently opened the box, her wide eyes reminded me of New Year's morning when she was a little girl. "Mama. I can't accept this! This is your silver star from Papa."

"No, my love, this is your star. I bought this star at a flea market a few months back. I couldn't believe my eyes when I saw it. I knew that one day soon you would get married, and I wanted you to have it. A few days ago, I had it engraved with Samuel's and your initials, and wedding date, similar to mine."

"I can't believe you found this! It looks so much like yours. Thank you, Mama, I will wear it with love."

"I wish you and Samuel the very best. I hope you have a happy and healthy marriage, like I had with your Papa. I'm sure Papa is here, looking down on us right now, glowing with joy." I smiled at Luba, through my tears.

My heart was brimming with excitement. My Luba had found the love of her life. Her Abraham. Most mothers would be nervous in this situation. Luba met Samuel only one week earlier, and today they were bound as one, but I had no hesitation. When she came home last week from the market, I knew something had changed. Her pale cheeks were flushed, and her smile lit the room as she talked about him, "Mama, I was walking to the market when I saw a young man walking towards me. I couldn't take my eyes off of him. Everything around me stopped moving, and all I could focus on were his kind green eyes. He stopped and said hello, and asked me my name. He joined me on my walk to the market, and after a few moments, I knew I had met a special person."

"Who is he?" I asked. "Do we know his family?"

"His name is Samuel Esterkin," she answered, her cheeks flushing a shade darker. "Mama, I think I am in love."

As she continued to tell me about him, I felt transported back to the moment I met Abraham for the first time. I knew exactly how she felt. "You know dear, I fell in love with your

Papa the moment I met him, so I know it is possible. Tell me more about him, I don't think I know his family."

"He seems smart, but not arrogant like some of the other men I have met. He made me laugh and I felt safe being near him. Does that even make sense?" Luba asked.

"It does make sense. Where is he living?" I asked.

"With a friend of the family. After serving in the army, he returned home to Minsk to discover that not even a single member of his family had survived the war. All eleven of his brothers and sisters, mother and father had been killed." Luba explained.

"That's awful. It must be very difficult for him." I said, putting my arm around her. The reality was that there were so many missing husbands, wives, and children after the war. Every single person I knew suffered loss. Over two million people were killed in Belarus alone during the three-year German occupation. But still, many of the survivors like us came back home to no husband, no home or possessions and tried to move on with our lives. For women, this was especially difficult since there was a shortage of decent single men after so many soldiers were killed. Finding a Jewish man was much harder, but it was necessary if you wanted to survive and live a simple life. When we came back to Minsk, I learned quickly that being alone wasn't an option.

The next day, Samuel stood in our doorway with two bouquets of flowers. He had asked around town and found out where Luba lived. They were soulmates, and it only took one glance to not only see it, but also enjoy it with them. After so many years of war and hardships, love was a nice change and I welcomed it with open arms. One glance into his honest green eyes as he proclaimed his love for Luba, and I knew that theirs was a love to embrace.

They didn't want to wait to marry, so I made all the arrangements in a matter of a week. It would be a small and simple wedding with only family and very close friends. When you have lived the past few years of your life not knowing what the next day would bring, or live to meet your other half, or even survive to watch another sunset, you learn to not take anything for granted, especially time.

◆ ◆ ◆

Joyful singing echoed through the house as the newlyweds twirled into their first dance as husband and wife. Luba's sandy brown hair was elegantly pinned back into a neat bun, leaving only a few curled strands of hair to frame her face. Her hazel eyes twinkled more than ever before as she gazed into Samuel's eyes. I watched the guests dance and smile happily into the late evening. Yury, my new husband sat next to me. His bushy eyebrows danced in unison with his intense dark eyes as he enjoyed the vodka, plov and other foods spread across the table. I cradled baby Mark as he slept through the loud sounds as if they were calming lullabies. I glanced down at him, sensing he was ready to eat as his lips searched for my breast.

As I sat in a quiet room feeding Mark, I thought about the last few years, and how much had changed since Abraham's death. In August, six months after his passing, news that the Red Army finally regained all of Belarus blared from the loudspeaker in the center of Kokand. When I heard, I wanted to enjoy the moment. I had hoped for it every day for the last three years, but now it felt bitter sweet. What would I be bringing my children back to?

As much as we had come to accept Kokand as our new home, it wasn't truly where we belonged. I knew we would be facing a new obstacle. The journey would be difficult knowing that we had no home left to go back to, but it still seemed like the right thing to do. A few months later we secured documents for our passage back to Minsk. My sister, Gita was able to get tickets for everyone through her connections at work. Without her, we would have most likely been stranded in Kokand. Most women were only allowed to return if they were summoned by their husbands or brothers, or through their job.

In December of nineteen forty-four, ten months after Abraham died, we boarded the train back to our motherland along with some other friends and neighbors.

As the train chugged along, I looked around at the faces of my family and friends. I thought about all the women who comforted and encouraged me throughout these difficult years. I may have reminded Abraham of one of his complicated clocks, but these women were like the facets of a diamond to me; each cut at a slightly different angle, flashing light in their own direction, but yet they come together to create something beautiful. Without them, I wouldn't have been able to continue, as they each played a unique part in my life.

I glanced over at Luba and Sofia, the most important girls in my life. They held the keys to my heart, and they have kept it beating even when I felt I could no longer continue. Having my Mama and sisters by my side quickly reminded me why we need family. They were my constants from the time we arrived in Bobruisk until now. I looked to them for advice and they never failed.

They weren't the only women that impacted me on this journey, as I thought back to Ester and Katerina. These two women I didn't know well, but their stories stuck with me, and I will carry them around forever. Ester was all alone running away from the Nazis, but she managed to stay strong and continue forward. Katerina, also alone after losing her baby, couldn't find the courage to continue. They each took a different path, and in doing so, led me to my own.

Then, there was Nina who took us into her home in Stalingrad. She cared for my family as if we were her own, and let us stay until we departed to the collective farm. On the farm, I bonded with Manya who taught me the hardships of farm living.

I can't forget my old friends, Klara and Lana, and my new friend, Feruza. They each taught me something different, and we held each other up in our own ways. These women truly understood what it felt like to be separated from someone you love. The constant worry and heartache that weighed us down also kept us alive, because we carried one another through the good and the bad times.

Considering what I lost over the years, it would be easy to feel sorry for myself. But then I think about how we survived and how we did it together. Like the woman that saved my bag said, 'We must support each other where we can, otherwise, what example are we giving our children? Don't worry about thanking me, instead keep the giving alive.' I have carried her wise words with me all these years, never forgetting how much more she gave me than just saving my bag.

♦　♦　♦

As we approached Belarus, I tried to brace myself and the girls for the devastation, but nothing could have prepared us for what took place in our absence. Not only were homes, buildings and entire cities destroyed, but so were the people.

When we arrived in Minsk, it had been three-and-a-half years since we had left, and it was like strolling through a new city. Nothing looked familiar, and nowhere looked inviting. Minsk lost eighty percent of its buildings to the war as well as many roads. We left the rest of our family in Bobruisk to settle into their new city and the three of us continued to Minsk, hoping for a clean slate to start over. I was among so many other women, on a journey to start a new life and leave the old one behind, for the sake of our children. Since most of the men had been killed during the war or they were making their way back to their wives, I worried about who was left to protect me and my girls.

I married Yury about six months after we came back. He was a soldier, like Abraham. He came home to Minsk in search of the rest of his family, only to find that they had all perished during the war. We met in the store where I was working, when we both grabbed the same potato from the pile. We began talking, and after he heard the girls and I were living under the staircase of a friend's home, he took us into his house. When he asked me to marry him shortly after, I knew that it was the best decision for the girls and me. I had already loved and been loved more than most people in a lifetime. Now it was time to survive.

NOTE FROM THE
AUTHOR

The years which followed were difficult ones as the city started to rebuild and the hatred for Jews spread. Some people blamed the Jews for the war and the shortages everyone suffered. There was a lack of everything, food, housing and goods. People lived in small communal apartments with three or four families sharing one kitchen and bathroom. Each family lived in one room with up to five people and sometimes more. Luckily, Yury had a good job and supported Raisa and her girls, and then Mark. He worked hard to provide food and clothes and anything else they needed to live a comfortable life.

Luba and Samuel lived together with Raisa and Yury for many years, and in 1951 they had a little girl, Alla. She was their only child. In 1979, she took a journey of her own in hopes of a better life. Together with her husband, Semyon and two daughters, Lena and Ella, she immigrated to St. Louis, Missouri with the help of the Jewish Federation. In 1985 they had me, their third and final child.

After ten years they sponsored all remaining family in Russia, from both Semyon and Alla's sides, and brought them to St.

Louis. Raisa and Yury were among those who made the transition to St. Louis.

Sofia also married and had one child, Adik, who had two children of his own and lives with his wife in Chicago.

Raisa passed away on May 12th, 1995 at the age of 89. Three years later, Luba passed away after celebrating 52 years of marriage with Samuel. Exactly one year later, he joined her, his heart broken without his soulmate.

I have always been an avid reader of WWII memoirs and historical fiction, but it wasn't until I started asking about my family history that I became interested in writing my own story. Unfortunately, when I learned about my family history, my great-grandparents and grandparents had already passed away. This left me with very little information from my mother. Once I had a rough idea of where my great-grandmother fled to during the war, I began to dive into researching archives and databases. After months of searching, I was able to find the original Tashkent registration documents for Raisa, Luba, Sofia, her sisters and her parents. I also found documents showing the medals and honors that Abraham received during the war, as well as the letter stating his death. At this point, I knew I had a story that I needed to write down. I wanted my two girls to know what their ancestors had to endure. I wanted her story to live on.

Soon after, Sofia's son sent me a collection of the original letters that Abraham sent to Raisa. They were only the ones from 1943 until his death in 1944, but they helped me to fill in much of the story. More importantly, they showed me what a true love story they shared.

Finally, I had enough pieces of the puzzle to start writing. I only had a rough idea of the journey they took, so many details were added based on the documented events during the time period. With that in mind, please note that several characters are fictional and added for the sake of the story.

Many stories however, are true. They either came from the letters or from stories my mother remembered. For example, Raisa did use her body several times to shield Luba and Sofia from falling bombs while they fled Belarus. Also, Luba was sick while in Kokand and Abraham did come to visit. Abraham was over 6 feet tall and often called Raisa his "feigele" or little bird, as she was just under 5 feet tall. My favorite story was how Abraham did in fact kiss Raisa goodbye every morning, and then circled around the house to kiss her through the window once more.

If you are interested in learning more about the history behind the story of Raisa and Abraham, please visit my website RachelZolotov.com to get a glimpse into the research that went into this project. There, you will find original photos, documents, full-color journey map, a family tree and more!

My goal in writing this novel was to tell a story that I felt could impact others. It is incredibly important that we keep the history alive, so that past mistakes won't ever repeat themselves. I hope *The Girl with the Silver Star* has enriched your life today with something that you may not have had yesterday.

◆ ◆ ◆

Thank you for reading *The Girl with the Silver Star*. I hope you enjoyed this novel as much as I enjoyed researching and writing it! Please take a moment to post a review on Amazon and/or Goodreads and tell a friend. Your feedback is so important to me, and will help other readers decide whether to read the book too.

Thank you again, I am truly honored to have been able to share this story with you!

Sofia, Raisa, Luba, 1940

Abraham, 1942

ACKNOWLEDGMENTS

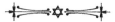

I am incredibly grateful to so many who have helped me shape this novel. I never would have been able to make this dream come true without the enormous support of my amazing husband, Andrey. I thank him for putting up with me all these years as I typed away into the late hours of the night. You are my Abraham.

To my daughters, Sasha and Lia - the two sweetest and kindest girls a mom could ask for, thank you for cheering me on and always being there to make me smile.

I must also name a few friends and family. Without their kindness and support I would not have made it to the end of this novel. I'd like to give a special thanks to my mother, Alla, for sharing her memories with me; Amy C. for being my #1 critique partner; Wendy G. for her attention to detail and always being honest; Cora K. for being my shoulder and rock when times got tough; my critique group circle for all the amazing suggestions; Leza I. for being my cheerleader and #1 supporter; Samantha P. for her expert creative eye; Susan M. for the outstanding writing advice; to my neighbor - known by my family as simply Baba Ira for being like a grandmother to me and spending weeks reading the Russian letters and postcards while I translated them to English; and Jenny J. for graciously helping with marketing and keeping me sane. Thank you to everyone else that helped and supported me on this journey, you know who you are! I owe you a huge debt of gratitude and I love you all dearly.

I would also like to thank my readers once again. Your continued support and feedback mean so much to me.

Last, but certainly not least, I would like to thank my incredible editor, Laurie Chittenden. Thank you for working your magic to help me shape my manuscript into the novel it is today.

Made in the USA
Monee, IL
18 November 2020